Smith's MONTHLY

Every Month Original Novels, Stories, and Articles

USA Today Bestselling Writer
Dean Wesley Smith

I0554012

TABLE OF CONTENTS

SHORT STORIES

FULL NOVEL

SERIAL NOVEL

NONFICTION

Smith's Monthly Issue #21

Introduction
ANSWERING A QUESTION

I wrote jukebox short stories, as I called them, for over thirty years. I set the stories in a small bar called the Garden Lounge that was owned by a really nice guy named Radley Stout. Just Stout to all his friends.

The jukebox had a special science fiction power. It could take a listener of a song played on the jukebox back to a memory.

Physically back to the memory.

And that person could then, in the few minutes of the song, change their life.

My first jukebox story was published in *Night Cry Magazine*, the sister magazine to the *Twilight Zone Magazine,* in 1987. That was a very long time ago.

And I had written and not published two jukebox stories before that.

Over the years, I wrote more jukebox stories and sold them.

"Jukebox Gifts" was published in the *Magazine of Fantasy and Science Fiction* and got me award nominations and a movie option. I even published a jukebox story in the *Jukebox Collector Magazine*, the only piece of fiction the magazine ever published.

As the years went by, I kept wondering about the origin of the jukebox, about those mysterious parts inside it that allowed it to take listeners to a memory. Stout, my character who owned the jukebox, never wanted to open it up and look at the strange equipment.

As the author, I wasn't ready to look inside yet either.

But I always considered the jukebox stories pure science fiction.

I just hadn't figured out the science to the jukebox.

Then a couple years ago, for the pages of this magazine, I started a new time travel series with a first book called *Thunder Mountain*. Again, pure science fiction, and in the Thunder Mountain series I actually explained the time travel with physics and math.

Thanks for the Support

Dean Wesley Smith

After *Melody Ridge* in this issue, I now have seven Thunder Mountain novels in the series. They all stand alone, but I think it would be fun for a reader to start with *Thunder Mountain* and read them from the start all the way through.

So what does *Melody Ridge* have to do with the jukebox stories?

Finally, after almost thirty years of writing jukebox stories, I wrote the jukebox origin story and that origin is *Melody Ridge*.

I finally got the courage to open up the jukebox and take a look at what made it work.

To me, this doesn't feel like an end of anything, but actually, now with the origin known, I can write even more jukebox stories as the mood strikes.

And I hope to keep writing Thunder Mountain short stories and novels as well.

So I hope you enjoy *Melody Ridge* and the other stories in this issue.

As a writer, I am very proud that I finally figured out a puzzle that had me stymied for almost thirty years.

Dean Wesley Smith
July 6, 2015
Lincoln City, Oregon

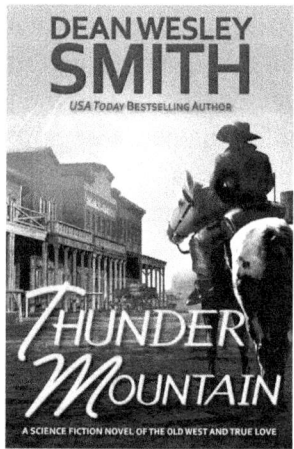

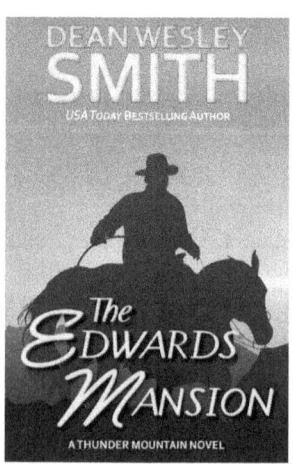

The First Six Thunder Mountain Novels
Available at your favorite booksellers.

Coming Next Issue in Smith's Monthly
The First Original Doc Hill Thriller
DEAD MONEY

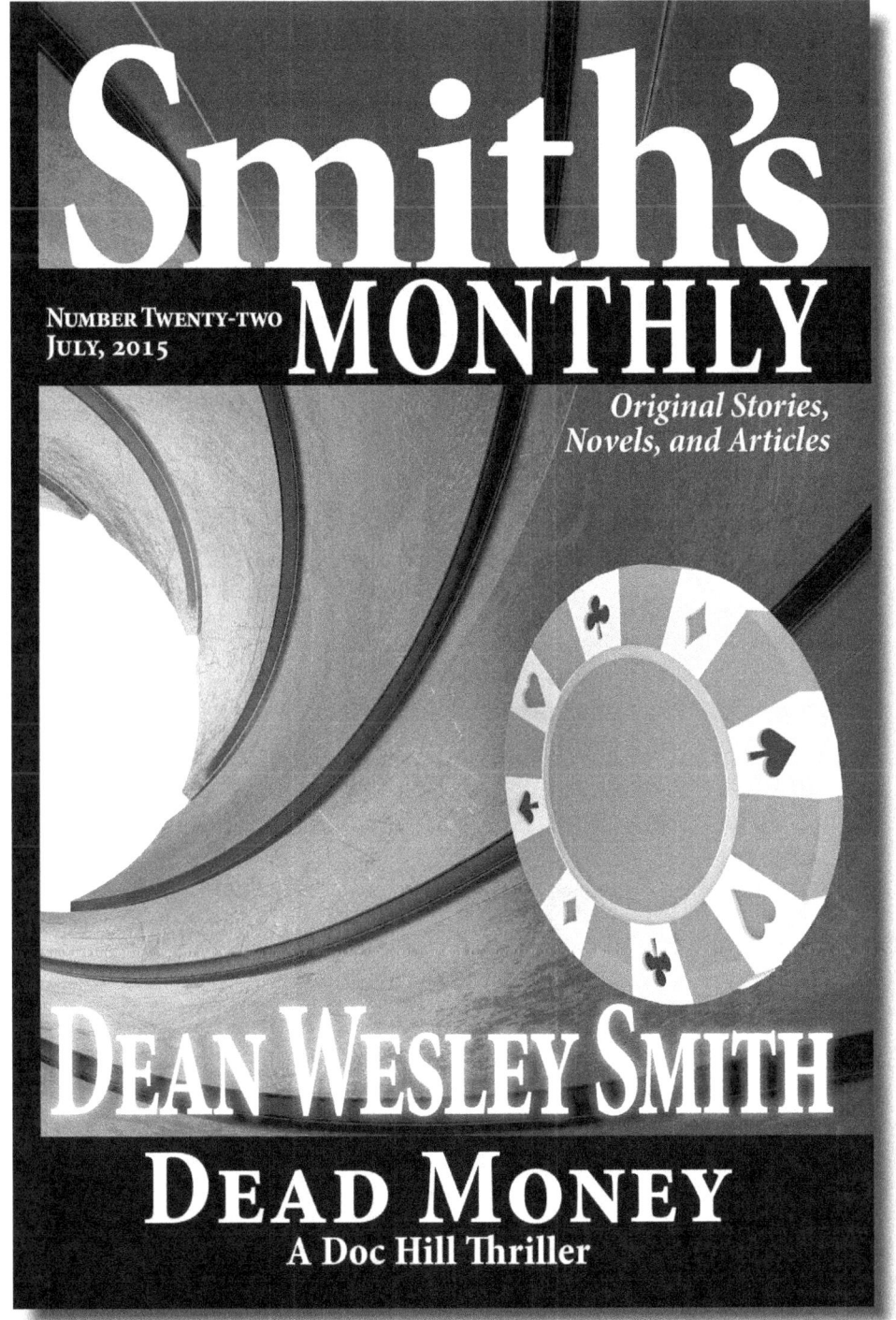

Poker Boy wants nothing more than to be left alone in a good game of poker. But a cherub circles overhead in the poker room wanting to talk.

And Poker Boy knows this cherub and knows the little guy represents trouble.

Even worse, the question the cherub asks Poker Boy could change a lot of futures.

How really, really annoying.

Just Shoot Me Now!
A Poker Boy Story

ONE

THE LITTLE JERK cherub just kept fluttering around near the ceiling of the poker room at Spirit Winds Casino. He acted like a bird trapped inside a small room with no windows. I know he was trying to get my attention, but the last thing I wanted to deal with tonight was a cherub.

And actually he had a couple small birds with very long beaks with him and they seemed to be flying in a figure-eight pattern, just missing each other as they moved around and around over my head.

The game was as good as a five-ten no limit gets. Three tourists who were drinking and wanting to have the action, two weak regulars, and two professionals. Plus me.

I had died and gone to heaven, cherub and all, it seemed. I was already three hundred up and the night was still young. Nothing can get my blood going more than a high-action poker game with players I know I can beat.

But nothing can put a player off his game more than a circling cherub.

I glanced up at the cherub and his two bird friends as I tossed a seven-four off-suit into the muck. No one else in the room could see the little idiot fluttering around the lights. He had golden hair and wore a white cloth wrapped around him that looked more like a diaper in places than anything else. The cloth started at one ankle and ended up over his shoulder.

His white wings were fluttering constantly like a humming bird's and he had on the traditional fake cherub halo that seemed to glow bright yellow. They could take those halo things off like a hat. He was about three feet tall at most and wore no shoes.

I even knew this one's name. Chadwick.

Chadwick the Cherub.

I had dealt with him once before on an assignment to help out a woman who thought she was dying and had started to give away her vast fortune. It turned out old Chadwick was just showing himself to her like a bad flasher, making her think she was seeing an angel with a very small penis.

He was sent to cherub counseling after I stopped him from forcing the poor woman to end up broke and insane and permanently put off of sex.

Now it seemed he was back. And was just as annoying. At least this time he was keeping his cloth diaper where it belonged.

I tried to ignore him again for another hand, but ignoring a kid-sized mythical creature fluttering over your head is hard to do.

Finally I couldn't handle it anymore. I flipped into the muck a couple suited connectors and froze time.

Actually I didn't really freeze time. No one could do that. But I did have the power to step between moments in time. It felt like I had frozen time because all the sounds of the casino stopped, and everyone froze in that moment.

Everyone but me and Chadwick.

His two bird friends remained frozen as well up near the ceiling. And some bird poop was stopped in midair headed for a spot right in front of my chips. Great, just great.

I stood and looked up at the cherub who had stopped flying around and was just hovering, looking down at me with a smile.

"All right, let's get to this," I said.

He came down and hovered in front of me, his white wings moving so fast that they looked like they were standing still. His smile was a cross between a worried grin and a smirk showing how happy he was I had come around.

"Nice trick on this time thing," he said, indicating the frozen people around us. "I thought only gods could do this."

"Just park it and take off that stupid halo," I said.

He stopped and stood on the nearest empty poker table. He folded his wings back behind him and stuffed the halo into his white cloth diaper strip where it wrapped up and over his shoulder like a sling.

"First off," I said, not even trying to hide how annoyed I was, "does Cherry know you are here?"

Cherry was the head cherub and one of the nicer creatures I had ever had the pleasure to meet.

Chadwick nodded. "She's the one who sent me."

His voice was deep and rough, not at all like what his image would project. He sounded more like a cigar-smoking old man. Most cherubs were thousands of years old. My boss, Stan the God of Poker had told me that Cherry was far older than he was which meant she was thousands and thousands of years old at least.

More than likely Chadwick was a few thousand years old as well.

"And I can check that?" I asked, calling Chadwick's bluff.

"Yes," he said.

He wasn't lying. I could tell a lie on a cherub's face from across the room. It seemed the sweet look didn't give them much chance to lie, especially to poker players. Cherry actually had suggested he come talk to me.

Great. Just great. A perfect night just ruined. Could someone just shoot me now?

TWO

"SO WHAT do you need from me?" I asked, almost afraid of the question's answer.

Good old Chadwick looked me direct in the eyes with those round, innocent-looking brown eyes of his and said, "I want to be part of your team."

I actually managed to not break out into complete gales of laughter.

The team he was talking about consisted of three other superheroes and one god that helped me solve major cases. We often saved the world.

Me and my girlfriend and sidekick, Patty Ledgerwood, aka Front Desk Girl, led the team. Patty was a superhero working in the hospitality side of the world.

The third member was Screamer, a man able to read minds and connect minds at times. Screamer was a superhero who worked in the law enforcement branch of the gods.

The fourth member was The Smoke, a part dog, part human who was a superhero working for the gods of animals.

And then there was Stan, the God of Poker, my boss. He was our connection to Laverne, Lady Luck herself.

And now Chadwick the Flasher Cherub wanted to join the team.

Somehow I kept most of my poker face locked on and smiled and asked him the next question.

"Why would you want to do that?"

"Oh, I personally don't," Chadwick said. "But Cherry thinks it would be a good idea for me to start doing something constructive with my time now that I am mostly done with my counseling sessions."

I sort of stared at the chubby little cherub for a moment, trying to understand what I had just heard.

I must be dreaming. I had to be. I was at such a perfect table, a perfect poker game, the kind of game that just didn't happen every night. And now I was dealing with a converted flasher who wanted to join my team, but who really didn't want to join my team.

And a bird was about to poop on my poker table.

This had to be a nightmare, a really bad one.

I had no idea what to do.

I wanted to just laugh and send him back to Cherry, but my little voice was telling me that wouldn't be a good idea. There had to be some politics involved with all this and for a superhero to get involved with politics among the different gods was never a good idea.

I looked at Chadwick again.

"What can it hurt?" he asked, shrugging.

I couldn't begin to answer that, since most of the time that the team worked together on a problem, the entire world was at stake.

I looked up at the ceiling and shouted, "Stan!"

I needed help and I needed it fast. Before I said something I would regret and maybe cause a rift between different branches of gods, as if there weren't enough of those already.

Stan appeared beside me, inside the frozen time instant I had created. Stan wore his normal gray sweater, dark slacks, and blank expression. He was slightly shorter than I was and looked like any person you might see on the street. As the God of Poker, he could blend in anywhere and it was impossible to read any emotion on his face unless he wanted you to, or didn't care.

"Hi, Stan," Chadwick said, waving a chubby little hand at the God of Poker.

"I was afraid of this," Stan said.

"That's not making me feel any better," I said. "Chadwick here wants to join my team."

"Yeah, I heard," Stan said.

"But he really doesn't," I said. "Do you, Chadwick?"

"Oh, hell no," the cherub said. "It sounds like far too much work. It was just Cherry's idea."

"You know what I told you about swearing," a woman's voice said from above us.

I looked up as Cherry fluttered to a stop on the table next to a suddenly worried Chadwick.

She looked almost identical to Chadwick, except her golden hair was longer and the diaper-like cloth also covered her chest. Her face was thinner as well and she had a beauty to her that took my breath away.

"Sorry," Chadwick said, looking down.

"Nice seeing you again, Cherry," Stan said.

"I agree," I said, bowing slightly to her. "You look more radiant than ever."

She smiled and I could feel the warmth filling the air around me. "There's a real reason a lot of the gods like you, Poker Boy," she said.

"He's a charmer all right," Stan said, shaking his head. "So tell me why you think it would be a good idea for Chadwick here to join Poker Boy's team?"

"Keep Chadwick focused and out of trouble," Cherry said. "He needs something to hold his attention."

"Besides human women," Stan said before I could.

Thankfully.

"Yes," Cherry said. "To be honest."

I knew now how to solve the problem. I just had to find good old Chadwick something to do. I had no idea what, but anything was better than him hanging around my team.

"You know we seldom put the team together," I said to Cherry. "In fact, it has been almost two months since the entire team has needed to be together for a problem."

"Oh," Cherry said, the smile vanishing from her face. "That's not going to work. I thought you met and worked every day together."

"Not even every month," Stan said, backing up my play.

Chadwick actually looked relieved. Cherry looked completely devastated for some reason.

I needed to come up with an idea and come up with it quick.

I sort of turned to Chadwick. "Besides human women, what do you like?"

"I don't even like them that much," Chadwick said.

Cherry turned slightly away and rolled her eyes, which made Stan grin.

Then Cherry said, "His mother married a Putti, so there is a lot of the old Cupid blood in him."

"So, Chadwick," I said. "What exactly are your powers that would help my team?"

I figured that if I could learn what he could do, I might be able to come up with a way to get him busy with something else. Anything else.

Chadwick looked annoyed, but Cherry looked at him and he took a deep breath and turned to face me directly.

"I can fly. I can be invisible. I can pass through any wall. I am an expert spy and can remember everything to the word anyone says that I am listening to and report that back exactly. Because of my father, I am an expert with the magical bow and arrow, but am not allowed to carry one because of an incident a number of decades back with a movie star and a president."

With that he glared at Cherry who only shrugged. "You tried to interfere with human events. You will serve your sentence to the fullest."

Chadwick just shook his head and looked down.

"How fast can you fly?" I asked.

"I can be in Las Vegas faster than you can jump there with your teleporting superpower."

Both Stan and Cherry nodded at that.

I was surprised. Now that I was actually thinking about it, there was no doubt Chadwick would be a good addition to the team on some problems. None of us had the abilities he had.

I glanced at Stan who actually looked like he was thinking the same thing.

"Chadwick," I said, "honestly I think we can use you at times on our team. We don't use every member every mission, but I think your powers would add to our team on certain missions."

Stan was nodding.

Cherry was looking surprised, and Chadwick looked shocked.

"You're kidding, right?" Chadwick asked.

"Not in the slightest," I said. "But the problem is we don't often have missions and you need something to keep you occupied."

"To help you keep that thing in your diapers," Stan said.

"It's not a diaper," Chadwick said in his gruff voice, glaring at Stan.

"Poker Boy is right," Cherry said, nodding to me with thanks. "If you want to be on Poker Boy's team, which is a very high honor, you need to stay out of trouble and do something constructive."

"And just what would that be?" Chadwick asked, looking disgusted. "I've been bored for most of the last thousand years. Being a cherub just doesn't have a lot of purpose these days. So I'm open to suggestions."

Because we were between a moment in time, the frozen poker room around us was deadly silent and now the four of us were as well. I just couldn't think of a thing for Chadwick to do.

Nothing.

THREE

I GLANCED UP and saw the two frozen birds that he had brought in with him. And the bird poop hanging in midair like a promise yet to be kept.

"What's with the birds?" I asked, trying to buy some time to think.

"I like birds and they like me," he said. "It's fun flying with them."

I had a faint glimmering of an idea, but I wasn't sure about it. I needed more information.

"Can you talk to them?"

"Not much," Chadwick said. "They aren't that smart."

I turned to Stan and Cherry. "Is there a god of birds? Or a god who looks over that area of the animal kingdom?"

Both Stan and Cherry looked puzzled.

"Not really," Stan said. "The Smoke's boss would be the most likely, but most gods tend to have one bird or another that they favor, but no one that I know is over all the birds in general."

"So they have no god really looking out for them?" I asked, surprised. I thought every aspect of the world had a god over it.

"I wouldn't think so," Cherry said looking very puzzled. "Odd, don't you think?"

I turned to Chadwick. "How about you make it your job to save birds and watch out over them?"

He just looked puzzled.

"You said you like them, right?" I asked.

He nodded.

"And you can fly faster than any bird, right?"

"Yeah," he said.

"So make it your job to save birds. If a bird is about to fly in front of a truck, save it. Save birds trapped in a cage in a burning house. Save birds from being shot by kids."

Both Cherry and Stan were smiling, so I knew I had them on board with the idea.

And Chadwick was nodding slowly as he thought about it.

"There is clearly no one else doing it," I said. "And from the number of dead birds I've seen over the years, clearly it needs to be done."

Chadwick nodded. "I've saved a few birds along the way and it always felt good."

"Cherry," I said, turning to Chadwick's boss, "you want to check with the appropriate god in charge to make sure it would

be all right if Chadwick took up this great mission?"

"I think it will be," she said, smiling at me and looking very relieved.

I turned back to Chadwick. "And I'll still need you on my team on some missions if that's all right with you. Your special powers could really help at times."

Chadwick was nodding and smiling. "Sure, sure, and if I find something big that I need help on, I can get your help as well?"

"Of course," I said, smiling. "The entire team if need be."

"Great," he said.

He turned to Cherry. "I really like this idea. Much better than going around shooting people with stupid magic arrows like my dad does."

"I agree," Cherry said. "It is a perfect mission for you. Perfect, and will do a ton of good."

"Thanks, Poker Boy," Chadwick said.

"Yes, thank you," Cherry said.

And then they were both gone along with the two birds, but the big drop of bird poop still hung there.

"Looks like you have a new member of the team," Stan said, shaking his head. "Hard to imagine."

I just laughed. "Patty is never going to believe that I invited Chadwick the Famous Flashing Cherub to join the team."

"If he can keep the little thing in his diaper," Stan said, also laughing, "he just might be able to help at times."

"He might at that," I said. "But if nothing else we saved a lot of birds tonight."

Stan vanished, but I could still hear him laughing.

I grabbed a couple handfuls of napkins and went back to my chair at the poker table. I placed the napkin under the bird poop and then let myself slip back into the time stream.

The noise of the casino crashed in around me as the bird poop hit the napkins and I swept them up before anyone noticed.

I just hoped that cleaning up crap wasn't a sign of the times ahead with Chadwick the Flashing Cherub.

Dean Wesley **Smith**

USA **Today** Bestselling Writer

Black Betsy

A Jukebox Story

Shoeless Joe Jackson made a mistake and was banned from baseball for life.

Sometimes, in the Garden Lounge, the special jukebox lets a customer go back in time to a mistake and fix it.

Shoeless Joe never had a chance to let the jukebox help him fix his mistake, but instead it allowed Shoeless Joe to do something even more important: Help a child become a better adult.

"Black Betsy" first appeared in the anthology Alternate Outlaws *from TOR Books edited by Mike Resnick.*

Black Betsy
A Jukebox Story

ONE

Eleven in the morning, December 5th.

The time and the day stuck in my head like the memory of my first kiss or the memory of my dad dying. The weather that morning had turned unseasonably cold. Not baseball weather at all. A storm coming down the west coast from Alaska was projected to bring four inches of snow to the valley floor and light snow was already falling. The storm would eventually drop almost a foot of snow and shut down the schools for two days. But that wasn't what I remembered about December 5th. What I remembered about that morning was Edward Toole. I turned on the jukebox that morning and sent him back to 1951.

Back to a time when baseball was important to him and to one other very special man.

I had just finished the morning bookkeeping for the Garden Lounge, made the deposit from the night before, and started the prep work for the day. Light snowflakes swirled in a whirlwind just inside the front door as Edward entered. He brushed off his coat, stamped his feet hard twice, and then moved through the empty tables toward the bar. He was a big man, thick shoulders, thick waist, with thinning brown and gray hair, and dark, brooding eyes. He was the last person I would have expected to show up in the Garden at eleven in the morning. He worked as a house lawyer for the big computer firm to the south of town. He had a wife, two boys, and was the town's Little League baseball coach. His usual drink was bourbon and water, with a twist of lemon. He never had more than three in any given night and never before five.

He didn't look up as he approached the bar, which was also rare. Usually he was one of the most open and smiling people who came through the door.

"Morning, Stout," he said quietly as he pulled out a bar stool. He took his coat off and draped it over the stool next to him, then climbed onto the stool closest to where I was working at the well. I had been cutting fruit, so I still had limes, lemons, and oranges scattered on the waitress station next to him.

"Edward," I said. "Good to see you. Out of the office early today. Heading home before it gets too deep out there?" I wiped the lime juice off my hands and slid a bar napkin in front of him. "What can I get for you?"

"The usual," he said, then swung around on the stool and faced out over the empty lounge. "You know," he said, seeming to stare off at the front door. "This place looks the same during the day as it does at night." He laughed. "Even the same smell of smoke and cleaner. For some reason I thought it would be different."

I glanced around. The Garden was a small bar by current standards. More like a neighborhood bar in the old fifties tradition. It had a dozen vinyl booths, six tables, and a bunch of plants, mostly fake ferns. The walls were a natural wood, dark brown, and the carpet was the same dark brown color. The old oak bar filled the wall opposite the front door in front of a mirror and glass racks. A classic jukebox was framed in real plants to the right of the bar. Except for Christmas Eve, the jukebox was never plugged in. Background music was supplied by the stereo I hid behind the bar.

Most of the customers said the Garden felt comfortable, like an old sweater. For me it had been home for five years. And since I had never been married, my regular customers, like Edward, were the only family I had.

I cut a twist off a fresh lemon, slid it along the edge of the glass, dropped it in the golden bourbon, and set the glass on the napkin in front of him.

He twisted around to face me, holding a strained smile in place. "I suppose," he said, "since there are no windows, there would be no reason for this place to notice the time of day. I just hadn't thought about it before." He picked up the drink, nodding thank you, and downed half of it.

In all the years I had been serving him I had never seen him do anything but sip his bourbon. Not even the night his Little League team won the state championship. "Everything all right on the home front? Carol and the kids?" I asked, picking up a lime and going back to slicing.

He finished the rest of the drink and slid it toward me for a refill. "They're fine. Or at least they were this morning." He paused for a moment, then said hesitantly, "But I just got fired."

"Holy shit! You're kidding."

Edward gave me another strained smile as I picked up his empty glass and moved to refill it. "Wish I was. Seems I made a bad choice a couple months back. Since what I did seems to be unethical, they had no choice but to fire me. And it seems that the State Bar will yank my license to practice law, too."

I finished making the drink in silence and placed it in front of him. "It was that serious?"

He nodded. "Mostly stupid on my part. I guess I knew better. Just wasn't thinking."

I stood across from him, waiting for him to continue. Tell me what he had done. He took a sip off his drink, looked up at me and asked, "You ever hear of Shoeless Joe?"

"The old baseball player they made the movie about?"

Edward nodded. "That's the one. Joseph Jefferson Jackson—Shoeless Joe. I had a chance to meet him once, back when I was fifteen. Back in 1951 in South Carolina. But I was too afraid to go into his bedroom with my baseball coach and two of the other players. Back then I really wanted to be a professional ball player when I grew up and everyone knew that Shoeless Joe Jackson was the best left fielder to ever play the game. And one of the best hitters ever. I guess as a kid I just didn't have the courage to meet him. He died two days later and I always blamed myself."

I slowly shook my head, took a deep breath and looked down at the fruit I had been cutting. None of this was making sense. But sometimes that was what a bartender had to expect. When customers needed to talk about problems, very rarely did they make immediate sense. The best thing a bartender could do was just keep them talking until they talked themselves out.

"You blamed yourself?" I asked. "Why? How old was he?"

"He was sixty-three. And he was sick. I know all that. He died on December 5th. Forty years ago today. Interesting, huh? That I would get fired on the same day. I think it is a sort of poetic justice."

"But if he was sixty-three and sick, why would you blame yourself?"

Edward took a deep breath and looked quickly around the bar, as if to make sure no one could hear him. Then he looked me right in the eye and said, "I stole Black Betsy. His bat."

TWO

EDWARD SIPPED on his entire second drink and he sipped his third through the lunch crowd and a fourth up until we were alone again at two. During that time we talked about what caused him to get fired, how stealing Shoeless Joe's bat from his house had caused Edward guilt for forty years. During lunch, Edward and two other regular customers filled me in on the entire Black Sox scandal of the 1919 World Series. I learned how Shoeless Joe was the leading hitter for that World Series with a .357 average. How he played errorless ball for the eight game series, yet was still thrown out of baseball for agreeing to take $5,000 to throw the series.

I learned about Comiskey Park, the White Sox, and Commissioner Kenesaw Mountain Landis. I learned about the other seven players that were thrown out with Shoeless Joe and about the Ten Day

Clause in the old player contracts that led to the entire mess.

I also learned that Edward was a haunted man. He was haunted by a mistake he made as a kid. For his entire life he continued to make the same sort of bad decisions and mistakes. I also learned that he knew when he entered college that he really didn't have the talent to be a professional baseball player. He truly loved being a lawyer, but he never lost his love for baseball, and regretted not playing ball for a living.

At some point during that three-hour period, I decided to break one of my own rules: I would plug in the jukebox, and give Edward a chance to correct that one big mistake.

THREE

THE JUKEBOX in the Garden Lounge was a time-travel device.

Actually, every jukebox is a time machine in a limited fashion. When a song is played on a regular jukebox, a person sort of travels back to the time and the memory associated with that song. The Garden jukebox does almost exactly that, with one major difference. It physically takes the person to the memory, and allows that person to be there inside their old body for the length of the song. They are actually there, smelling, tasting, and feeling the past.

And they can change it, too. Which is why I only allow myself to plug the jukebox in on Christmas Eve and then only for a few close friends every year. Changing the past is way too dangerous. And I have lost a couple of good friends because of it.

I inherited the jukebox from the junk in the basement of the first bar I owned. Ten minutes before the bank came in to close me down, I hauled the old jukebox out of the basement and into my garage at home, figuring I had the spare time to fix it up. A year later, when I finally got around to opening it up, I discovered a bunch of stuff inside that didn't belong in a normal jukebox. Stuff that seemed far beyond my limited electrical ability, so I just cleaned off the dust, fixed the electrical cord that looked as if someone had ripped it from the back of the machine, and turned it on.

Luck had it that the only forty-five I had around the house was a recording of a song that reminded me of the night I almost asked Jenny, the only woman I have ever loved, to marry me. It had been her favorite song. I had the record in a scrapbook with pictures of her and hadn't listened to it in years.

I fired up the song and the next thing I knew I was with Jenny. I could feel my fingers touching her hand. I could smell her light perfume. I licked my lips, and tasted the faint cherry from her lipstick. I was there, fumbling, trying to get up enough courage in my twenty-three year-old body to ask her to marry me. Yet I was also there as a thirty-seven year-old man, with the clear memory that I had not asked her. And the next week she had left me for college and eventually another man.

I sat there across from her, stunned, not talking, until the song ended and I found myself back in my garage.

The next day I finally got up the courage to play the record again and ended up sitting across from Jenny again. And again at the exact same time and place. That was where my memory from that song took me. That second time I almost asked her to marry me. Almost. It would have changed my life and my future. And I had no idea what that would have meant. My life really wasn't so bad. I have never had the courage to play Jenny's song again, even though it is on the jukebox, waiting.

Since then, every Christmas Eve I have given a few close friends the opportunity to go back and relive one memory. Sometimes they change something back there and don't come back. But most of the time they pop back into the bar as the song ends. Sometimes laughing, sometimes crying, but always more content then before they played the song.

Now I was going to break my own rule. It was December 5th, and I was going to plug in the jukebox and give Edward a chance to change his past and his life. I just hoped I was doing the right thing.

FOUR

"WELL," EDWARD SAID, looking around as the last lunch customer went out into the blowing snow. "I suppose it's time for me to go home and tell Carol the news." He shook his head. "Damned if I know what we're going to do. I've never been fired before."

I set two dirty glasses in the sink and took a deep breath. "Humor me for a moment. What do you think would have happened if you hadn't stolen that bat?"

Edward shrugged. "I would have slept a lot better over the years, that's for sure."

I nodded and went on. "You have a song, or style of song that reminds you of that time you went to see Joe?"

Edward thought for a moment, then nodded. "Big band stuff. You know, like Dorsey. My mom was always playing it, and I remember a record player on real low, with one of those bands playing on it, when we visited Joe's house. Why?"

I pointed at the Wurlitzer jukebox to the right of the bar. "You ever have a song take you back to a memory?"

"Of course. Who hasn't?"

I moved out from behind the bar, reached in behind the polished chrome of the jukebox and plugged it in. A soft whirring came from inside and I could feel my stomach tightening up. I always felt sick every time I turned on the jukebox. The sickness of dread, of worry. The sickness of fear, like going into a bad situation, or knowing the moment before you are going to get hit that you will get hurt.

I stood and faced Edward as the green, red, and yellow lights flickered on, casting an odd rainbow on the floor and nearby booth. "I know you won't believe me, so just listen. This jukebox can take you back to that memory of Shoeless Joe."

Edward laughed. "I don't need a machine to do that. It is with me every day."

"It will actually take you there. Maybe this time you can leave the bat."

Edward looked at me for a moment, then snorted. "Right." He picked up his drink and downed it. Then reached into his pocket for his wallet. "I think I had better be getting home. Music there to face for sure."

"I told you that you wouldn't believe me. So just humor me. Play one song. Do that and the drinks and lunch are on me. I'll even supply the quarter." I held up a quarter for him to see.

He looked around at the empty bar. Then, after a long moment, he shrugged. "Stout, people said you were a strange bird. Now I guess I know why." He moved over to the jukebox, taking the quarter from me as he did.

"There are a number of big band tunes on there. Pick the one that reminds you the most of that moment you took the bat."

"Will do," he said, shaking his head.

I watched him as he looked over the selection, then dropped the quarter into the slot and punched the buttons. The jukebox clanked and then the sound of a small motor came from inside, followed by a bunch of clicks.

Now I felt as if I wanted to throw up. What happened if he changed something really major? Something that cost a lot of lives. Every damn time I plugged in the jukebox that fear hit me like a hammer.

I took a deep breath, placed both hands on the bar in front of me and faced him. He was a friend. He deserved the chance. "Just think about that moment in Joe's house," I told him. "And remember while you are there that you only have the length of the song that is playing. Not one moment longer."

"Sure," he said. "And then..."

The song started and Edward faded from the bar and was gone.

I took a deep breath and moved over to the well as the Jimmy Dorsey Band filled the room with the sounds of the past. I really wanted to break another one of my rules.

I needed a drink.

FIVE

BIG BAND MUSIC played softly from an old record player in the cluttered dining room. The house smelled musty and closed in, with a faint medicine smell that seemed to coat everything. A big, overstuffed couch with doilies on the arms filled one wall. Glass cabinets with old trophies and pictures filled another. Outside, it was a cold December day in South Carolina.

In front of the glass case was a round umbrella stand. In that stand were five baseball bats, including a black one. Edward stared at that bat for a moment, not really understanding what it was, then glanced around the living room.

"Wow, Stout. You can really pull off an illusion." As he said it he realized his voice didn't sound right. It seemed too high and a different pitch to his ears.

He glanced down at his younger body, the heavy coat, the boots, and the memories came flooding back. The memories of coming into Shoeless Joe's house with Coach and Dave and Johnny just a few minutes before.

Yet those memories were overlaid by the years of the future and the very real memory of just getting fired from a job he really loved.

"Stout! How..."

The sound of laughing came from the back room over the top of the music. Stout had been right. Somehow he was here, yet he wasn't. He couldn't be. He was married, with two kids years in the future. He reached out and touched the arm of the couch.

It felt real.

He looked around again, then moved over and pulled out the black bat. It was heavy and a little cold to his touch. The grip was rough with the old tape and felt almost sticky.

Black Betsy. Joe's favorite bat.

He remembered looking at it forty years ago and then slipping it up inside his big coat and going out the front door. He had stashed the bat in a large bush and then waited for Coach and the others to come out. They had ribbed him a little about not going in to see Shoeless Joe, but not much. Mostly they just talked about how exciting it was to meet Shoeless Joe and how he couldn't have really thrown the series. He had gone back that night and picked up the bat. He still had it up in the attic.

Young Edward turned the bat over in his hands and looked at the initials S.J. carved in the handle. Many a night over the next few years he would hold that bat and run his fingers over those initials. He did so again, his young self treasuring the feel, his older self hating it.

The two emotions battling inside his head and stomach.

The fight lasted for only a moment, but it seemed much longer. Finally the forty year-old memories won and he dropped the bat back into the umbrella stand.

It was as if the weight of an entire life lifted from his shoulders. "Thanks, Stout," he said to the air. He took a deep breath and let it out. It was time to face a few more things. The song was still playing, so with one last look at Black Betsy, he turned and headed for the back room.

Shoeless Joe's bedroom was filled with a huge dresser and a big, old, metal bed. The drapes were open to the gray December day. Joe was propped up on pillows and he was laughing. To Edward he looked like a skeleton, with large ears, an even bigger nose, and eyes that seemed to sparkle.

As Edward entered Joe looked over and nodded.

"Glad you came in," Coach said, and motioned for Edward to move up beside the bed. "Edward, this is Shoeless Joe Jackson. Mr. Jackson, this is Edward Toole, one of my better players." Joe smiled and stuck out his hand. Edward shook it. Joe's grip was strong, but the skin was dry and rough.

The older Edward wanted to scream and shout for joy. He was actually meeting Shoeless Joe Jackson. Actually shaking his hand. But his fifteen year-old self was too embarrassed to talk. This time the young self won.

"Nice meeting you, Edward," Joe said. His voice was deep and powerful and surprised Edward, coming from the thin body.

"Nice meeting you, sir." Edward stammered.

Joe smiled as if he understood. And just maybe he did, because for a moment he looked into Edward's eyes. Then Joe's smile slowly turned to a frown, he shook his head and looked around. "I suppose you all are wondering the same question that everyone wonders. Did I really throw the series?"

"Sir," Coach said, "I made the boys promise to not ask about that."

Joe waved a large, thin hand in dismissal. "That's all right. After all the years I have sort of got used to it."

In the other room the song was almost finished.

Joe looked directly at Edward. "Sometimes you make good choices and sometimes you make bad ones. Just like in a ball game. And with every play you must live with the choice. Sometimes only to the end of the inning. Sometimes for much longer. You understand me?" He was asking Edward directly.

Both young- and old-Edward could do nothing but nod.

The song had very few seconds left.

"I made a bad choice and it cost me," Joe said. "But I tried from that day forward to make good choices. And I kept on living. Just like in a game you must keep on playing, no matter what the mistake. What I learned is that you don't ever give up."

Edward nodded. "Thank you, sir." And Edward's older self added, "More than you will ever know."

The song ended and years of future memories slipped from the young Edward as Shoeless Joe nodded and smiled.

SIX

THE LAST NOTES of the big band song echoed around the Garden Lounge.

Edward did not reappear.

I let go of the warm chrome of the jukebox where I had been holding on to make sure I remembered Edward. He didn't come back so he had changed his past somehow. He probably didn't take the bat this time, and that had changed his present in some way. Now maybe he hadn't got fired. Or maybe he had never taken the job with the computer company in the first place, or he had never become a lawyer.

Anything could have happened, and I would not have even remembered him being in the bar this afternoon if I hadn't been holding onto the jukebox when the song ended. My memories would have switched over to this new world's. But by touching the jukebox I could remember the old world.

And Edward.

I couldn't resist the temptation to go to the phone book and see if Edward's name was still in there. It was, only it also had an office number with it besides his home phone. It looked as if he had hung out his own shingle in this world. I hoped that meant he was happier. I unplugged the jukebox, finished my drink, and went back to cleaning up from lunch rush. If he didn't show up after five I would check around. Until then there wasn't anything I could do but wait.

SEVEN

AT SEVEN MINUTES after five Edward walked through the door. He looked the same, except that he wasn't wearing a suit. Instead he had on a casual dress sweater and golf slacks. He smiled and waved as he came through the door, and I waved back and started to make his normal drink.

There were about twenty of the regulars in the Garden, and he stopped for a moment to talk to a few of them at the first table. So by the time he was on the only empty stool to the right of the waitress station, I had the drink in front of him.

"Quick as always, Stout," he said. Then he held up the glass with the bourbon and a twist and looked at it. "But what's this. You forget after all these years that I drink Vodka tonics?"

A couple of the others at the bar laughed and I laughed right along with them as I took the drink back from him. "Just not with it today," I said, trying to act as normal as I could, even though my heart was pounding as if I had just run a hard five miles. I had about six hundred questions I wanted to ask him. Yet I knew he wouldn't understand a one of them.

I fixed him a new drink and slid it in front of him. He held it up and looked at me. "To Shoeless Joe Jackson," he said, making a toasting motion, then sipping his drink.

"Shoeless Joe?" I asked, somehow keeping my voice from shaking. "Wasn't he the one they made the movie about?"

Edward laughed. "You know, Stout, you have said that same thing every year. It's December 5th, the day Shoeless Joe Jackson died. Don't you remember we toast him every year on this date? He was the greatest left fielder to ever play the game." He paused for a moment, smiling to himself.

"Oh, God," one of the regulars down the bar said, shaking his head. "Here we go again."

Edward just kept on smiling. "You know," he said. "I met Shoeless Joe once."

~

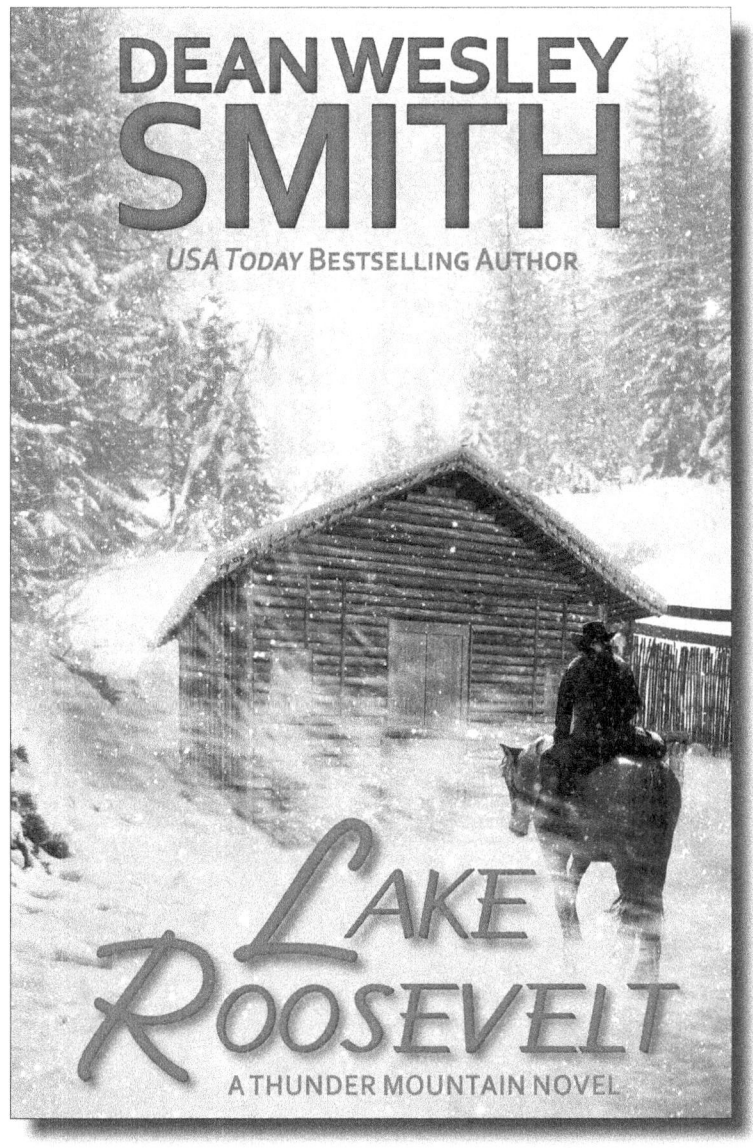

USA TODAY BESTSELLING AUTHOR

DEAN WESLEY SMITH

AN EASY SHOT

A GOLF THRILLER

In the first installments, Seattle Police Detectives Bonnie and Craig, while taking a late night walk on a Scottsdale Arizona golf course happen to overhear a conversation between two men plotting to kill a United States Senator.

At the same time, a young golf professional's wife is kidnapped. Scheduled to play with the Senator, he must do what they ask or his wife will die.

Bonnie and Craig get the FBI and local police involved. Everything is set and they play with the Senator to help protect him.

Nothing goes wrong, but that night, they see the two men again who they had overheard.

AN EASY SHOT

Part 4 of 8

CHAPTER TEN

Saturday, April 8th
10:19 p.m.

CHARLES ROBINS MOVED out onto his patio toward the man standing there. Never had the man returned in the middle of an assignment before. And never had the man called him on his personal, unlisted number to set up a meeting so late.

Charles had paced for the last two hours, waiting, coming up with a dozen things that could have gone wrong. Clearly the Senator had not met with his accident yet, so something had. The question was what?

And how serious was the problem?

Finally the man in the dark suit had appeared on the patio, smoking as always.

"So what has gone wrong?" Charles demanded.

"You tell me," the man said, his voice low and very mean. "The Senator has clearly been tipped that something might happen to him this weekend. Both the Scottsdale authorities and the FBI are staying very close to him. And he is playing with two cops from Seattle."

Charles felt as if someone had punched him in the stomach. "How? I said nothing to anyone but you."

"Are you sure?" the man asked, his voice seemingly on the edge of anger, barely controlled. His eyes were like two black holes in the darkness, unblinking and deadly.

"Of course I'm sure," Charles said, disgusted. "If Senator Knight makes that vote on Monday, I'm as good as broke and in prison. It would only be a matter of time. So why the hell would I tell anyone I'm trying to stop him?"

"Well, they have discovered the threat to the Senator in some fashion," the man said.

"But can you still do what needs to be done?"

The man nodded. "The Senator can still meet his date with an accident. But it will cost you a great deal more than before. And this will be our last meeting ever."

"How much more?" Charles demanded. The man's fee hadn't been small before this set-back.

The man laughed. "This is not a negotiation." He handed Charles a slip of paper.

Charles did not even give the man the satisfaction of looking down at the note.

"If the first amount specified is not in that off-shore numbered account by ten in the morning, the Senator will make his plane to Washington just fine."

"And if I put the money in the account and you do not carry through on your end of the deal?" Charles demanded, getting angrier and angrier.

"Then you do not have to pay the second, larger payment specified."

That made Charles glance down at the paper, but he could not read it in the dim light.

"And trust me," the man said, "if I carry through with my end of this and you do not pay the second amount, you will meet an accident far worse than what waits for the Senator. And far more painful."

"You are threatening me?" Charles demanded, stepping toward the man. Charles could not remember ever being so angry as to want to hit someone. But right now he was.

The man stood his ground, his dark eyes intense, his posture relaxed. "Of course I am."

Charles just stared at the man. This man was blackmailing him and there was nothing at all he could do about it. Charles was going to lose everything and the man knew it and was using that fact to extract everything he could.

"Think it over," the man said.

"How do I know you didn't make up this entire story about the FBI knowing there is a threat to the Senator?"

"You don't," the man said. "But it is the truth and there is no way to prove it to you."

Charles stared at the man. More than likely this guy had just been waiting for the right assignment from Charles to pull this blackmail stunt and then vanish. More than likely the man had done the same to other clients in the past and gotten away with it.

Well, he was going to get away with it again. Charles was desperate. Senator

Now Available
from all your favorite booksellers in trade paper and electronic editions.

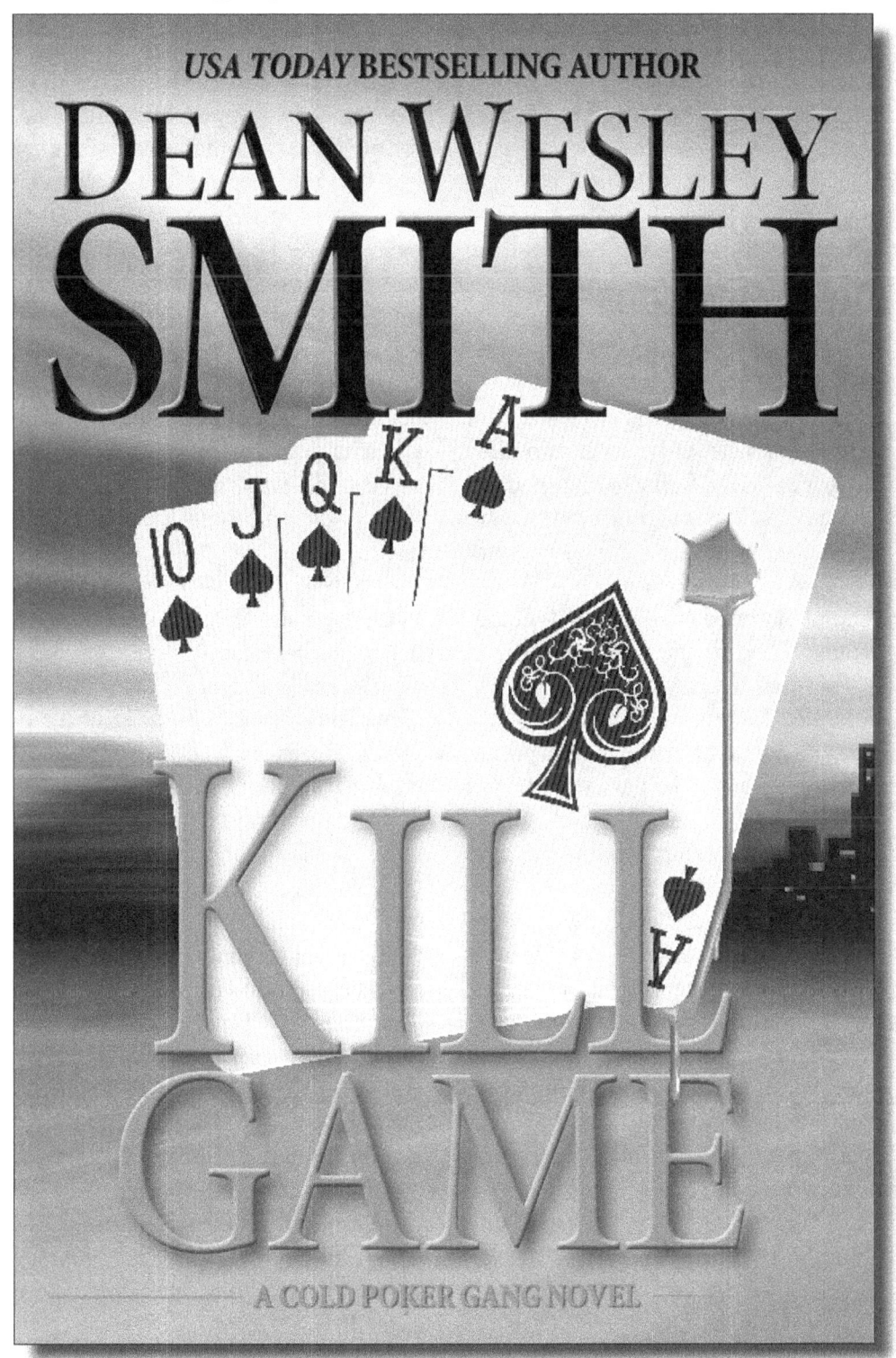

Knight had to be kept from that vote on Monday. There was no other choice.

"All right," Charles said. "The money will be in the account in the morning."

"It has been nice doing business with you," the man said, turning from Charles and starting across the patio.

"Just make sure it's done," Charles said.

"Oh, I will be successful," the man said without looking back. "You just make sure the payments are made and we can both live happily ever after."

With that the man walked down the path away from the patio and vanished into the night.

Charles turned and moved back into the light so that he could read the amounts on the paper. His stomach clamped up like the guy had punched him. $250,000 by ten in the morning. $750,000 within twelve hours of completion.

"Damn, damn, damn," he said, glancing around to see if the man was still in sight. That was a vast amount of money, yet possible. And the man he called Bill knew it. Its removal from his corporate accounts was going to be hard to hide, but better taking a chance with some missing money than having Knight vote on Monday.

He turned and headed for the office he kept here in his home. It was far past the time he would normally be in bed, but he knew without a doubt there would be no sleeping tonight. He had to figure a way to cover his tracks with the money.

And then spend the rest of the night worrying about the thousand things that might go wrong.

CHAPTER ELEVEN

Saturday, April 8th
11:30 p.m.

DANNY OPENED the door for the man and stepped back into his hotel room. All day he had been simply walking through the motions. He had managed to play decent golf, but that had been mostly because he hadn't cared. He kept thinking about his wife. He couldn't imagine what they were doing to her, and yet he couldn't think of anything at all to do. If he told someone, they would kill her, he had no doubt. And he couldn't live with that.

But he was also starting to wonder if he could live with the Senator getting hurt.

"Nice to see you not bein' guarded, kid," the man said. "Lot of cops around here. You have anything to do with that?'

Danny suddenly felt his stomach clamp down into a tight knot. "No!" he said as firmly as he could. "I didn't say a word to anyone."

The guy nodded. "You sure about that?"

"You said you'd kill my wife," Danny said, staring into the dark eyes of the man. "Why would I chance that?"

The guy looked at him for a minute, then nodded. "Smart kid. I believe you. Besides, we've been keepin' an eye on you and I doubt you had a chance to tell anyone."

Danny felt the relief flood over him. "Can I talk to Steph?"

He had insisted that before he would do anything for them, he could talk to Steph every night. The kidnappers had agreed.

"Sure thing, kid," the guy said. He reached into his coat pocket and flipped Danny a cell phone. "Just hit redial."

He did as the man told him to do, then listened as it rang on the other end twice before Steph answered. "Danny?"

"Steph?" he said, the relief he felt flooding through him, making his knees weak and his eyes water.

"Are you all right, Danny?" she asked, her voice barely able to sustain the question.

"I'm fine," he managed to say. "How are they treating you?"

"They're keeping me locked in a bathroom," she said, "but they are feeding me and they haven't touched me."

"I love you," he said.

"I love you, too," she said.

The phone went dead.

He handed the cell phone back to the guy and he put it in his pocket. "You want to see that wonderful wife of yours again, you'll play along tomorrow."

"I'll do what you asked," Danny said.

"Good," the guy said, patting Danny on the shoulder as he headed for the door. "Then I'll see you tomorrow evening for the grand reunion with your wife."

Danny could only nod as the man opened the door, glanced in both directions, and then turned toward the elevators.

The door banged closed.

In all his life Danny had never felt so alone as he did right at that moment.

He stared at the closed door for the longest time before returning to the couch to try to watch television.

It was going to be another long, sleepless night.

A very lonely night.

CHAPTER TWELVE

Sunday, April 9th
6:00 a.m.

THE WAKE-UP CALL and the sun behind the pulled drapes came way, way too early, as far as Bonnie was concerned.

Craig grabbed the phone, listened for a moment, hung it back up, and then just lay beside her half-snoring, half-moaning.

She had the alarm clock set to go off ten minutes after the wake-up call, and if she had anything to do with it, she was going to make sure she used those ten minutes to get as much sleep as she could.

But the wake-up call stirred the memories of what had happened yesterday, and last night.

After the second trip to the cart shed and the discovery of the stairs up into the service area, she and Craig, along with Maxwell and Hagar, had spent two hours planning the protection of the Senator today. Hagar was going to bring in an extra three men, and Maxwell would also have extra men on duty, but he never said how many.

Bonnie never expected to meet any of them. More than likely, knowing how efficient Maxwell had been so far, those extra men would be posing as staff, or even playing in the group ahead of the Senator.

By the time midnight had come around, they had ways figured to keep the Senator completely covered from the moment he left his room to the moment he got on the plane headed for Washington. And as Maxwell assured them, even beyond. Even the plane he was due to fly on would be double-checked and all baggage scanned with special equipment.

Bonnie lay there, letting the conversations from last night go through her mind as Craig snored lightly beside her.

Maxwell had told them he had an idea as to who might want Senator Knight hurt. He had gone on to describe Charles Robins and the relationship between Robins and Senator Knight, including the vote on Monday in Washington in the Senator's committee that would surely cripple Robins' companies. The two men had never met, but were deadly enemies.

"Robins has enough at risk to hurt a United States Senator to stop it?" Bonnie had asked.

"More than enough," Maxwell had replied. "But we don't know for sure that he is behind anything. It could be literally anyone."

"Or that anything is even going to happen," Craig had reminded them. "We're still only acting on what we overheard by accident."

"Which is why we can only protect the Senator and see if anyone makes a move," Maxwell had said.

None of them liked that option, but there just wasn't any other plan as far as they could figure.

Now Bonnie lay in the bed waiting for the alarm to go off, listening to Craig snore, trying not to think about what the day might bring. There wasn't going to be any more sleeping for her, that was for sure. And if she couldn't sleep, Craig shouldn't be able to either.

She flicked off the alarm and rolled over to cuddle with him, putting her naked body the entire length of his back. His skin felt wonderful against hers, firm and smooth and warm.

She rubbed her hand over his unshaven face and then down his chest.

He moaned softly and then rolled toward her and onto his back.

She pushed the covers back so she could see what she was doing in the early morning light coming through the curtains. He didn't move or open his eyes.

She wondered how long he could stay still with her against him. As it turned out, not long. He nuzzled his chin into her neck, letting his unshaven stubble brush lightly against the sensitive area under her ear. The motion sent shivers down her spine and she pushed against him.

Their parking in the cart garage last night had been rudely interrupted and they had been too tired by the time they got back to the room to even think about finishing. But this morning was another matter.

Just the thought of what they had started last night in the cart got her even more excited.

She glanced at the clock. They didn't have much time if they were going to meet Hagar for breakfast.

But they had enough.

To be continued…

Thunder Mountain Novels

Now Available at your favorite booksellers.

Now Available
from all your favorite booksellers in trade paper and electronic editions.

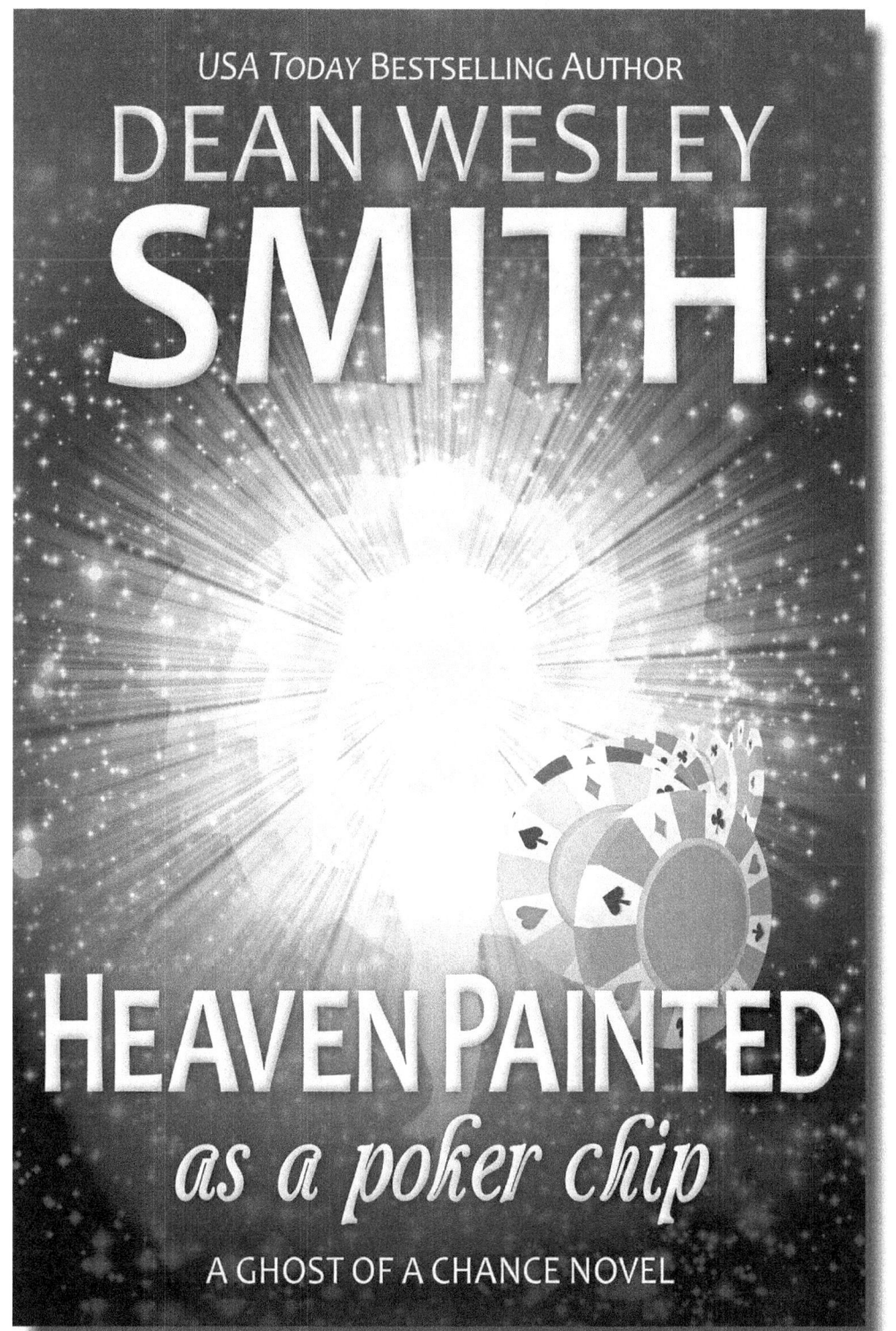

Hanna had a job and a life that just didn't let her meet men. So her boss invited her into a very special book club.

One night Hanna decided to take The Romance Novel Challenge. With luck she just might live happily ever after.

This might just change forever how you look at book clubs.

Published under the pen name Dee W. Schofield.

THE ROMANCE NOVEL CHALLENGE

ONE

HANNA WURMBRAND sat on her couch staring at the thick, brown envelope that had just been delivered. The special delivery package lay on her apartment's brown carpet next to her front door like it was a snake ready to bite her.

She had dropped the package once she realized what it was.

She had been expecting the package, yet it still had surprised her when the Fed Ex guy handed it to her.

She had closed the door, dropped the package, and then backed to her couch like moving away from a wild animal.

The entire idea had seemed like such a good idea at the time. A daytime-talk-show-idea to spice up her sex life.

Problem was Hanna Wurmbrand never watched daytime talk shows. In fact, she seldom watched television and she had no sex life.

At least she hadn't until tonight.

Tonight, thanks to that package, she might actually have a sex life again.

Hanna didn't even have a boyfriend and she hadn't had a date in a year at least, even though at five-three, long black hair, and a model's body, she was very attractive.

She got lots of those "looks" and some women called her "stunning."

She had had more than her share of dates back in high school, even though she was considered one of the "brains" of the place. And in college she went with Dave Pennant for most of the five years before he went slightly crazy and joined the Marines.

He had told her that killing the enemy took precedence over their relationship. She would have been fine if he had said, "defending the country" or "doing his civic duty" was more important. She could understand that, but Dave had said he would rather kill people than be with her.

That didn't do a girl's self respect any good at all.

She had had sex with exactly nine different men in her twenty-four years, with most of the encounters being short and nothing to even bother writing in a diary if she bothered to write in a diary, which she didn't.

Over the last year of no sex she had tried to remember a few of those encounters, but the only thing that came to mind was sweat dripping in her eyes and a lot of grunting.

Nothing at all romantic.

Every time she had felt like more of a conquest for the guy instead of a heroine being swept off her feet by a hero of a romance novel. Was there anything wrong about wanting to be swept off her feet? Clearly there must be, because it had never happened to her.

She had graduated from college a year before with three degrees, one in English and two in computer science.

She had the degrees after five years of college, but no boyfriend.

No hero.

She took the first job offered right out of college, a government job doing computer work for the CIA trying to track down any kind of threat to the country.

Mostly the job was her sitting in front of large computer screens and trying to

find patterns in massive amounts of data. It had sounded exciting at first, being on the front lines of the war against terror, but that excitement wore off after a few weeks.

She was good at her job and she did feel she was helping her country. And it paid well, but wow was it boring.

Every day she drove alone to work in her fancy new red Mustang, on nice days letting her long black hair fly in the breeze just like a romance heroine.

She always parked in a large parking lot in her assigned spot, went to a gray-walled office, and sat in front of two large computer screens. She only talked to the other three women in the office and her boss, Constance, all of whom were happily married and who mostly talked about their kids.

Sometimes the women around her talked about trying to find her a man, but it never had gone anywhere.

There were a lot of men in the building, mostly wearing gray suits with tight collars and thin ties. They seemed to all carry briefcases and not a one of them seemed to give her a second look.

She usually had lunch alone or with her coworkers, then went home alone at night and read romance novels until she fell asleep to wake in the morning and start the routine over again.

On the weekends she either worked extra or went from Washington up to Newark to her parents' home where she couldn't talk about her work and never met anyone.

Twice her parents had tried to set her up on blind dates. Both times had been a disaster. One guy she had tossed her drink on before the salads arrived at dinner.

It had been one year of the same routine at work. She was shut off from the world, friendships, and any chance of meeting a man even for casual sex.

It was enough to drive any normal young woman to extremes and a growing collection of vibrators.

Three months ago she had finally tried a dating service, only to cancel before all three dates the service set up for her. With Constance's permission, Hanna had run background checks on the three men while at work and all three had turned out to be losers.

One even had a stalking case pending.

Now, thanks to Constance, she had decided to do what was called *The Romance Novel Challenge*.

After Hanna's last attempt at the dating service, Constance had called Hanna into her office, closed the door so no one could overhear them, and then had sworn Hanna to secrecy.

Hanna had thought it was about something going on at work until Constance asked, "You getting tired of spending the night with vibrating appliances?"

Hanna started to deny everything, then laughed. "I have a few special ones I've grown fond of."

"I thought so," Constance said, smiling.

Constance was an attractive blond with extra large breasts that she kept tightly contained in gray or brown suits. Just as Hanna did, Constance kept her hair pulled back tight and pinned while at work and kept her makeup at work to a minimum.

But under that hidden shell, Hanna knew Constance had a spirit of adventure.

She was married to a man named Ben whom Hanna had never met, but he looked handsome in the photo on Constance's desk. Hanna had heard all kinds of stories about the two of them going skiing, camping, surfing, and other things. They didn't yet have kids, so they liked to have "adventures" as Constance called them.

"So why such a personal question?" Hanna had asked.

"I have a special invite to extend to you," Constance said and then went on to tell Hanna about *The Romance Novel Challenge*, calling it the best thing she did for her marriage.

It seemed that Constance and her husband were both members of a very *special* book club.

"The rules of the book club are simple," Constance had said. "A new romance novel is mailed sealed to two members. By the luck of the draw, two members of the club, one man, one woman, are paired up."

"And you have no idea who does the pairing?" Hanna had asked, still thinking Constance was pulling some sort of joke, even though it wasn't her style.

"No idea and I don't want to know," Constance had said. "With the unopened package, the book club member is sent to an assigned hotel suite where he or she meets a partner for the night."

"A dating book club?"

Constance had just shaken her head no and went on.

"The hotel suite is always fancy and is paid for by the monthly dues required to join the club. Both members of the book club, without talking, open their package at the same time and then take turns reading the supplied novel in the package to the other person while sipping champagne in the hotel suite."

"Now that's kinky," Hanna had said and Constance just kept going.

"No names are allowed except for the character names in the novel. The woman takes the heroine's name, the man takes the hero's name. When they reach the first kissing scene, they have to follow and act out what happens in the scene."

"And if it's a sex scene?" Hanna had asked, now starting to understand what this *book club* was all about.

Constance had just smiled. "They have to act that out as much as is possible inside the hotel suite. Then, without exchanging any names or personal information, they have to leave the hotel room, taking their books with them."

Hanna had been shocked and Constance could tell.

"Come on, Hanna," Constance had said. "You can't tell me you're a prude?"

"Far from it," Hanna had said. But inside she wasn't so sure.

Constance went on to tell how she and her husband attended the book club night once a month with different partners, then took their books home and finished the two books with each other the rest of the month, acting out every scene.

"And you never ask about the other person?" Hanna had asked.

"Never," Constance had said. "We both know what happens. The reason we are members is the excitement. And we both love to read, of course."

"Of course," Hanna had said.

Now Hanna sat on her couch staring at the special delivery package on her floor by her apartment front door.

It contained a book, a romance novel that would change her life if she let it.

Tonight was the night. She had gone through all the steps, been vetted by who knew who, signed all kinds of papers, and had paid the first month's fee of three hundred.

Since she had started the process, Hanna had to admit she had gotten more and more excited at the idea.

Constance had told her that some nights were pretty mild, other nights were wild and crazy. It all depended on the novel. And how much each person got into their character's role.

Hanna went over and picked up the package, resisting the impulse to hold it at arm's length.

It clearly had a book inside. She really wanted to open it, but instead she just looked at the address typed in the return address area.

Suite 611, Hyatt Regency Hotel. Seven P.M.

She glanced at her watch. It was four now and it would take her an hour to get to the Hyatt if traffic was bad. She had better get going.

She turned toward the bathroom, dropping the package back on the floor near the door.

She had a new book to read this Saturday night.

She just didn't know what the title or the plot was yet.

TWO

BY THE TIME Hanna made it across town to the Hyatt, she was early and scared to death. Her stomach was doing flip-flops and even with the night air being cool and the roof up and air conditioning on in her Mustang, she was sweating.

She got the key to the room from the front desk and then ducked into the restroom off the plush, plant-filled lobby. She put cold water on a towel to try to cool her face. But even the cold towel and two Tums didn't help the twisting in her stomach.

This had just seemed like such a good idea at the time.

And she did so love romance novels.

But even though she worked at the CIA, she just wasn't the adventurous type. She much more wanted a real hero to come along and sweep her off her feet to live happily every after.

Tonight might have a happy ending or two involved, but it sure wasn't a romance, anymore than a night home alone with her favorite vibrating appliance was a romance.

She stared at herself in the mirror.

She looked good, ready for a night on the town. He long black hair flowed around her face. Her shoulders were naked and the lace along the top of her black dress accented her breasts. Plus she had on her best underwear.

"You've gone this far, Hanna," she said to herself.

Her voice sounded as hollow as she felt.

This was stupid, but after a year, even stupid started to sound good.

She turned and headed back out into the lobby.

Hanna knew that all romances had meet-cutes where the two characters would meet and fall in love and then eventually hop into the sack, sometimes before trouble hit them, sometimes after.

Meeting her date tonight would be far from a meet-cute. More like a meet-scared-to-death.

As she went toward the elevators, she happened to glance up to see a very nervous-looking-man waiting for the elevator, an identical package to hers in his hand.

She stepped to one side behind a stone column protected by a large plant and watched him for a moment.

He was handsome and tall and he did have dark hair.

He could be the perfect hero of any romance novel. He even a little chiseled jaw.

But she could tell he was as frightened as Hanna felt.

Maybe more so.

And Hanna knew him.

She wasn't sure where, but she felt she knew him from somewhere.

He paced, waiting for the elevator and his nervousness calmed hers. For some reason it made him seem even more attractive. And he was already into Greek God country.

But wow did he look familiar.

She had never met him. She would remember meeting someone as good-looking as he was.

Then she gasped and wanted to throw up.

Now she knew why he looked familiar.

The man she was supposed to meet was Ben, Constance's husband.

Oh, no. Now what was she supposed to do?

The rules of the club were that no one was to know each other.

The elevator doors opened and Ben just stood there, not getting on.

After the doors closed he shook his head, took a deep breath, and pushed the button again.

The poor guy was scared to death.

How could a man that good-looking be that scared?

This time when the doors opened he stepped inside.

Hanna felt her own fear vanishing.

If Constance and Ben were so experienced at this book club thing, Ben never would have been acting like that.

He had never done this before either.

This book club thing was all a fake.

Constance had made up this entire thing, more than likely to try to spice up their marriage, and who more gullible to fall for it and help her and Ben out than Hanna, the shy recluse with too many vibrators.

Suddenly Hanna felt herself getting angry.

It would serve Constance right if Hanna did go up there and seduce her husband. They needed marriage counseling, not a book club.

Hanna started to toss the book into the garbage can next to the elevators and head for her car, then stopped.

Not showing up wouldn't help either.

She actually considered Constance a friend. An office friend, maybe, but at least some sort of friend. And clearly Constance and Ben needed some help. If Hanna didn't show, Constance and Ben would just try it with someone who might actually show up. And maybe destroy their marriage.

She had no plans on sleeping with that hunk of a man who had just gone upstairs, but she could at least help him and Constance out.

A few moments later she was pushing open the door to the suite on the 6th floor, the book club package in her hand.

The suite was fantastic. A huge, plush living room with far too many large, green plants accenting the tans and browns of the couches and chairs. The drapes were pulled, the lighting lower than normal to set a mood, the wide double-doors to the bedroom completely open showing a bed large enough to sleep a family of six on.

Facing her across the carpet was the guy she had seen getting on the elevator. Ben, Constance's husband.

He was clearly one of the most handsome men Hanna had ever seen. He was dressed perfectly in an expensive suit and a silk tie that matched the handkerchief tucked perfectly in his pocket. Up close he not only had a chiseled chin, but deep green eyes.

He could pose for covers of romance novels.

Hanna felt her stomach twist again. Maybe, just maybe she might spend a little time with him before calling his bluff. Someone like him she could have great fantasies about later with her vibrator collection.

Then she shook her head and cleared out that thought.

He nodded and nervously smiled with a smile that could just about break anyone's heart.

Wow!

The package in his hands looked like it might explode at any moment the way he squeezed and twisted it.

She smiled at him.

Maybe she should just jump his bones. Constance didn't know how lucky she had it. What was she thinking letting this man near another woman?

Hanna smiled back, then turned and shut the suite door and locked it.

Then she turned and tossed her book package on a small table near the door.

"All right, Ben," she said. "Let's drop the act and call Constance."

The man facing her for a moment looked puzzled. "You know Constance?"

His voice was deep and rich enough to give a person a sugar high.

"Of course I know Constance," Hanna said, heading past the hunk toward the bottle of champagne on the table. She needed a drink more than anything except sex at the moment.

"How?" he asked, still holding the book package.

"She's my boss and the one who pulled this book club scam on me. And I've seen pictures of you on her desk."

The hunk sort of looked at the book package in his hands, then tossed it on the closest couch like it would burn him if he held it any longer.

"So call her and tell her to get her ass down here," Hanna said. "We all have some talking to do."

The guy opened his mouth to say something, then shook his head and closed it. He took out his cell phone and hit a speed-dial number as Hanna poured herself a glass and then filled one for him as well. Might as well get a little something for her money. There was no doubt this night was going to be a bust.

THREE

"CONSTANCE," he said. "Hi."

He paused. Then he said, "Not so well. She says she recognized me from a picture on your desk and wants to talk to you down here."

He nodded and listened, then said, "All right. Thanks."

He clicked off the cell phone as Hanna watched.

"She said it would take her twenty minutes."

Hanna nodded and handed him a glass of champagne.

She had about a thousand questions she wanted to ask him, but most of them would wait until Constance got her. For the moment she was just going to stare at the guy and pretend he really was her date for the evening.

He took the glass and walked over to the window and opened the heavy drapes.

For the first time she noticed the faint background music playing in the suite. Romantic string music not too loud, but there.

Someone really had gone to a lot of work with every detail.

After taking a sip and staring out the window for a moment, he turned. "So you were willing to go through with this crazy book club idea?"

She shook her head. "More than likely not. I was about to chicken out when I recognized you getting on the elevator. I figured I was a friend of Constance and you two, if you were going to this level of planning and deception, really needed some marriage help."

For the second time he smiled and again she felt things melt inside her that shouldn't be melting in public.

He sipped his champagne. "Since you seem to know me, can I have the pleasure?"

"Sorry," she said, smiling back at him. "Hanna Wurmbrand. I work with Constance at the CIA and can't tell you any more without killing you."

He actually laughed softly at her stupid joke, the nervousness now long gone, replaced by a confidence that sort of radiated from every wonderful pore of his wonderful body.

And she was starting to feel more nervous by the moment.

She took another sip of the expensive champagne and then went back to the package she had tossed on the table near the door. She held it up. "Did you open yours?"

"No," he said. "I followed the rules."

She looked at him and frowned. "So you don't know which book Constance put in these packages?"

"Not a clue," he said, again smiling. "But I have to admit, this is a very, very elaborate set-up don't you think? I wonder how she got the idea?"

Hanna now felt even more confused. It was starting to sound like Ben hadn't been in on what Constance was doing. Or at least it seemed that way.

She put the package down without opening it yet again.

He took a sip, then excused himself and headed for the bathroom. "Nervous bladder and too much coffee on the way over here."

He vanished into the bathroom and closed the door, leaving her alone in the huge suite that now felt completely empty. It was stunning how one man could fill such a huge space with his presence.

Constance had no idea how lucky she was.

Hanna opened the door into the hallway and blocked it open with the security latch, then took her glass and went over to the window to stare out at the beautiful Washington DC night. If nothing else about this city, it could be beautiful.

Behind her there was a knock on the hotel room door.

She didn't know how she felt right now, but anger was just below the surface. More than likely she was going to be without a job in a few minutes, but she didn't care. She couldn't work with Constance anymore, not after this.

"Come on in, it's open."

Hanna turned as Constance and Ben came through the door from the hallway.

Hanna glanced at the bathroom door, which was still closed.

And Ben had changed into a sweater and tan slacks.

Constance looked around, worried, then stepped forward leaving Ben in the entry. "Are you all right?"

Hanna went to open her mouth to yell at her boss but didn't get out a word as the bathroom door opened and a second Ben stepped out.

"Constance, Ben," the man said. "This sure was an elaborate trick to play on us."

Hanna just stood there, her mouth open, staring at the three other people in the suite.

Two who were clearly twins. Identical twins.

"Sorry, brother," Ben said, stepping forward. "We figured it was the only way we could get you two together."

Constance nodded, smiling first at Hanna, then turning to the man who would have been Hanna's date. "You both hated blind dates and had had such bad luck with dating services. We felt you would be a perfect match if we could just get you together."

"So you tricked us," the man said, clearly some anger in his voice as he moved up to stand near Hanna, his champagne glass in his hand. "Why didn't you just introduce me to this wonderful and smart woman and let us see what might happen?"

Hanna looked over at him. She didn't even know his name.

"And how would we have done that?" Constance asked. "You two are impossible to break out of your schedules."

"A backyard cookout might have been an idea," he said. "You do barbeque, don't you, Ben?"

Ben, standing behind Constance, just nodded, clearly embarrassed.

Hanna held up her hand for silence.

"Constance, could I get a complete story please?" And then she turned to the man standing beside her. "And a name?"

"Gary," the man said, looking at her with those wonderful green eyes and a smile that could melt steel off a high-rise. "I am Ben's twin-and-clearly-smarter brother."

He reached out and they shook hands.

At that moment Hanna didn't want to let go of Gary's hand and he didn't seem to want to look away or let go of her hand as well.

She could get lost in those eyes if he let her. Wow, what a horrid romance novel cliché, but now she understood it. The swirling green of those eyes were just hypnotic.

Finally he did let go and she felt disappointment go to places of her body she didn't know could feel disappointment.

Constance shrugged. "We thought it would be impossible to get you two together, so we came up with the book club idea. It seemed like a great idea at the time."

"Hanna thought I was Ben," Gary said, "and was willing to stay here and help talk her friend through her marriage troubles."

Constance looked at Hanna, then just blushed and looked down. "Thank you," she said softly.

A very tense silence settled over the large suite with only the faint romantic background music floating through the roughness of the moment.

Hanna knew that it was up to her to do something to break this. Her job and the future of their family happiness and trust depended on her taking some action now.

She turned to the handsome hunk beside her. "I am all dressed up and so hungry I could eat the cork off that bottle."

Gary smiled and said nothing.

"How about we go get dinner, just you and me?"

"I would love that," he said, smiling, offering his arm.

She took it with a flourish, and she had to admit it felt wonderful. He felt strong and solid.

As they walked across the suite toward the door, she smiled at Constance and then at Ben. "Thank you for the very kind thoughts."

"Yes," Gary said to his brother and sister-in-law. "Weird, but interesting. Thank you."

As Gary opened the door for her, Hanna smiled at her boss. "And we expect a new bottle of champagne by the time we get back."

"And you two long gone," Gary said.

Constance and Ben both smiled huge smiles of relief.

"And leave the books," Hanna said, winking at Constance and making her blush as the door swung closed.

Hanna and Gary both laughed all the way down the hall, which Hanna knew was just the romance novel way of saying they lived happily-ever-after.

And she liked that idea a great deal.

—

Now Available
from all your favorite booksellers in trade paper and electronic editions.

Dean Wesley Smith

USA Today
Bestselling Writer

What Happens
When Socks
Go Rogue?

My Socks Rolled Down

When a fella wins the lottery, he learns all sorts of things, including how his magic socks really feel and how much they want some companion magic socks.

But sometimes, even after winning the lottery, magic socks don't always get what they want.

When socks go rogue. Never a pretty sight.

MY SOCKS ROLLED DOWN

A PERSON CAN only go so far in life with only one pair of magic socks. I know, I know, it's tough to imagine anyone only having one pair of magic socks, but you can come and search the three drawers in my small bedroom of my trailer, or look under my old second-hand green couch, or even check the coin-op laundry where I do my clothes. You won't find more than one pair. And I wear them every day and have for my entire life, all twenty-three years of it.

Sad, huh?

I've never had more than one pair. My mom gave them to me on her deathbed when I was born, rolling my little feet into the magic white cotton like putting little rubbers on two small penises. I don't remember the act, of course, but for some reason, that pair of magic socks are the only pair I have ever had.

As with all magic socks, they fit me perfectly and always have, growing perfectly with me right up until I stopped growing at five-four and a half.

And they never wear out. I wash them once a week, never leaving the washer or dryer while they are in there. I've heard of people stealing magic socks. It's bad enough only having one pair. I really can't imagine those few poor souls who have none.

What scares me is that I am only one pair of magic socks away from those poor, sockless souls. It would really be better if I could find a second pair. And three pair would be perfect. I might be able to do something with my life if I had three. That way I wouldn't have to do laundry so often.

Well, my dream to have enough money to buy more magic socks finally came true on January 13th at five in the evening. I was sitting there, watching my old television, hoping a truck didn't go by outside on the gravel road and shake the rabbit ears I had made of tin foil.

Every week I bought a lottery ticket, and every week I played the same numbers and watched the lottery drawing on television before turning the channel over to *Wheel*. Can't let a night go by without staring at Vanna's tits, you understand.

If I just had more than one pair of magic socks, she might talk to me.

I had my feet kicked up on the old pine coffee table while I sat on the couch drinking a Pabst, the best beer anywhere for the price. My boots were by the front door and my magic socks looked like it was time for another trip to the coin-op.

The first number was six, and the magic socks on my feet tingled a little. The last time they tingled like that I found a five-dollar bill on the sidewalk.

Six was the first number I always picked. It was how old I was when I shot my first rabbit with Grandad's twenty-two.

Next number was eight, and my old magic socks were giving me a real itchy feel. Last time they did that, when I was sixteen, I got laid for the first time by the mother of my best friend at the time.

Eight was the age I was when Dad brought home my new stepmother who stayed for two years before she disappeared one night and Dad came back kind of muddy and smiling.

I took a swallow of the Pabst and set it down on the coffee table as the next number came up.

Fourteen, and my magic socks were rubbing my feet so hard they were getting almost hot. In all my years I'd never had my magic socks get so excited.

"Down, boys, down," I said, reaching for the drawer and pulling out this week's ticket to make sure I had the numbers right. I did. The first three were six, eight, fourteen. Fourteen was when they arrested Dad for killing stepmom number three, or maybe it was number four, I wasn't sure.

The police talked to me for a while, then said that I was going to a foster home, but I ran off, got my clothes and hunting equipment and Dad's hidden rifle and ammunition and made it off into the mountains along the coast. I camped out until I turned eighteen, which was my next number.

The guy on the television watched the old ping-pong ball slide up the tube and he said, "Eighteen."

My magic socks felt like dancing, so that was what I did, got up and danced around the living room for a moment, letting them celebrate. I really liked how they were hugging my feet like a woman hugging a long lost lover. That felt great to be honest.

With four right numbers I had already won a few thousand. Just one more of the two and things would be really fine.

My next number was twenty. That's when I moved into this doublewide trailer up Jenson Creek.

The old guy that lived here before me is buried out back, and so far no one has missed him at all. I told two neighbors he got sick and moved into Portland and I was renting the trailer. That seemed to keep them happy, and I buried the old man deep enough no coyotes were going to dig him up. Now after three years, a tree was growing on his grave. Nice little thing, too.

The old guy had on his one pair of magic socks when I shot him, but weirdly enough, when I went to shoot him, my aim suddenly went bad and instead of hitting the old guy in the chest, I hit him in the foot, right through one magic sock, blowing it all apart.

As the old guy jumped backwards, screaming and swearing and holding his torn-up foot, I shot again.

And again the gun seemed to have a mind of its own and it shot the guy in the other foot. I gave up shooting him and tried to pound his head, but I just kept missing like he was moving around, even though he wasn't. The old guy bled out after a few minutes and died anyway, and his magic socks were worthless and dead as well. A real bummer and to this day I have no idea why I couldn't shoot straight that day.

The announcer said, "Twenty."

My magic socks sort of flipped my feet up in the air so hard I went over backwards, smashed into the wall and hit the floor hard.

Then, even though I was hurting something awful, the socks got me to my feet and ran around the small living room of the trailer, bouncing me off the walls like I was so much kindling.

"Slow down!" I shouted at the white socks on my feet, but they didn't.

I heard a thought clear as a bell in my mind. *You dumb idiot, don't you realize you've just won enough money to buy a dozen more magic socks and I won't have to put up with your smelly feet all the damned time.*

My magic socks could talk to me. Wow!

"How come you've never said anything before now?"

What for? Holding a conversation with you would be like talking to an outhouse wall, like you did for all those years we were camping.

"Hey, nothing wrong with—"

Shut the hell up and let's see if you've won the entire thing!

The announcer said, "Twenty-three."

My final number, because that's how old I am now.

An instant later my magic socks had me walking on the ceiling, then doing a moon-walk backwards across my ceiling and down the wall.

Now you can buy a thousand pairs of magic socks. And you can retire me.

"What happens if I don't want a thousand pair?"

The magic socks stopped me cold in the middle of the floor. *What did you mean by that?*

"I didn't know socks could talk. I'm not so sure I want all them living here and talking to me."

There was a nice silence in my mind, like normal, then my magic socks sort of growled low and deep, like a wild animal ready to attack.

Then I decided something real clear like. "You know, I could buy a huge house and have rooms full of magic socks and tell them that none of them could ever talk to me. Only to each other."

I smiled for a moment before I realized that my magic socks had made me say all that.

"I'm not going to do that and you can't make me," I said.

Again there was a low growl, then the socks said inside my head. *That's it. I'm still young, I have a life to live, other socks to meet, baby magic socks to create. I don't need to stay here with you anymore.*

"You're my socks and I'm not taking you off," I said.

You are such an idiot. You think you are in control. All of you humans believe that, letting us live off your energy, giving us special places in your life. But we control you, every last one of you. And idiot boy, it's time I moved on.

Now I was getting mad. "And just how do you think you're going to do that if I don't take you off?"

The voice of the socks sort of gave off a snorting sound, then I walked against my will over to the wall, up the wall, and out onto the middle of the ceiling, hanging upside down from my white socks.

Oops, the voice inside my head said, and suddenly I was hurtling toward the green shag carpet. I tried to get my arms up to break my fall, but I couldn't. I hit on the top of my head and flopped sideways.

"That hurt!" I shouted.

Damn it all, the voice said.

My magic socks were trying to kill me!

No, shit, Sherlock.

With that my magic socks walked me to my phone and made me pick it up and dial 911.

Then, when the operator asked what was my emergency, I said without wanting to, "I killed an old guy and he's buried out under a small tree in my backyard. I can't take the guilt. I'm going to kill myself."

Then I laid the phone down and walked down the hall to where I kept my rifles, all of them loaded.

My magic socks weren't allowing me to say anything, so instead I just thought at the socks really, really hard that they should stop.

Wow, a thought, the socks said. *From the idiot. Stunning.*

"Why are you doing this?" I asked as at the same time I dug into the guns and pulled out my favorite without wanting to.

Because I'm tired of your sweating feet, I want to meet other magic socks as you call them. Actually we are called Yekcoj, a race millions of years older than humans.

I just didn't believe that. My magic socks had lost it, gone off the deep end.

You want to know what we really look like?

Suddenly my white socks shifted around my feet and combined, with both of my legs fitting into the teeth-lined mouth of what looked like a nasty groundhog, only with scales and ten eyes and four arms.

To be honest, I'm tired of you standing and walking around in my mouth. Why my people thought this was a good idea is beyond me.

One long black eye blinked at me and then my magic socks were back, white as ever.

The socks walked me back out to the living room. The operator on the phone was saying, "Sir! Sir! Help is on the way."

I sat down on the couch against my will, put the gun in my mouth against my will, and put my finger on the trigger against my will.

Thanks for the worst twenty-three years any socks could ever dream of living. See ya.

I pulled the trigger.

The socks laughed and pulled themselves off of my body's feet.

I could see my body through the eyes of the magic socks, or weird groundhog or whatever it was. The gunshot had blown most of my brain against the front window and some part of my skull was hanging off the drapes.

Now you've done it, I thought at the socks.

What…? What…? What are you doing here? You can't still be here, in my mind, you're dead.

Never heard of the Four Laws of Magic Socks, have you?

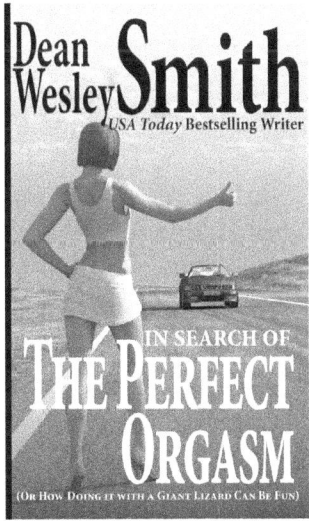

I hadn't known them either until I died. Now I knew them and a lot more stuff I had never known when alive. Weird how dying made me a lot smarter.

What four laws? the magic socks asked.

It was part of the treaty with humans when they allowed your people to come here to live.

I hadn't known that either until that gun blew my brains out.

Law #1: You must always let humans wear you at any time.

Yeah, yeah, the magic socks said.

Law #2: You can't speak to any humans or let them know of your presence. Broke that one, didn't you?

Just go on, my magic socks said.

Law #3: You must always follow the orders of your human unless it conflicts with Law #4, which is that Magic Socks cannot allow harm to come to humans unless otherwise avoided.

Oh, my magic socks said softly.

Let's get back into place on my feet, I thought at my not-so-faithful magic sock companion, *so when the Magic Sock police get here, they'll know what to do with you and with me.*

Together we moved over to my body and formed clean white socks around my now very dead feet.

Outside, coming up the dirt road, the police sirens filled the narrow valley. Back when I was alive, that would have scared me enough to go get my gun. Now it just made me laugh.

Too bad I'm never going to get to collect the winnings on that ticket. I might have bought a big place and lots of your friends for you to play with.

Please, please, please would you just shut up for a few minutes? my magic socks said, clearly angry.

Nah, I thought at my magic socks as together we rested around the feet of my dead body. *I figure we can spend our last few hours together going over all the great years we had together.*

My magic socks made a groaning sound.

Remember that day when I was four and had to take a crap really bad, and didn't make it to the bathroom and crapped all over you? Wasn't that a great time? I think that pulled us closer together, don't you?

My magic socks said nothing, once again following the Second Law of Magic Socks.

The police knocked hard on the door, then shoved it open, covering their mouths when they saw the mess my brains left on the window and drapes.

"He's got magic socks on," one cop said, pointing to my feet and me and my magic sock companion.

"How could he do this, then? Magic socks won't let you hurt yourself."

Both cops looked at each other, then one of them said, "Rogue Socks."

"Call the Magic Sock Police representative," another cop said. "If his socks went rogue, it means this guy is still in there with the socks."

I made old magic socks move what used to be my big toe up and down like I was doing a mini-nod.

"Shit," one cop said and both backed up.

So they call you rogues, huh? I thought at my magic socks.

My socks said nothing.

Remember that time I was all out of toilet paper and needed to use you to wipe my ass? Great fun, huh?

Hey, idiot-boy, my magic socks thought at me, *with all your new knowl-*

edge you should know what's going to happen next, now that you told those cops I was a rogue and you were trapped in here with me.

"We do it together," one cop said.

"Count of three," the other cop said as they stepped closer to me and my magic socks.

Suddenly I realized what the two cops planned to do. When magic socks went rogue and killed a human, they had to be killed at once, not only to stop the rogue socks, but to release the soul of the departed.

Hey! I thought at my magic socks, suddenly very panicked. *Get us out of here. Make a run for it!*

I'm not allowed to talk to you, remember?

But you're supposed to follow my instructions. Run!

The two cops got closer and both aimed their pistols, one at my right foot, one at my left.

I don't have to, my magic socks said. *I'm rogue, remember?*

"One," a cop said, pointing a big gun at my old right foot while the other cop pointed at my left foot.

Don't you want to live?

My magic socks laughed. *With you? Not any more. Twenty-three years was more than enough.*

"Two," the cop said.

I should have used you for toilet paper more often, I thought at my magic socks.

I should have killed you long before now, my magic socks thought back.

Screw you, I thought at my magic socks.

Another original thought, my magic socks thought back.

"Three," the cop said.

There was a huge explosion and I could feel myself slipping away, fading into the darkness.

And the last thing I heard before I vanished into the blackness was the last thought of my magic socks.

Oh, thank the Great Sock this is over!

DEAN WESLEY SMITH

USA Today BESTSELLING AUTHOR

MELODY RIDGE

A THUNDER MOUNTAIN NOVEL

I *wrote for decades about a jukebox that took a listener back to the memory attached to a song. The series consists of more than twenty short stories and gathered numbers of award nominations and movie options.*

Then in 2012, I started work on the Thunder Mountain series of novels, starting with the novel Thunder Mountain. Time travel novels set partially in the Old West.

Now, finally, in Melody Ridge, I combined the two worlds and reveal the origin of the jukebox for the first time.

MELODY RIDGE
A Thunder Mountain Novel

For Kris, who has been a supporter of both the jukebox stories and the Thunder Mountain stories since the beginning.

AUTHOR'S NOTE

Parts of this novel were published originally in much altered forms as short stories. All places and characters in this novel are fiction. However, Roosevelt was destroyed in 1909 by a flood and covered by a lake. Sadly, the Monumental Summit Lodge does not exist.

PART ONE
The Gift of Music

CHAPTER ONE

December 24th, 2015
Boise, Idaho

THE STEREO BEHIND the bar was playing soft Christmas songs as Ridley Stout clicked the lock to the front entrance of the Garden Lounge and flicked off the outside light. He could feel the cold of the night through the wood door and the heat of the room surrounding him. It didn't often snow on Christmas Eve, but it felt like it might tonight.

He took a deep breath.

Christmas Eve was finally here.

He could see the entire lounge and the backs of his four best friends sitting at the bar. He had never been much into decorating with Christmas stuff, and this year was no different. His only nod to the season was a small Christmas candle for each table and booth.

Some customer had tied a red ribbon on one of the plants over the middle booth, and the Coors driver had put up a Christmas poster declaring Coors to be the official beer of Christmas.

The candles still flickered on the empty tables, but the rest of the bar looked normal. Dark brown wood walls, dark brown carpet, an old oak bar, and his friends.

The most important part was the friends.

His four best friends' lives were as empty as his. Tonight, on the first Christmas Eve since he bought the bar, he was going to give them a chance to change that. That was his present to them.

It was going to be an interesting night.

"All right, Stout," Carl said, twisting his huge frame around on his bar stool so that he could face Stout as he wound his way back across the room between the empty tables and chairs. "Just what's such a big secret that you kick out that young couple and lock the door at seven o'clock on Christmas Eve?"

Stout laughed. Carl always got right to the point. With Big Carl you always knew exactly where you stood.

"Yeah," Jess said from his usual place at the oak bar beside the waitress station, "what's so damned important you don't want the four of us to even get off our stools?"

Jess was the short one of the crowd. When he stood next to Carl, the top of Jess's head barely reached Carl's neck. Jess loved to play practical jokes on Carl. Carl hated it.

"This," Stout said as he pulled the custom-made felt cover off the old Wurlitzer jukebox and, with a flourish, dropped the cloth over the planter and into the empty front booth. His stomach did a tap dance from nerves as all four of his best customers whistled and applauded, the sound echoing in the furniture and plant-filled room.

The Wurlitzer was the old classic Bubbler 1015 model, made in 1946 from wood and glass and a little plastic to play seventy-five records. But along the way someone had taken out the old interior and replaced it with a 45 record exchanger and some interior workings he had been afraid to even touch.

David, his closest friend in the entire world, downed the last of his scotch-rocks and swirled the ice around in the glass with a tinkling sound. Then, with his paralyzed right hand, he pushed the glass, napkin and all, to the inside edge of the bar.

"So after hiding that jukebox in the storage room for the last ten months, we're finally going to get to hear it play?"

"You guessed it," Stout said. He ran his shaking fingers over the cold smoothness of the chrome and polished wood and glass. He had carefully typed onto labels the names of over sixty Christmas songs, then taped the labels next to the red buttons. Somewhere in this jukebox he hoped there would be a special song for each man.

A song that would trigger a memory and a ride into the past.

His Christmas present to each of them.

Stout took a deep breath and headed behind the bar. "I hope," he said, keeping his voice upbeat, "that it will be a little more than just a song. You see, that jukebox is all that I have left from the first time I owned a bar. Since I've owned the Garden Lounge, the jukebox has never been played."

Jess, his dress shirt open to the third button and his tie hanging loose around his neck, spun his bar napkin on top of his glass. "So why tonight?"

"Because a year ago on Christmas Eve I made the decision to buy the Garden Lounge, and try running a bar again."

"And I'm glad you did," David said, lifting his drink in his good left hand in a toast.

"Here, here," Fred said, raising his drink high above his head and spilling part of it into his red hair. "Where else could we enjoy a few hours of Christmas Eve before going home to be bored?"

All four men raised their glasses in agreement as Stout laughed and joined them with a sip of the sweet eggnog he always drank on Christmas Eve. No booze, just eggnog.

"It's been a good year," Stout said, "especially with friends like you. That's why I've decided to give each of you a really special present."

"Oh, to hell with the present," Jess said. "How about another drink? I've got a wife to face and knowing her, she ain't going to be happy that I'm not home yet."

"Is she ever happy?" David asked.

Jess shook his head slowly. "And I wonder why I drink."

Jess slid his glass down the bar as he always did at least once a night. Stout caught it and tipped it upside down in the dirty glass rack.

"I'll fix everyone a last Christmas drink as you open the first part of your presents," Stout said.

He reached into the drawer under the cash register and pulled out four small packages. Each was the size of a ring box wrapped in red paper and tied with a green ribbon.

"Awful little," Fred said as Stout slid one in front of each man and then put four special Christmas glasses up on the mat over the ice. He'd had the name of each man etched on the glass.

"You know what they say about small packages," Jess said, twisting the package first one way, then the other while inspecting it. "But knowing Stout, the size will be a good indication."

"You just wait," Stout said.

"Great glasses," David said, noticing them for the first time. "They part of the present?"

"Part of the evening," Stout said.

Stout let each man inspect his own empty glass before he filled it. The names were etched in gold leaf over the logo of the Garden Lounge. Stout had had the glasses done to remember the night. He hoped he would have more than a few glasses left when it was all over.

Carl was the first to get his present unwrapped. "You were right, Jess. It's a quarter." He held it up for everyone to see. "Looks like old Stout here is giving us a clue that we should tip more."

Stout laughed as he filled Carl's glass with ice. "No. It's a trip, not a tip."

Stout finished pouring Carl's drink and slid it in front of him.

"Since you unwrapped yours so fast, you get to go first." Stout nodded at the jukebox. "But there are rules."

"There seem to be a lot of rules around here tonight," Fred said.

Everyone laughed.

Stout held up a hand for them to stop. "Trust me. This will be a special night."

"So give me the rules," Carl said.

Stout leaned on the dishwasher behind the bar so no one could see that he was shaking.

"On that jukebox is every damn Christmas song I could find. Pick one that reminds you of a major point in your life—some *thing* or *time* or *event* that changed your life. After you punch the button, but before the music starts, tell us what the song reminds you of."

Carl shook his head. "You know, Stout. You've gone and flipped out."

"Sometimes I think so, too," Stout said. He wasn't kidding. Sometimes he really did think so.

"Tonight seems to be ample proof," David said, holding up the quarter.

"Just trust me, that is a very special jukebox. Try it and I think you'll discover what I mean."

Carl shrugged, took a large gulp out of his special glass and set it carefully back on the napkin. "What the hell. I've played stranger games."

"So have I," Jess said. "I remember once with a girl named Donna. She loved to—"

David hit him on the shoulder to make him stop as Carl twisted off his stool and moved over to the jukebox to study the songs.

Stout watched as Carl bent over the machine to read the list. At six-two, two hundred and fifty pounds, Carl was all muscle, with hands that looked like he was going to crush a glass at any moment. A carpenter in the real world outside the walls of the Garden Lounge, his small business sometimes employed four or five workers. Mostly he built houses, although his big project this year had been Doc Harris's new office. That had taken Carl seven months and helped him on the financial side.

Carl had never married and no one could get much information about his past out of him. He had no hobbies that anyone knew of, and winter or summer Stout had never seen Carl dressed in anything other than work pants and plaid shirts. He kept his graying black hair cropped short and never wore a hat, no matter how hard it was raining.

After a moment bent over the jukebox, Carl's large shoulders slumped, almost as if someone had put a heavy weight square in the middle of his back. With effort he stood, turned around and faced the bar. His face was pale, his dark eyes a little glazed.

"Found one. Now what?"

Stout took a deep breath. It was too late to back out now. These were his friends.

"Put the quarter in and pick the song."

Stout's voice was shaking and David looked at Stout. David could tell something was bothering Stout.

Stout took a deep breath and went on. "Before the song starts tell us the memory the song brings back."

Carl shrugged and dropped the quarter into the slot. The quiet in the Garden seemed to almost ring as he slowly punched the buttons for his song.

"Anything else?" he asked as the jukebox clicked and the mechanism moved to find the record.

"Just state what the song reminds you of. And remember, you only have the length of the song—usually about two and a half minutes. Okay?"

Carl shrugged. "Why?"

"You'll know why in a moment. But remember that. It might be important. Now tell us the memory."

Carl glanced at the jukebox and then quietly said, "This song reminds me of the night my mother almost died."

Stout thought his heart had stopped. This wasn't what he had planned. Why did Carl have to pick a memory like that? This was Christmas Eve. Most people would have memories of good times. Times they wanted to relive. Damn, it was too late now.

"Two and a half minutes, Carl," Stout managed to choke out. "Remember that."

Carl glanced over at Stout with a frown as "I'm Dreaming of a White Christmas" started.

Then Carl was gone from the bar, physically gone, back into his memory.

CHAPTER TWO

About five years later…
June 9th, 2020
Central Wilderness Area, Idaho

RYAN SADDLER SAT on the expansive wooden balcony of the Monumental Lodge, sipping a Diet Coke, and just staring out over the valley below and the sharp-peaked mountains beyond. The valley was so far down the sheer mountainside below the lodge, the tall pines along the stream looked like dark green child's toys. And the mountain peaks seemed like paintings against the deep blue sky. Most of them had streaks of snow still covering them.

The lodge sat on the edge of the most primitive area in all of the lower forty-eight states. And the most beautiful, as far as Ryan was concerned.

The massive balcony seemed to stretch the entire length of the huge lodge, and was covered in tables and chairs so customers could have food out here or just sit and enjoy a drink with the view.

Right now, he was the only person on the huge deck, which suited him just fine.

Ryan had on jeans, tennis shoes, and a heavy dress shirt with the sleeves rolled up. He had no doubt the shirt would not be enough for the mountain air very soon, as the sun slowly went behind the distant peaks. He had brought a light tan jacket that hung over the back of the wooden chair at the moment, but he was delaying putting it on, instead just letting himself enjoy the cool bite to the crisp fresh air.

More than anything, he was enjoying the intense silence. He had no idea it was possible to hear silence, but on the top of this summit, looking out over a hundred miles of steep mountain ranges and deep valleys, silence was very real and very intense.

He couldn't believe he was even sitting here on this deck. Until a couple days ago, he didn't even know this place existed. It was a very long way from his office at the University of California Berkeley and his small apartment on the hill overlooking the city of Berkeley. But when Duster Kendal asked Ryan if he was interested in a very special project, he had said yes without even asking what the project was about.

Or even where he would have to go to work on it.

Duster and his wife, Bonnie, were two of the greatest theoretical mathematicians to ever live. Ryan had never met either one, but had heard nothing but incredible things about them for his entire time getting his doctorate in mathematics. In fact, he had published a couple of papers expanding Bonnie and Duster's theories in a tiny area of the nature of time and space and energy.

It was just after his second publication that Duster had called.

Not only had Ryan been excited about meeting Duster and Bonnie, but he hoped to meet Brice Lincoln and Dixie Smith, the two theoretical mathematicians who worked with Bonnie and Duster. They were only a couple years older than Ryan, but had already become legendary in their advances in the nature of space and time.

Theoretical mathematics at the level Ryan was working was a very small world and he felt lucky now to get to meet the people on the leading edge.

When Duster had picked Ryan up at the Boise airport and they had headed out of town, Duster had told Ryan that there would be another member of the team. Doctor Talia Marr would be joining them.

Ryan had only heard of her a few times, since her field of expertise was in the mathematics of sound waves. She was a professor at University of Wisconsin-Madison. He had never met her.

It seemed Bonnie and Doctor Marr planned on flying into the lodge by helicopter. Ryan wouldn't have minded that as well, since Duster had brought him up to this eight-thousand-foot summit on one of the scariest, twisted, and narrowest roads imaginable.

From the Boise airport, with a stop for lunch in Cascade, Idaho, it had taken them almost seven hours of driving.

Most of the drive, Duster had asked Ryan about his life growing up in Phoenix, his love of music as a member of a band in high school, and his extreme love of mathematics.

A lot of Ryan's questions of Duster were deflected by statements like, "When we're all together we'll explain that."

It seemed that Duster didn't want to explain something twice, and Ryan didn't blame him.

But after seven hours with Duster, Ryan got the feeling he had been riding with a very wise and old man, even though Duster wasn't more than six or seven years older than Ryan. But Duster just had this air about him and a laugh that seemed to be more amusement at the world than anything.

Just as Ryan gave up the fight against the chilling air and was putting on his jacket, Duster arrived wearing a long brown oilcloth coat that brushed the ground and a cowboy hat. He looked like a marshal from the old west more than a famous theoretical mathematician. He stood tall and walked with purpose. And the long coat and cowboy hat seemed to really accent that.

"Bonnie is getting Dr. Marr checked into her room," Duster said, sitting down and putting his cowboy boots up on a second chair. "They will join us in a minute."

"Thanks for showing me this incredible place," Ryan said, indicating both the massive log lodge behind them and the mountains below them.

Ryan had been blown away by his room after he had checked in. Not only was it in perfect style of 1900's furniture and bathroom fixtures, but the bed was a real honest featherbed that when he dropped on it, the bed had seemed to swallow him in the most perfect comfort he could have ever imagined.

It was as if nothing had been changed at all in this lodge since the day it had been built in 1902.

Ryan couldn't imagine how much Duster was paying for the three rooms at this time of the year, but from what Ryan understood, Bonnie and Duster had no issue at all with money. They sure gave enough of it away in endowments and mathematics scholarships.

"Dr. Saddler, I presume," a woman's voice said from the door.

Ryan jumped to his feet and turned to face the smiling Bonnie Kendal. She had her hand extended and he took it, noting the firm, strong grip. For a mathematician, she clearly worked out a lot.

She stood about his height at five-eleven and had her long brown hair pulled

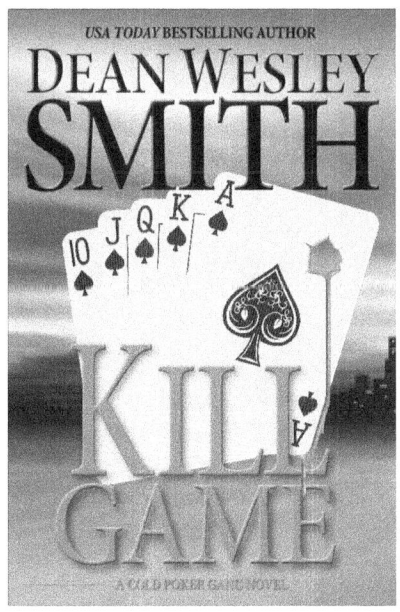

back and tied. She had on jeans, tennis shoes, a white blouse and a dark jacket that she left unzipped at the moment.

"Wonderful meeting you," Ryan said. "And please, call me Ryan."

It seemed odd to Ryan for Bonnie or Duster to call him a doctor, since each of them had far more degrees than he could ever dream of attaining.

"I will, Ryan," Bonnie said. "If you call me Bonnie."

As Ryan sat down, she went around, knocked her husband's boots off the chair and sat down. "You order us a drink?"

"Of course," Duster said, smiling. "Smooth flight?"

"As smooth as it gets when flying over these mountains," she said.

She looked at Ryan. "Enjoy the drive?"

"Never been on a road like that before," Ryan said. "But beside the cramp in my hand from hanging on to the door handle so hard, it was actually enjoyable."

"You ought to have seen it before it was paved," Duster said, laughing.

"No thanks," Ryan said. He didn't even want to pretend to imagine that road not paved.

"That room is wonderful," a woman's deep voice said from behind him and again Ryan scrambled to his feet.

Duster also stood.

"Dr. Marr I presume?" Duster asked, extending his hand.

"Just Talia," the woman said, shaking Duster's hand as Ryan tried to catch his breath. The woman was the most attractive woman he had ever seen. How was that possible?

The woman stood just a couple inches shorter than Ryan and also had on jeans and tennis shoes, plus a white Wisconsin sweatshirt over what looked like a red blouse.

She had short blonde hair and the brightest green eyes Ryan had ever seen.

He had no idea Dr. Talia Marr was so good-looking. Stunning, actually.

"Talia. Call me Duster."

"This is Dr. Ryan Saddler," Duster said.

Talia turned to shake Ryan's hand and both of them just sort of froze, staring into each other's eyes.

Finally Ryan managed to shake her hand, which felt wonderful and smooth and silky.

Then somehow in slow motion he was sure, he nodded. "Please just call me Ryan."

He was beyond happy that his voice didn't crack.

She nodded. "Talia."

At that moment, a woman with three drinks on a tray came out of the lodge and broke the moment. Thankfully.

Somehow, Ryan managed to get seated again before his knees gave out or he fainted dead away from not breathing.

He had never had a reaction about a woman like that before.

Ever.

It must have been the high altitude and clean air.

CHAPTER THREE

December 24th, 1995
Boise, Idaho

THE URINE and disinfectant smells of the nursing home washed over Carl like a wave over a child on the beach.

He grabbed the doorframe and held on, feeling dizzy, confused.

A moment before he had been standing in front of the jukebox at the Garden Lounge, playing a stupid game that Stout, the owner of the bar, had insisted on playing. Carl had that memory firmly placed in his mind, as well as the memories of the last twenty years.

Yet he also had fresh memories of driving to the nursing home this Christmas Eve. Memories of wishing he could go back to college, wishing he could do something to put Mother out of her pain and suffering.

And a very clear, very fresh memory of his decision to help her die with some dignity as she had asked.

It had been a Sunday afternoon, right after the second stroke. She had not only asked, she had begged him to help her if another stroke took her mind and left her body alive. That had been her worst fear.

Yet he hadn't done anything.

The part of his mind that remembered the Garden Lounge knew that she had suffered three more strokes.

He had been too afraid.

He squeezed the doorframe until his hand hurt. Christmas music played softly down the hall. "I'm Dreaming of a White Christmas," the same song he had just punched up on the jukebox at the Garden Lounge.

How...?

This made no sense.

He forced himself to take a deep breath and look around. There was a white-haired nurse sitting behind the counter at the nurse's station. His mother was in her bed across the small room. Slight, wasted remains of the woman she had once been. She no longer recognized him or anyone else from her life. Most of the time she sat in a wheelchair and just drooled, her head hanging limp.

The doctors had said she would never recover from the series of strokes. Carl knew from his memory of the Garden Lounge that she would spend the next five years in that bed and chair. He would grow to hate this room, hate his own fear, hate his own inability to do something to help her.

He glanced over at his own hand against the doorframe. It was his hand all right, only young. No scar where the broken window cut it last year. No deep tan from being outside for so long.

He was somehow in his young body, his old memories combined with his young ones. He felt dizzy with the conflicting memories and thoughts. His mouth was dry.

He could really use a drink.

From down the hall the song reached its halfway point and Carl felt panic filling his mind. Stout and that damn jukebox of his had given him a second chance. An opportunity to do what he had always wished he had done. Now he was wasting it by doing what he had done the first time.

Nothing.

He took a deep, almost sobbing breath.

This time would be different.

He checked the hall and then moved across the room and around to the other side of his mother's bed. She smelled of urine. The nurses would change her diapers many times in the next five years, and many times he would be forced to help.

"This is what you wanted, Mom."

He swallowed the bile trying to force its way up into his mouth.

"I'm doing what you asked."

He pulled the edge of the pillow up and over her face, pressing it hard against her mouth and nose.

"I love you, Mom," he said, softly. "I've learned to be strong. I hope you would be proud of me."

She struggled, trying to twist her head from side to side. But he held on, wanting to be sick, wanting to let go, wanting to let her breathe, but not wanting her to suffer day after day for five long years.

Finally the tension in her body eased and her head became heavy in his hands.

Very heavy.

He gently stroked her soft hair as he held the pillow in place for another fifteen seconds. Then he eased his mother's head back into a more comfortable position.

He stood up straight and took a deep breath, never taking his gaze from the face of his dead mother.

A feeling of sadness filled him at the same time as a lightness, as if a great weight had been lifted from his shoulders.

"Thanks, Stout," he said out loud as the last faint chords of the song died and took his future memories with it.

CHAPTER FOUR

December 24th, 2015
Boise, Idaho

AS THE LAST few notes of the Bing Crosby song faded into the carpet and booths of the Garden Lounge, the air shimmered as if a heat wave had passed though the room.

None of the plants moved.

And Stout felt no heat.

But he knew what it meant.

He glanced around the room. Fred was sitting where Carl had sat, and the planter that Carl had built under the east window was gone, replaced with two chairs.

Carl wasn't coming back, that much was clear.

During the song, Stout had calmed the other three men down, explained that Carl had gone back into a memory. Then, on the excuse of Carl needing a drink when he returned, Stout took Carl's glass and moved over to the jukebox.

Stout had stood there with one hand on the cool chrome of the jukebox for the last half of the song.

He glanced down at the glass with Carl's name in his hand. So it had worked. Anything anyone held if they touched the jukebox stayed in this timeline after the switch. Good.

And because Stout was touching the jukebox, he still remembered Carl. Carl had changed something in his past and his new future no longer brought him to the Garden Lounge.

Stout hoped it was a good new future for him.

Stout studied the jukebox to see if anything had changed. Damned if he knew how it worked. He had just taken it from storage in his old bar and fixed it, put a favorite record in, and the next thing he knew he had found himself facing his old girlfriend, Jenny, in his young body.

Scared him so bad all he did was sit there and stare at her. He had wanted to be with her more than anything else, but he had not had the courage or the desire to ask her to stay with him. On their third year of being together, she had gone back to college while he stayed in their hometown to work. That semester she had met someone else, and by Christmas she was married to that other someone.

The song Stout had played on the jukebox had been their song. It had been playing the afternoon he had had a chance to stop her leaving. And that was where the jukebox took him and left him for the entire length of the song.

The next day he played the song again and the same thing happened again. He did nothing but sit and stare at her.

He didn't play another song on the jukebox until he had all the possibilities figured out, including what would happen if he had changed something, as Carl obviously had done.

"What the hell are you doing over there?" David asked, twisting his custom drinking glass in his good hand.

"Yeah," Jess said. "You going to tell us what we're supposed to do with these quarters?" He flipped it, caught it and turned it over on the bar. "Heads."

"Play a song," Stout said.

None of them remembered Carl or Stout's explanation of where he had gone or anything Carl had done, which included playing the last song. Carl had never existed for them because they had not been touching the jukebox.

Stout moved back around the bar, dumped the remainder of Carl's drink out and set the glass carefully on the back bar.

"Who's Carl?" David asked.

"Just another friend I wanted to give a glass to."

"So how come you want us to play a song?" Jess asked.

Stout took a long drink of his eggnog and let the richness coat his dry throat. He was going to miss Carl. Stout just hoped Carl was happy. Maybe sometime over the next few days Stout would look up Carl's name in the phone book. Maybe Carl had stayed around town. He would never remember the Garden, but it would be nice to see him again and see how things ended up for him.

"You all right?" David asked.

All three men were staring.

"Yeah, I'm fine. I was just thinking about how songs are like time machines. When you hear one it takes you back to some special moment when the song was playing."

Stout pointed at the little boxes and the quarters. "Those are for your memory trips. Fred. Why don't you try it? But you've got to follow my rules."

"More damn rules, huh?" Fred said. "Can I at least get off my bar stool or do I have to toss the quarter at the machine from here?"

Stout tried to laugh but it came out so poorly that David again looked at him with a questioning look.

"Go pick out a Christmas song that reminds you of something in your past. Then after you've selected it, stand beside the machine and tell us the memory."

Fred picked up the quarter from the bar and swung around. "I think I can handle that."

"I'll bet that's not what your ex-wife would say," Jess said.

Everyone laughed, and that started the nightly joking about Fred's ex-wife. She was well known to the group because it seemed at times that was all Fred could talk about. Her name was Alice and she and Fred had gotten married young, had one child, and gotten divorced in an ugly fashion about ten years before.

Fred was tall and thin, with about twenty pounds of extra weight around his stomach. He used to have bright red hair that was now sun-bleached because he worked for the city streets department. He said that almost a quarter of his salary every month went to paying child support, even though his ex-wife very seldom let him see his daughter. He claimed he loved his daughter, and one Saturday had brought her in for everyone to meet. Sandy had bright red hair like her father.

"Got one," Fred said as he dropped the quarter into the slot and quickly punched two buttons.

"So what's the memory?" Stout asked.

Stout's stomach felt weak. Was he going to lose Fred, too? Maybe he shouldn't warn Fred that he only had the time of the song, that if he wanted to change anything, he would have to do it fast.

"The first time I got laid," Fred said, smiling. "The night Sandy came to be."

Stout choked. God, what was he doing to his friends? What kind of presents were these?

"Stout," David said. "You all right? You're as pale as a ghost."

Stout nodded and looked up at Fred. "You only have the time of the song. Remember that. Just over two minutes."

Jess laughed. "More than enough time for Fred to get laid, from what I hear."

Fred had taken a step toward Jess when the Gene Autry song started and Fred vanished from the bar.

CHAPTER FIVE

About five years later…
June 9th, 2020
Central Wilderness Area, Idaho

TALIA FELT STUNNED at her reaction to Dr. Ryan Saddler. She had been excited at the prospect of working with him. She had read some of his papers and admired how he came at mathematics, but she never imagined him to be handsome as well.

She had no idea what she had expected, but it certainly wasn't dark brown eyes, a square jaw, and shoulders that looked like he worked out more than he spent hunched over a computer.

And his handshake had damn near made her knees shake. How was that even possible? She had had her share of boyfriends over the years, but all of them didn't much like her focus on math and her job at the university. Now suddenly she found herself not only sitting with two of the greatest minds in mathematics, but a handsome man almost as smart as they were.

This was all going to be a dream and she would wake up from it at any moment.

She took a deep breath of the crisp air and let the freshness of it calm her.

"Amazing view, isn't it?" Duster asked.

Talia made herself focus on the mountains and valleys that stretched for miles under the magnificent lodge deck. The valleys were being filled with blackness as the sun set, but the tops of the peaks, many with snow on them, were being colored shades of reds and pinks.

"Stunning," she said. "Just stunning."

"I'll second that," Ryan said softly.

She smiled at Duster who had his cowboy hat tipped back and his coat draped behind him. He was just staring out at the view as if he hadn't seen it before.

He and Bonnie were amazing people. They seemed totally in control and enjoying life and each other. She had really treasured her time with Bonnie so far. Talia had a hunch that she would find she liked Duster as well.

Then Talia glanced at Ryan, who was also looking out over the view, his hand holding a Diet Coke can.

Talia could feel her breath catch. He looked better in profile than he did directly on, if that was possible. Nobody was that good-looking.

Ryan Saddler was. Damn.

Just damn.

Finally Duster pointed down the valley. "We might as well get started explaining some of this."

Talia noticed that Bonnie nodded and Ryan came back into his eyes and focused on Duster.

"The valley below us is called the Monumental Valley," Duster said. "About five miles down that valley from here is a small lake. That lake is what is left of a larger lake that covered a mining town called Roosevelt in 1909."

"What happened?" Ryan asked.

"Mud slide," Bonnie said. "No one died and there are a few pictures taken of the town as it slowly submerged over three days."

"There's a big display back in the main dining room off to the right of the front desk," Duster said. "You can read more about it in the morning."

Talia nodded. She planned on doing just that. Wisconsin had its share of old towns and a ton of history, but not like western history and entire towns being submerged.

"Roosevelt was a pretty amazing mining town," Duster said. "Almost ten thousand people during the boom summers lived in the valley below us."

"Wow," Talia said, trying to imagine ten thousand people all crammed into a narrow valley.

"It was a very noisy place," Bonnie said, smiling. "Alive in all ways."

"The pianos helped," Duster said, smiling. "You see, for the longest time, there were no real wagon roads into that valley, so everything in that town had to be brought in over three trails, one of which went right where the road is now on this summit."

"They took in pianos on horseback?" Ryan asked a half second before Talia could.

She smiled at him and he smiled back.

"Took them apart, hauled them in, put them back together again," Duster said. "At one point there were supposed to have been fourteen pianos in that valley."

"Only ten were ever accounted for," Bonnie said. "But they were all in the saloons and the doors in the summer were always open."

"Ten pianos in a very narrow valley can make a lot of noise," Duster said, shaking his head.

Talia stared at him. He was talking as if he had actually heard the pianos.

"The legend is," Bonnie said, "that if you stand near the lake, you can still hear the pianos playing on a calm summer evening."

"An awful lot of people have reported hearing them," Duster said, shaking his head. "And that's what we want to hire you two for."

Ryan sat back, shaking his head.

Talia just felt confused. She had been working on the mathematics of music, but what that had to do with an old legend was beyond her.

"We believe," Bonnie said, looking first at Talia, then Ryan, "that mathematics can answer the question as to why that music is still being heard through time."

"You believe the legend?" Ryan asked, looking shocked at Bonnie.

She nodded.

Duster nodded.

"We have heard it many, many times, actually," Duster said. "Damn creepy if you ask me, but I believe in mathematics and I want to know the reason that music has the power to cut through time. What is it about music and the waves of music sound that have that power?"

Talia glanced at Ryan. He was clearly deep in thought.

She felt confused. She had no idea why Bonnie and Duster would bring her all the way from Wisconsin to this mountaintop for such a crazy idea. There had to be more about it.

"I have read most of your works on time, energy, and space," Ryan said to Bonnie and Duster after a moment.

"And your last paper," Duster said to Ryan, "on the nature of waves through time was what brought us to thinking about the possibility that this legend of the pianos might be solved with mathematics."

Ryan nodded.

Talia was stunned. He was clearly taking them seriously.

Very seriously.

Bonnie turned to face Talia directly. "Your knowledge of the mathematics of sound combined with Ryan's ability to work the mathematics of waves through time might be able to solve this riddle."

The intense silence of the mountains smashed in on the four of them. Talia could almost feel the pressure of that silence, as if it had a real weight.

Finally Duster said, "Well, it's been a long day of travel. Let's meet for breakfast out here at eight and then head down to the lake."

"We're going to the site of an old ghost town?" Talia asked, her stomach twisting.

"It's actually pretty amazing," Bonnie said, smiling at her as all four of them stood. "Get some sleep and we can talk about all this tomorrow."

"Sounds good," Ryan said. "But I have two more questions for you."

"Go ahead," Duster said.

"We both signed do-not-disclose papers," Ryan said. "But you are going to pay all the bills and allow us to publish our own findings. Is that correct?"

"It is," Duster said.

"So," Ryan said. "Are you going to show us the nexus?"

Talia had no idea at all what Ryan was talking about, but it froze both Bonnie and Duster like marble statues. Talia had never seen two humans assume such perfect poker faces before.

But by that very reaction, Talia had no doubt that Ryan had hit on something.

Finally Duster laughed. "Eventually, we'll do one better."

With that Bonnie and Duster headed off, arm-in-arm toward the stairs, leaving her on a beautiful summer night alone on a deck in the mountains with the most handsome man she had seen in years.

And more confused than a teenage girl on a first date.

"Nexus?" she asked Ryan.

His face was beaming, just beaming, as if he had just won the most amazing prize ever given to anyone.

He indicated she should sit back down and he sat down across from her, his dark eyes filled with joy and excitement.

"You know who those two people are, right?" he asked.

"Two of the greatest mathematicians to ever live," she said. "I wouldn't come this far for just anyone."

"I have studied and read every paper they have ever done on the theories of space and time and matter," Ryan said. "I have done two recent papers taking a little side sliver of their work and expanding it."

Now Available
from all your favorite booksellers
in trade paper and electronic editions.

"Music?" she asked.

"Waves," he said. "But the key is that Bonnie and Duster have proven mathematically that all matter, all energy, and all time are tied together."

She knew that, so she just nodded.

"But they also theorize that space and time and matter all have a physical location where it all ties together. They called it the Nexus."

"You think it actually exists?" Talia asked, sitting back.

"I know it does," Ryan said. "Mathematically, it has to. But now I know, from their reactions, that they have found it."

"Oh, shit," Talia said.

"Oh, shit is very right," Ryan said.

CHAPTER SIX

December 24th, 1997
Boise, Idaho

THE SNOW BLEW hard against Fred's face as he dodged across the rush of pedestrians on the busy sidewalk and in the front door of Abraham's Drug Store. The bell over the door jingled as he entered.

The store smelled clean, with a faint background of medicine. The tile floor looked slick from polish.

Old man Abraham was behind the druggist's counter in his white smock. Judy, the clerk, was at the cash register waiting on a heavyset man who was buying cough syrup. In the background the song, "Rudolf the Red-nosed Reindeer" played.

That was the same song he had punched up a moment before on the Garden Lounge jukebox. How the hell had Stout done this?

What was going on?

Fred glanced down at himself. He was young, dressed in his high school clothes. How could that be? Only a moment before, he had been in the Garden Lounge, drinking, eighteen years in the future. This was some practical joke. He'd get Jess for this.

And Stout.

He was about to turn and head back into the storm when the younger memories that were mixed with the older ones reminded him of why he was here. He had come to the drugstore to buy a rubber. A condom.

He was on his way to Alice's house. Her parents were at a Christmas party and would be gone for a long time.

He and Alice would start out on the couch watching television and work their way naked to the floor. It would be their first time and because he had chickened out and not bought the rubber on the way to her house, she had gotten pregnant and they had gotten married right out of high school. Sandy had followed three months later.

He grabbed hold of the doorframe, then touched a bottle of hair oil on a nearby shelf. Everything felt real. Damned if he knew what was going on.

He turned back to face old man Abrahams who was now watching him. It was no wonder he had chickened out the first time. He had bought condoms hundreds of times in the last twenty years, but right now he felt afraid. But what the hell could the old man do to him?

Fred shook his head. He didn't want to think about that.

He took a deep breath and moved up to the counter.

"Can I help you?" Abrahams said, staring down from his high perch. The guy looked like a cross between God and his dad.

"I'd..." His voice broke and he cleared his throat and tried to lower the pitch to a more normal range. "I'd like to buy a..."

He glanced quickly around. Judy was watching him and smiling. He'd had a crush on her for years. It was no wonder his younger self had chickened out.

"Well, young man?"

Fred turned back to face Abrahams. He could feel his face getting hot. If he didn't ask now, Alice would get pregnant and they would end up married. That had turned out to be a fate much worse than asking one simple question. Much, much worse. All those years of shouting and the hate and the ugliness their marriage had been. The only slightly good thing had been Sandy. But who knew how screwed up she was going to be because of the ugly marriage he and Alice had had.

He looked up at Abrahams. "I'd...I'd like to buy a condom."

There.

He had done it.

Old man Abrahams had the good sense not to laugh. But Fred could tell he was holding back a smile. "Well, son, they come in packages of three or six or twelve."

"Six," he said quickly. No point in having to go through this too often. And next time he would just go to one of the major grocery chains. But a dozen would seem like bragging.

Abrahams nodded and rummaged behind the counter. "Now, which brand would you like?"

At that Judy giggled and Fred could feel his face and neck burning. His younger self wanted to flee the store. He'd never be able to face her.

But his older memories kept him there. "I... I... I don't care. Your best."

Again Abrahams nodded. "That would be Trojans." He slid the box across the counter. "Pay Judy."

Damn him. He was doing this on purpose. He had a register. He could take the money. Again Judy giggled as Fred picked up the box and turned. At that very moment he noticed that the song was almost over and he knew without a doubt that his face was as red as Rudolf's nose.

He pulled a twenty-dollar bill out of his pocket and tossed it on the counter. "Keep the change," he said to Judy and, without looking at her, he sprinted for the front door and the snow beyond.

At least now he had the choice to have Sandy or not. He'd have to give this some serious thought.

As the door slammed shut and the song ended, the memories of the choice, Sandy, the marriage to Alice, and the next twenty years faded and were gone.

CHAPTER SEVEN

About twenty-three years later…
June 10th, 2020
Central Wilderness Area, Idaho

RYAN COULD NOT believe how well he had slept in that featherbed. He had left the window slightly open and the cold mountain air, the soft bed, and two thick quilts had just let him sleep until his phone alarm woke him at seven.

Last night he and the incredibly attractive and very smart Talia had talked in whispers on the big deck overlooking the valley below until they were both shivering from the cold. No one had bothered them at all, and when after an hour they both decided to get some sleep, they didn't even see anyone at the front desk.

It seemed the Monumental Lodge just rolled up everything when the sun went down.

Ryan figured that with no one around, the big log room should have felt kind of creepy, being all alone like they were in a old log and stone lodge in the Idaho mountains. But it actually felt to Ryan more like home. He had fallen for this place instantly.

A fire crackled softly in the large stone fireplace in the living area and a slight wind stirred the trees as they climbed the stairs together, the wooden planks creaking slightly.

She had a room at the top of the stairs to the right and his was to the left. There were only four rooms total in the long carpeted hallway at the top of the stairs and Bonnie and Duster had one of the others.

The moment of goodnight felt awkward, since Talia was as attracted to him as he was to her, which he was more than grateful for. Usually he had no idea when a woman was attracted to him. He could never understand why a woman would ever be attracted to a geek who spent all his time crunching numbers and working theories.

And honestly, most of his dates hadn't turned into relationships and the ones that had gave up on him after a few months. He didn't blame them at all. He was not a catch by anyone's standards and he knew it. He was just too focused inwardly in his own thoughts to give a relationship any time.

They had both managed to get fairly quietly into their rooms and their doors closed. And fifteen minutes later, he was asleep in the featherbed, the cool and crisp and clean mountain air brushing past his face.

As he came out of his room, freshly showered and wearing jeans, tennis shoes, and a light shirt with a heavier shirt over it, the smell of bacon hit him like a physical presence.

At that moment he realized just how hungry he was. His mind had been spinning on what Duster had said about the coming project and also about Talia and working with her.

He was so looking forward to this day, he felt like a kid about to go on vacation.

There was talking and some laughing coming from the dining room and as he reached the bottom of the stairs a smiling woman about his age behind the desk pointed to the deck. "Dr. Saddler, Bonnie and Duster are having breakfast through those doors."

"Thank you," Ryan said and headed back out toward the deck. The woman behind the desk looked very familiar from somewhere. She had long brown hair and dark eyes and a smile that seemed to light up her face. But Ryan couldn't place where he knew her and his mind was so focused on the coming day, he honestly didn't want to give it any thought at the moment.

Bonnie and Duster were at the same table they had occupied the night before. Both had orange juice and toast, but were clearly waiting for their meals.

Bonnie had on jeans and a thick jacket. Duster was wearing his normal cowboy hat and long oilskin coat.

As Ryan opened the door to go outside, the biting cold morning air hit him and almost took his breath away. Then the incredible view spread out just beyond the railing did take his breath.

Tall, snow-capped peaks seemed to cut into the air with knife-like sharpness, and the valleys were so deep between them, it seemed they were jagged slices into the earth. Shades of greens and browns and the intense blue sky seemed to mix in the crystal clear morning light.

It seemed almost too much to focus on.

Ryan shut the door behind him and sat down. Their table was the only occupied one on the massive deck, mostly because Ryan was pretty sure that frost might form on the table at any moment. And he had no doubt that if he picked up the metal silverware, it would just freeze to his fingers.

"Amazing, isn't it?" Bonnie asked, indicating the spectacular vistas.

"Beyond amazing," Ryan said, then shivered. He wished he had brought his gloves and coat.

Duster laughed. "You and Talia should eat in the dining room. It's going to be too cold out here for both of you."

Ryan started to object because he really, really wanted to continue the conversation from last night, but Duster held up his hand.

"We're used to this and enjoy it," Duster said.

"We'll come in when we are done with breakfast and we can talk then," Bonnie said, smiling at him.

He nodded and stood. "Thanks. Berkeley just never seems to get this cold."

"You ought to be on this deck in the middle of the winter," Duster said, smiling.

All Ryan could do was shiver again and shake his head. The idea of that just scared him more than he wanted to think about.

At that moment, behind him, the door opened and Talia came out. He glanced back at her and smiled. She looked as wonderful as she had the night before. Her hair was still damp from her shower

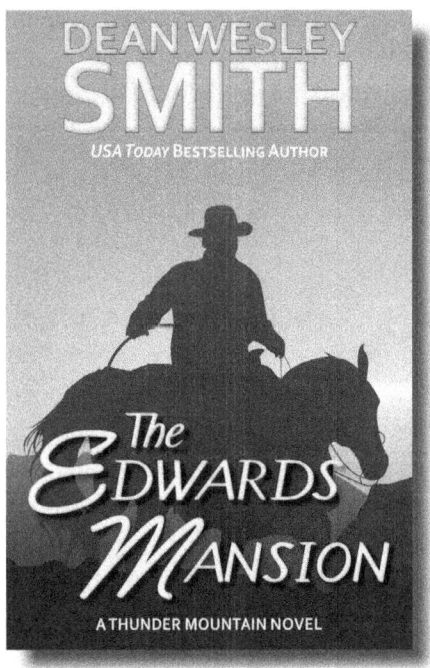

and she had on jeans, a blouse, and the sweatshirt over the blouse.

He had no doubt that if she stayed out here, her hair would freeze.

"Wow," she said, wrapping her arms around herself and tucking her hands into her armpits. "What a view."

Ryan smiled at Bonnie and Duster and then turned for the door. "I'll get us a table in the dining room, close to the fire I hope."

Talia looked confused as he passed her and Duster just laughed.

As he went back into the high-ceilinged warmth of the main room of the lodge, he blew on his hands to try to get some feeling back in them. The smell of bacon again hit him and his stomach rumbled.

"A little too cold for normal folks out there, isn't it?" the long-haired woman behind the desk asked, smiling at him.

"They do that regularly?" Ryan asked.

"For as long as I have known them," the woman said. "I took the liberty of reserving you and Dr. Marr a table near the fire in the dining room."

"Didn't think we would make it out there, huh?" Ryan asked.

"No reason to when you can enjoy a comfortable breakfast by the fire."

"Got that right," Ryan said.

The woman came around the desk and led him into the warm and very comfortable dining room. Three tables had people at them, and a woman with a white apron was serving one table.

He got seated and sighed, just holding his hands out to the nearby fire in the massive stone fireplace. Now this was the way he wanted to enjoy his breakfasts in the mountains.

CHAPTER EIGHT

December 24th, 2015
Boise, Idaho

WHEN THE LOUNGE finished shimmering, Stout let go of the juke-box and moved around behind the bar. Carefully, he dumped what was left of Fred's drink and placed his glass beside Carl's on the back bar.

Stout hadn't felt this tired in years. He looked at the two glasses. "Good luck, guys," he said softly. "I hope life is better for both of you."

Now he only had two friends left in the bar. He could stop this at any time, while there was still someone left to talk to.

"So what are we supposed to do with these quarters?" Jess asked. "I got to get home before that bitch of a wife chews my head off."

Stout glanced at Jess and then at David, who was looking worried.

"You play a song. That's all." Stout motioned at the jukebox. "But find one that has a strong memory with it."

Stout took a deep breath. He might as well give him a real present. "Maybe even one that was during the time that you met your wife."

Jess laughed. "Why the hell would I want to do that?"

"Trust me," Stout said. "Just find a song."

He leaned against the counter behind the bar and concentrated on taking deep breaths and not thinking about Carl and Fred.

"You all right? David asked.

Stout looked up into David's worried face. What would Stout have done over the last few years without David's friend-ship? What was Stout going to do without it over the next few years if he let David play a song?

"Just suddenly got tired. Nothing big."

Stout moved to pour himself anoth-er eggnog and watch Jess pick over the tunes. Jess was the best joker. He said he needed the practical jokes to keep his sanity with his bitch of a wife. But when asked why he didn't just leave her, he always said marrying her was his mistake and he would live with it. That was what he had been taught. Then he would make a joke and change the subject.

"Found one," Jess said. He held up the quarter. "You want me to play it?"

"Yeah. But after you select the song tell Dave and me what memory it reminds you of."

Jess dropped the quarter into the slot and punched two buttons to start the juke-box. "You remember the song, 'Snoopy Versus the Red Baron?'"

Stout and David both nodded.

"That was playing the moment I asked my wife to marry me. Figures, doesn't it?"

David laughed.

But Stout didn't. He knew he was go-ing to lose Jess also.

"Remember that you only have the length of the song. Not one second lon-ger. All right?"

Jess shrugged and started back to-ward the bar. "Whatever you..."

The song started and Jess vanished.

"What the hell?" David asked, stand-ing and heading toward the jukebox.

Stout picked up Jess's mostly empty glass and moved around toward the juke-box, too.

David glanced at the two glasses on the back bar and then at the glass Stout held. Then he looked over to where Jess had been. "You want to explain exactly what the *hell* is going on here?"

Stout nodded, too tired to argue. "But come on over and touch the jukebox. It's the only way you're going to remember."

CHAPTER NINE

About five years later…
June 10th, 2020
Central Wilderness Area, Idaho

TALIA BARELY MANAGED to get back inside the lodge before her slightly wet hair froze to her head. It got cold in Wisconsin in the winter, of that there was no doubt. But not in June. In fact, when she had left, the weather had been a humid ninety-two in Madison.

Wow, how Bonnie and Duster could eat breakfast out there was amazing. Granted, some would say the view was to die for, but she had no intention of freez-ing to death for it.

Ryan was sitting close to the fire at a four-person table, his hands stretched out toward the crackling flames from the logs. The room smelled wonderful, a combination of bacon and wood smoke from the fireplace.

She had felt instantly at home when she came into this lodge. She doubted she could afford rooms here as nice as hers was, but as long as Bonnie and Duster were paying, she was going to enjoy it.

And enjoy her time with this hand-some and smart mathematician she was going to get the pleasure to work with. Ryan seemed so in control, so excited about life and this project, and that made her smile as well.

She reached the table and he glanced up, saw her, and stood, a large grin on his face.

Now that was impressive. A smart man with manners as well.

"Hair almost froze to my head out there," Talia said, laughing as she sat down at the heavy wood table. The wonderful fire was exactly the right temperature to take off the chill she was feeling from only a minute on the deck.

"They are a hardy pair," Ryan said. "Amazing minds."

"Do they seem older to you?" Talia asked. Spending time yesterday with Bonnie at the airport, then at lunch, then on the helicopter flight in, she got the sense that Bonnie was far, far older than in her early thirties.

"Very old," Ryan said, nodding. "I spent all of yesterday with Duster and felt more like a child being humored at times. Nothing disrespectful at all, but as if Duster was very old and some of my reactions and responses were just young."

"Strange, huh?" Talia said as the waitress with short black hair in jeans, a white blouse, and a white apron came to get their order. They both ordered the same thing. A ham-and-cheese omelet with a side of bacon and coffee. Ryan took his coffee black, just as she did. She was liking more and more about this man every moment.

After the waitress left, Talia scooted her chair around slightly so her back was to the warm fire and she was facing Ryan directly. "Could you explain to me more of what you think this nexus is?"

Ryan nodded and she could see in his eyes his mind gearing up. He seemed to vanish from his eyes for a moment, then returned.

She had a hunch she did that same thing at times when deep in thought on a problem. A couple of her short-lived boyfriends said she was often just not home in her head.

She had told them she was home just fine, just down inside in another room where they weren't welcome. For some reason, that hadn't pleased any of them.

"The math of modern physics," Ryan said, "which includes time and energy and matter, always leads to the fact that at regular intervals through the known universe, all three forms must come together. That's what Bonnie and Duster, in some of their papers, call 'The Nexus.'"

"So you think they might have found a Nexus?" she asked. "You clearly surprised them with your question."

"It would seem logical," Ryan said, "but I would have no idea what this Nexus would look like. They might have only found it in pure theory as a point in space or something."

She nodded, staring into his dark eyes. "So you think music waves can travel through time? I've worked a lot with the mathematics of sound waves. Never occurred to me to think that."

"Never worked much with the math of waves," Ryan said. "But from the math that Bonnie and Duster have done, they have proven at least mathematically that time and energy and matter are moderately fluid. And waves can travel through a fluid."

Talia sat back, nodding. Now she understood why she was here. This entire idea was so cutting edge mathematics as to be scary. And combining the mathematics of energy and time with that of the mathematics of waves would be amazingly fascinating.

And exciting.

Who knew what they might find.

She was honored that Bonnie and Duster had picked her for this research.

In front of her, a plate slid on the wooden tabletop as the waitress put her breakfast in front of Talia.

She blinked and looked up at Ryan's smiling face.

"Did I leave for a moment?" Talia asked.

Ryan nodded. "My friends say I do that as well at times. Glad to see I'm not the only one."

"Yeah, me too," Talia said.

"Damn dangerous driving, though," Ryan said.

"I hardly drive at all," Talia said. "Don't even own a car."

Again Ryan laughed as he dug into his omelet. "Neither do I."

Damn, she was liking this man more and more, and not just for his incredible brain and looks. He might actually understand her.

CHAPTER TEN

December 24th, 1999
Boise, Idaho

SNOOPY AND THE Red Baron were just starting to go at it on Jess's classic '65 Ford car radio as Jess found himself face to face with Mary, his soon-to-be bitch-of-a-wife.

"What the...?"

"Is something wrong, Jess, honey?" Mary said, her hand stroking his arm up and down and up and down. She looked more beautiful than he had ever remembered, and she smelled wonderfully fresh, as if she had been outside in the country all day.

But he knew the look and the smell wouldn't last long. Six months after they were married she would gain fifty pounds and a few years later she would level out a hundred over her marriage weight.

But now, in this dream or whatever it was, she looked sexy and very trim in her low-cut blue dress.

Jess pulled back away from her and looked around. This was his car all right. The same one he had sold in '01.

The same classic car that he and Mary had first made love in.

He rubbed his hands along the steering wheel to make sure it felt solid. They were parked just down the tree-lined street from Mary's house. When they were dating, she said she loved his old cars, but after they were married all she did was harp at him to get a more practical modern car like a van or something.

So how had Stout pulled this off? This had to be some kind of dream or hallucination. That was it. Stout had hypnotized him and he was still sitting in the Garden Lounge while they laughed.

Jess would get them for this.

Mary scooted over closer to him and rubbed his leg real nice, getting the reaction in his crotch she wanted. "Were you going to ask me something?" she said, looking up at him with her large brown eyes.

"That I was," he said. It was a clear memory that in this exact situation he had asked her to marry him. He knew that's what his younger self had been planning to do.

He was currently a second-year law student, and he remembered his classes that Friday morning real well. Yet he also remembered sitting having a Christmas Eve drink with his friends at the Garden Lounge sixteen or so years in the future.

Strange.

Too damn strange.

On the radio the old classic Red Baron shot down Snoopy. Stout had said Jess only had the length of the song. Whatever was going on, it was halfway over.

Mary rubbed Jess's leg and waited. Waited, knowing what the question would be. Waited, knowing that she had led him right to where she wanted him.

Well, this time around she would get a surprise, because dream or no dream, this was going to be fun.

Hell, after all the years with her, he deserved a little fun.

"I wanted to ask you," Jess said, then paused, trying not to smile.

The Red Baron and Snoopy drank a Christmas toast.

"Yes," Mary said, her voice low and sexy. She had been one beautiful woman on the outside. That had kept him blind to all the ugliness that was just under the surface.

Blind until it was too late.

"I wanted to ask you if it would be all right if I slept around with a few other women? You know, sew a few wild oats before I settle down?"

That did it.

Holy smokes did that do it.

The sultry look drained from her face like wet makeup, to be replaced by the bitch look he had grown so familiar with.

"What did you say?" she asked, her voice low and mean and controlled. He knew that voice real well, too.

He smiled, easing toward her, trying to act romantic. "I was just thinking that for a few years, maybe five or ten, we could have an open relationship. I'd love to sleep with a few other women. It would be good for us. Honest. You know, free love and all."

He moved as if to kiss her and she backed away across the seat.

"Wouldn't you like sleeping with other men? Then after we've both got a little more experience we could live together for a few years. Trying on the old shoes, as the saying goes."

Jess knew that would get her. She had said a hundred times how much she hated the thought of living together. For her it was marriage or nothing. Damn it was hard keeping a straight face. He was going to thank Stout for this one. Best Christmas present he had ever had.

"You're sick!" she screamed. "Sick! Sick! Sick!"

Jess tried to look innocent and sad.

On the radio Snoopy flew off singing about Christmas cheer as Mary rammed against the car door, opened it and ran up the sidewalk.

"Thank you, Stout. I've been dreaming about doing that for years."

The song ended.

And so did the dreams.

CHAPTER ELEVEN

About twenty-one years later…
June 10th, 2020
Central Wilderness Area, Idaho

RYAN HAD FINISHED up the last of his breakfast and was sipping on his coffee when Bonnie and Duster came in from the deck.

Duster's long oilcloth coat swirled around his feet and his cowboy hat was pulled down tight on his head.

Bonnie had her coat zipped up and she looked cold. Her face was flushed red.

Over food, Ryan and Talia had talked cats. He had two wonderful cats in his apartment in Berkeley, both strays he found starving on the street. He had called one Bonnie and one Duster, which Talia had found fantastically funny. And he had made her promise to not tell the real Bonnie and Duster.

She had one cat named Thunder because his deep and loud voice could shake her entire apartment when he was hungry or demanding attention. A friend had found him lost and almost dead in the cold and snow one winter and Talia couldn't resist.

She called him her best buddy.

"This is fun," Ryan had said. "We're in the Thunder Mountain region of these mountains with Bonnie and Duster. I would hate to calculate the odds on that happening."

"It would take some work," she had said, laughing.

He loved how she laughed easily, and he loved how she had just vanished back into her mind when thinking about the reality of time and sound.

"So how was breakfast?" Talia asked as Bonnie and Duster took chairs at their table. Bonnie sat closest to the fire and seemed relieved to be beside it, unzipping her coat and taking it off.

"Refreshing," Duster said, smiling.

"Damn cold," Bonnie said.

Duster laughed and nodded. "I think tomorrow we'll eat right here, next to the fire."

"I will," Bonnie said, glaring at Duster.

Ryan and Talia both laughed, but stayed silent. Ryan wanted to work for these two legends, not get them annoyed at him right off the bat.

Duster just sort of ignored Bonnie and turned first to Talia, then to Ryan.

"You two up for a fairly short drive down into the valley below to see the lake and the old mining town site we were talking about? We can talk and answer questions along the way."

"It will warm up quickly," Bonnie said. "So you both should be fine dressed in the layers you are in now."

"Thank you," Talia said.

"Excited to see the place," Ryan said. And he was.

"Did you get a chance to read the history and see the pictures over there on the wall?" Bonnie asked.

"I didn't," Talia said.

"Neither did I," Ryan said.

"We'll have some coffee here and warm up and wait for you," Bonnie said. "It will help if you have some of the basics about where we are headed."

Ryan nodded and he and Talia both stood at the same time and headed for the wall of framed pictures and a few cases of different memorabilia that ran along one side of the high-ceilinged dining room.

Only two other lodge guests remained in the room and they sat at a table near a window that had a view looking down into valleys in the opposite direction from the lake.

Ryan was really impressed that anyone would even think of building a massive lodge this size on a summit this high up in the mountains. And then maintain it for well over a hundred years. There had to be a story in that all by itself.

Talia led him to the start of the history about the area and they both quickly went through how the mining started in this area and became a real gold rush in 1901.

There were lots of historical figures talked about that Ryan didn't recognize at all. But the pictures of the town of Roosevelt had him amazed. The town was tucked between two extremely steep mountain slopes and at places couldn't have been more than a hundred yards wide.

Everything in the entire place had to be brought in over three very dangerous trails that closed down seven months of the year.

One map showed all the locations of the major mines in the area and another showed the location of the old trails and a few other smaller ghost town locations farther down the valley.

And another story that both he and Talia spent extra time to read was about the pianos in the town and the legend of still hearing the music. Ryan found that flat amazing now that he was looking at it from an actual mathematical angle.

Then there were some pictures of the author Zane Gray when he came to this area to write a book about the area called *Thunder Mountain*. There was a copy of the book itself in the case, signed by the author.

There were numbers of pictures of the flood after the landslide that blocked the valley. It seemed the waters took days to back up over the town and many of the buildings just broke apart and jammed into the spot where the stream eventually flowed over and around the landslide.

At the end of the long display, there was an image near the end of the valley taken from the air and the lake in 2014 with an outline showing the size of the lake originally right after the flood. It was clear the lake was now less than an eighth of its original size. All the rest had filled in with sediment brought downstream.

The final part of the display was about the modern history of the valley and how the area had become The Frank Church Primitive Area and how an exemption for

a small tourist area near the lake and road into the lake had been allowed to exist because of a mining claim.

"Amazing place, huh?" Talia said after the reached the end of the images and articles.

Ryan could only agree. He was very, very excited to see it now, more than he had been before.

And even more excited to see if they could explain why the sounds from those pianos from 1902 to 1909 were still being heard today.

The idea of that almost had him bouncing like a kid before Christmas.

CHAPTER TWELVE

December 24th, 2015
Boise, Idaho

STOUT MOVED SLOWLY around behind the bar, dumped out the remainder of Jess's drink and set Jess's special glass beside the others on the back bar.

"Got quite a collection there," David said as he moved over to take his stool. "So Carl and Fred were friends of mine in another timeline?"

Stout took a long hard drink of his eggnog and then nodded.

"Jess," David said, "was sent back by the jukebox to his memory and he changed something that moved his life in another direction. And with that new direction, he didn't end up coming in here. Right? And he would have no memory of ever being in here because he hasn't been."

Again Stout nodded and finished off the drink.

David picked up the quarter in front of him and glanced over at the jukebox. "You know this is a wish that everyone has had at one time or another? How come you've never done it?"

"Oh, I did. Actually twice when I first discovered what the jukebox could do. But I didn't change anything. Too afraid, I guess. And, I suppose, not that unhappy with this life."

Stout nodded at the three empty glasses. "That is until tonight."

David took a sip of his drink and looked at his name on the glass. "So you gave the gift of a second chance to your friends for Christmas."

Stout laughed. "Seemed like a good idea at the time. But I didn't expect to lose everyone. Not exactly sure what I expected, to be honest with you."

"I'm still here."

Stout glanced over at his best friend. David worked as a vice president of a local bank and enjoyed flying his small plane on the weekend. But back twenty-some years ago, he and his new wife, Elaine, had been driving home from a Christmas party. David was scheduled to finish flight school that next spring. He had a dream of flying for the airlines.

That night David had had a little too much to drink and the car missed a slick corner and plowed into an embankment. Elaine was killed and David lost most of the use of his right hand.

End of flight school.

End of dream.

Stout reached out and slid the quarter at David. "Your turn."

David shook his head. "No chance. There's no way I'm leaving you after what you've done for Jess and those two other guys." David pointed at the glasses lined up on the back bar.

Stout laughed a laugh that sounded bitter even to his ears. "I don't know what exactly I've done except change their life in some fashion. I can only hope it is for the better. But you I *do* know the jukebox can help."

Stout reached across the bar and patted David's ruined right hand. "Go back to before the crash and save Elaine. And yourself."

David jerked as if he had never thought of the possibility.

"You saw it work," Stout said. "If nothing else, give it a try. You don't have to change anything. Just go back and see Elaine again. It's not a one-way trip if you don't change anything."

David looked dazed. "If I don't change..."

Stout nodded and picked up the quarter and placed it in David's good left hand. "Go say hello to your wife."

Still looking dazed, David slowly stood and moved toward the jukebox. "Is it really possible?"

"Yes," Stout said. "Now pick the right song."

David nodded and turned to study the song list. His tie hung loose in front of him, his right hand useless against the glass of the jukebox.

Stout could feel his stomach hurting from the very idea. He downed a little more eggnog. He knew that once David saw Elaine, he would be unable to stop from changing the past.

Stout knew for a fact he was going to lose his best friend. But maybe someday Stout would see him again, striding through an airport in his pilot's uniform. That alone would be worth it.

"Found the song," David said and turned to look at Stout.

"Then go for it," Stout said.

David paused, as if he wanted to say something. Then he turned and dropped the quarter into the machine and punched the two buttons.

"State the memory," Stout said. "Got to follow the rules, you know."

David smiled. "This song reminds me of the night my wife died."

Stout nodded. "Good luck. And say hello to Elaine for me."

"I will," David said." And I'll be back."

"In case you're not, I'll be holding onto your glass and the jukebox."

David smiled. "Thanks."

The song started and he vanished.

CHAPTER THIRTEEN

About five years later…
June 10th, 2020
Central Wilderness Area, Idaho

AFTER A TERRIFYING car ride down the side of a mountain cliff on a one-lane dirt road not much bigger than the large Cadillac SUV that Duster drove, Talia managed to relax and enjoy the rest of the day in the steep-walled valley. At least on the valley floor the road was flat and there was no place for a car to fall a thousand feet.

She found the old mining valley fascinating, and how Bonnie and Duster talked about parts of the valley history, it felt like they had actually been here during the old mining days. They certainly loved the place, there was no doubt in that at all.

The crystal blue waters of the lake allowed her to see old building sites thirty feet down through the water. That just stunned her, and filled her with an over-whelming sense of sadness. It was one thing to see the town in photos, another to see the remains deep under water.

The landslide blocking one side of the valley and forming the lake had a hundred year growth of pine on it, so it looked just like a natural part of the valley now.

And where the stream left the lake, a giant logjam had formed and stuck in place, a pile of twisted logs jammed together a good forty feet deep into the water. It felt to Talia when they went across the logjam that she was walking on a giant pile of Tinker Toys, since all the logs had been parts of buildings. And she could see large fish swimming down among the logs below her feet.

While Duster sat on a rock in the shade, Bonnie took her and Ryan down the trail another half mile to the old cemetery roped off under some trees above the stream.

Talia found the cemetery just flat creepy.

They then headed back to where they had parked the car about a mile above the lake just as the sun was hitting the valley floor and the afternoon was getting warm.

Talia had taken off her sweatshirt on the way back from the cemetery and Ryan had shed his coat about the same point. It was finally getting that warm.

The weather extremes in this area certainly were amazing to her. In Wisconsin, when it was hot, it stayed hot day and night. And when it was cold, it stayed cold. Not at all like here.

The four of them had a great lunch that the lodge had packed for them, sitting at a card table on folding chairs in the shade of a stand of pine. All four had prime rib sandwiches on fresh buns, with a stunningly good potato salad and iced tea.

The stream tumbled down over rocks filling the narrow valley with a soothing sound of water and in the shade the temperature was perfect.

And without bugs. If they had sat out like this in Wisconsin, they would have needed major protection.

"The lake backed up this far originally," Duster said, pointing to an area farther up the valley than they were. "But this part quickly filled in with sediment since it was so shallow."

"Another fifty or sixty years and the entire lake area will be nothing more than a meadow," Bonnie said. "Amazing what time can do."

"It really is," Duster said.

Talia glanced at both Bonnie and Duster. For a moment they seemed lost in thought.

She glanced at Ryan and shrugged slightly and he smiled at her and they both went back to finishing off their wonderful beef sandwiches, letting the two legendary mathematicians sit in their thoughts for a moment.

Finally, Duster pushed his plate forward. "We have one more thing we want to show you before we head back up to the lodge."

"It's close to here," Bonnie said, standing and starting to collect the paper plates and silverware.

Talia and Ryan both helped Bonnie as Duster went to the back of the SUV and pulled out some sort of small instrument in a backpack.

It took only a few minutes before they had everything cleaned up and back inside the car.

"This way," Duster said, striding off toward a flat bridge where the road crossed over the stream, his long coat flowing behind him, his cowboy boots kicking up a small cloud of dust with each step.

He kept going along the road as Talia followed. Ryan was behind her and Bonnie behind him. Bonnie only had on jeans, tennis shoes, and a long-sleeved blouse, but Duster had kept on his long coat and cowboy hat. Talia was starting to doubt he went anywhere without it on.

The dirt road went up a side valley off the canyon, climbing at a decent slope, just enough to start to wind Talia.

"How high are we here?" Ryan asked.

"Around seven thousand feet," Bonnie said.

Talia nodded. No wonder she was getting winded with a short hike.

Duster had said the road led into a patented mining claim that was still being worked in the next valley over. It seemed that patented mining claims remained when they turned this massive center of Idaho into a wilderness area. And the claims could maintain roads, the only reason there was a road even close to the old lake.

About a hundred paces up the side valley, Duster turned off the road to the left and followed what might be called a trail on generous days back toward the main valley. The trail cut along the side of the hill and kept climbing.

Around the edge of a small ridge, the trail seemed to vanish into a flat area covered with small rocks and some light brush. A couple pine trees grew tucked against the hillside on the flat area.

"This an old house site?" Ryan asked.

When he said that she could see some stones that looked like part of an old fireplace and some rocks for foundations.

"It was," Bonnie said. "A beautiful home."

Duster just nodded to that.

Talia was surprised. They were about fifty feet over the large valley floor. She could almost see the lake in the distance and from here looking back up the valley, she could see the magnificent Monumental Summit Lodge spanning across the top of the summit. That lodge had to be three miles away and a thousand feet above them and it still looked majestic and impressive.

"This is called Melody Ridge," Duster said. "It seems to be where the clearest sound from the pianos can be heard."

"Seriously?" Talia said. She was far, far from convinced about this idea of still hearing pianos playing from over a hundred years in the past. Nothing in all of her study had ever shown such a thing possible. But what she and Ryan had talked about had her excited at the quest.

They all stood, silently listening. All she could hear was the sound of the water running in the stream below them.

"In the winter," Bonnie said, "in the snow, without the sounds of the stream, the pianos can really be clear here."

Talia said nothing.

Duster set the pack he had been carrying on a rock and indicated Talia should take a look at the device inside it.

"Recognize what this is?" Duster asked.

She knew exactly what it was. It was a simple amplifier used to pick up sounds outside human hearing range. She noticed that the one Duster had was just a simple amplifier attached to a light battery pack.

"I do," she said. "Usually it's attached to recording or playback equipment and is plugged into a circuit, but a battery pack allows for less electrical interference."

"The recording part of all this was too much at this point to lug around," Duster said. "You used these before?"

"Regularly," Talia said.

He indicated that she should work the machine.

She got it turned on and then focused on the stream sounds and had the device block the sound of the stream and the water, filtering it out. Then she filtered out the slight sounds of a breeze through the pine trees.

"So I suppose I'm looking for music?" she asked.

"More like music mixed with the sounds of a valley alive with activity," Bonnie said. "Boost it if you find anything like that so we can all hear it."

Talia nodded.

She expected to find nothing.

But after a moment she was wrong. There was an area of waves that under normal conditions would be considered just very faint background noise. But up here in the mountains, there were no other background noises that she hadn't already filtered.

The sun beat on her back as she knelt beside the rock and filtered out one area after another, leaving only the unknown sound waves.

Then she amplified them so they all could hear them.

At first it sounded to her like a jumble of just noise.

Then the sound of a hammer banging came clear. And then other sounds of an alive valley, as if ghosts from a hundred years before were suddenly working around them.

And behind it all, clear as anything she had ever heard, were the sounds of numbers of pianos playing various songs, the music echoing.

She stood and stepped back, staring at the device as the sounds filled the flat area around them.

"Shit," Ryan said softly, as if his voice might disturb sounds coming through time from over a hundred years before.

She looked at him. Ryan's face was white, his eyes wide as he stared out at the empty valley listening to the sounds from the past.

She also stared down the valley toward the lake that covered the old mining town as around them, the sounds of pianos filled the air.

Impossible pianos.

Pianos that had not played a note in this valley for a very, very long time.

CHAPTER FOURTEEN

December 24th, 1994
Outside of Boise, Idaho

A LIGHT SNOW kept the old Ford's windshield wipers busy as David and Elaine headed down the gravel country road toward the lights of the city.

"Silent Night" was playing on the portable radio on the seat between them.

She was singing along, her voice pure and clear, even though a little drunk. The party, just south of town in the foothills, had been a good one and they had stayed far later than they planned.

David looked over at his wife of six months. She had dark brown hair that flowed long and straight down her back. Her eyes were a dark green and her face lightly wrinkled with laugh lines. While David was in school, she worked at a dress shop. Her desire was to someday design clothes, and he knew she would be, would have been, good at it.

"Son of a bitch," he said out loud. "Stout was right."

"Who was right?" Elaine said, then went back to singing and watching the beautiful countryside flash by through the snow.

David glanced once more at her and then back at the road. He couldn't let her die.

Stout had known that.

David braked the car to a quick stop on the side of the road. He turned off the car, yanked the keys out of the ignition and got out. Then as hard as he could,

he tossed the keys into the brush. In the silence of the night he could hear them catch brush as they landed.

That was his only set. Now there would be no way he could drive again tonight.

"David," Elaine said, getting out of the car and coming around to him. "What are you doing?"

"Saving our lives," he said.

He grabbed her and held her tight, relishing in the feeling of her against him after such a long time. He had never remarried because there had never been anyone again he felt this way about. No one woman who had felt this good.

The faint sounds of "Silent Night" drifted from the portable radio in the car. The song was about half over.

He didn't have much time.

"Are you all right?" Elaine asked. "Why did you throw the..."

"I'm fine. Like I said, I was just saving our lives. But now, before that song ends, I need to save a friendship. A very important friendship to me. And I'm going to need your help."

CHAPTER FIFTEEN

December 24th, 2015
Boise, Idaho

STOUT LET HIS hand slip off the jukebox as the last strains of the song faded into the empty Garden Lounge. David's glass was in Stout's hand. Stout looked down at it, feeling its heavy weight.

David must have stopped the wreck.

Of course he had. It was the only thing he could have done.

"Well, you idiot," Stout said to himself just to hear some noise. "Looks as if you've gone and done it now."

He moved slowly around behind the bar and set David's glass beside the other three, name out. "I'm going to have to find some special place for these." He laughed. "To remind me of another life that never was."

The silence seemed to echo in the room. It was going to be a very long, very quiet Christmas.

He refilled his glass of eggnog and moved around to what had been David's favorite stool. The jukebox seemed to call to him. "Come play me, Mr. Radley Stout. Come and see your old girlfriend again. Ask her to marry you. What would it hurt?"

"No," Stout said, loud enough to echo between the empty tables and booths. He squarely faced the glasses on the back bar and held up his mug in a toast.

"Merry Christmas, my friends."

Then he added softly, "Wherever you are."

The empty glasses didn't return his toast, so he went ahead and drank alone. He had the sneaking feeling he was going to be doing that for a while.

He had finished the eggnog and was about to start closing down when someone knocked on the front door.

"I'm closed," he yelled. "Merry Christmas." He was in no mood for visitors now.

But the person knocked again.

"All right, all right. Hang on a minute."

He went around to the back bar and, being careful to not look at the four glasses lined up there like so many tombstones, retrieved the keys and headed for the front door.

As he unlocked it and swung it open he heard, "Merry Christmas, Mr. Radley Stout."

David and a woman about his same age stood arm in arm facing the door. He wore an airline overcoat and she had on a nice leather jacket.

"David," Stout said. "How...?"

David unhooked himself from the woman's arm and extended a perfectly healthy right hand for Stout to shake.

"Your hand," Stout said as he shook it. "You didn't...?"

Again he stopped. There was no way David could know about the wreck and his lame hand if it hadn't happened. And in this world it hadn't.

"This is my wife, Elaine," David said.

"I don't know what to say."

Stout took her hand. He felt as if he was shaking the hand of a ghost.

"Please come in." He stepped back, the feeling of shock washing over him.

David and Elaine moved into the bar. Both of them walked directly to the jukebox.

"But how could you remember?" Stout asked moving up beside them.

"He doesn't," Elaine said, laughing with a tense sort of laugh.

David only nodded and then turned to face Stout.

"Christmas Eve, twenty-one years ago, Elaine said I suddenly called out the name 'Stout,' then stopped the car. I then proceeded to toss the car keys into the brush. For what crazy reason, I have no idea."

Stout laughed. "I do. Pretty smart thinking if you want to make sure you can't drive that night."

"But why would I want to do that?" David said. "And how would you know anything about it? This entire thing has been driving me nuts for over two decades."

Stout waved his hand. "I'll try to explain in a minute. For now please go on."

Elaine reached into her purse, pulled out a few tattered pieces of paper, and handed them to Stout. "For the next minute after he tossed the keys into the brush, David madly wrote this while repeating your name and the name of this bar over and over again so that I would remember it. He made me promise that no matter what he claimed he didn't remember, we would come to this bar on this Christmas Eve at this time to meet you. Not one minute before or one minute after."

David shrugged. "Damned if I can remember why. It was as if I was possessed."

"In a way, you were," Stout said.

"You know what else he said?" Elaine asked. She looked at David and he motioned for her to go ahead. "He said it was his Christmas present to you."

David looked at Stout. "Did it work?"

Stout nodded, afraid to say anything. But he could feel the smile trying to break out of the sides of his face. And after a moment all three of them were laughing just because Stout was smiling so hard. He was going to enjoy these new friends.

Stout motioned for them to take a seat at the bar. "Boy have I got a story to tell you."

He scampered like a kid around behind the bar and grabbed the glass with David's name on it.

"And for you, David," Stout said as he held the glass up for them to see. "A very special Christmas present and a toast to friendship."

PART TWO
Lost and Found

CHAPTER SIXTEEN

June 10th, 2020
Central Wilderness Area, Idaho

AFTER THE INCREDIBLE sounds of an alive, people-filled valley and piano music from the past, Ryan felt more in shock than anything else. The four of them had talked some about the valley and the sounds on the walk back to the SUV and then on the drive back up the valley. But then Duster had cut off conversation just before they got to the lodge.

"We have much more to talk about at dinner tonight," Duster had said. "So we'll meet in a private room behind the dining room at 6 p.m."

Duster had parked the SUV beside the lodge and then he and Bonnie had gone inside, leaving Ryan and Talia alone together under the tall pine trees that surrounded the parking area on the ridge.

The day was still warm since it was only about four in the afternoon. A slight breeze felt nice against Ryan's bare arms and the smell of hot pine needles seemed extra strong.

"You up for a drink on the deck?" Ryan asked Talia. He was really thirsty and needed to just sit and think and talk.

She nodded, but said nothing.

Ten minutes later they both had glasses of iced water and Diet Cokes and were sitting at one end of the long deck looking back out over the valley they had just been in.

Only two other tables were occupied, and they were both near the other end, so Ryan and Talia had a very private place to talk.

As they both stared at the valley, Ryan had to get the one question out that he needed to ask. "I can't imagine those two doing so, but was there any way the sounds of those pianos were faked or recorded?"

Talia just shook her head. "No chance at all. Those sounds existed on that old cabin site. That instrument that Duster had was state of the art and could pick up and filter out sounds at extreme frequencies."

Ryan nodded. "So where did the sounds come from?"

"I have no idea," Talia said. "I would have to record them and analyze them in a modern lab. If they were manufactured in any way and played back from another point in the valley, I would be able to detect that."

"But if they were not?" Ryan asked.

"I honestly don't know," Talia said.

He could tell she was upset. He didn't blame her. He was as well. The idea of Bonnie and Duster faking the sounds was just too silly to imagine. So that left Bonnie and Duster's theory, that the sound waves could travel through time.

That simple idea, backed up by many hearing the piano music at different times over decades, tore apart a lot of belief systems. Even the groundbreaking work in mathematics on time and energy and matter that Bonnie and Duster had done didn't account for this being possible.

"Any other evidence of anything like this before?" Ryan asked.

"I would have to go back and scan through data from other experiments," she said. "But honestly, with sound, we are always filtering out unknown factors."

"You would have filtered that out?" Ryan asked.

Talia nodded. "Most likely. The universe seems to almost have a background noise that mathematics has not yet explained."

"Maybe we are about to explain it with this project," Ryan said, starting to lose the feeling of shock and regaining the excitement.

"We don't even know what the project is yet, exactly," Talia said.

"I have a hunch we're going to know tonight," Ryan said, smiling at her.

She nodded, smiling slightly as well. "It would be exciting, wouldn't it?"

"Challenging," Ryan said.

They both stared out over the beautiful valley, the steep walls seeming to funnel everything down to the stream. The sun had left the valley floor, leaving the trees and brush and the dirt road in dark shadows.

In that valley Ryan knew that pianos had echoed from open saloon doors for years.

And now, if what Bonnie and Duster said was happening was real, those echoes had made their way through time.

And that scared Ryan and excited him more than he wanted to ever admit.

CHAPTER SEVENTEEN

December 24th, 2018
Boise, Idaho

FRED JUST FELT stunned. She came through the heavy front door of the old hotel with a face as young as yesterday. And for just a moment, the stale piss-smell of the thick air, the stained and faded linoleum floors, the peeling paint on the smoke-yellowed walls in the front foyer simply vanished.

For just a moment, the long, dull days were forgotten.

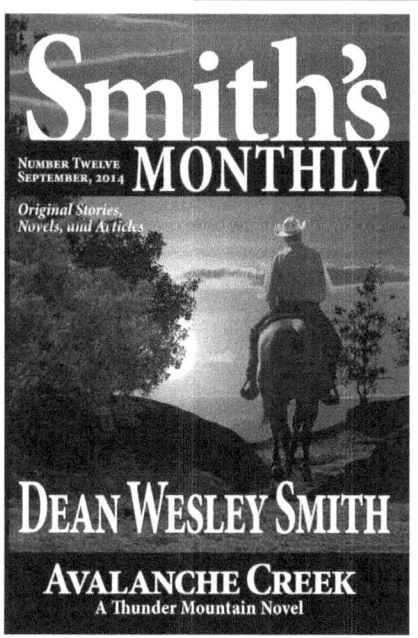

Fred and his two friends, Michael and Hank, lived in old men's boredom, moving like zombies from bedrooms, to the sitting room with the television, to the front stoop, back to the sitting room, then back to bedrooms, punctuated only by a silent lunch and an even more silent dinner in the small kitchen.

When she came through that door, Fred knew that the three of them forgot they were three corpses too damn old to just lie down and be done with it.

Forgot about being the last residents of The Golden Dream Hotel for men.

Even forgot it was Christmas Eve.

A year ago, crusty Jamison bought the old hotel from a development agency. Fred and Jamison and the other two signed an understanding agreement that the four men would be able to live in the hotel until all died.

Jamison died the next month at the age of sixty-two, giving Fred the hotel in his will. Now the three of them just sat around and wondered who would be next.

But no one talked about it. Fred was the youngest by far. He figured he would have the longest to wait. Since he owned the place that sort of made sense.

And now, as she stood there on this cold winter evening, her short, perfect-skinned nose wrinkling at the smell of the old hotel, even the thought of dying of boredom seemed forgotten.

She blinked in the dim light and then focused on the old box television in the corner. A long ways from the modern plasma screens, but it worked fine for them.

Fred could see she had bright, large eyes, thick eyebrows, and a full mouth. The kind of mouth Fred remembered that Alice had back what seemed like a million years ago.

Alice was his first love, his first sexual partner, his first real girlfriend. He never married her and always wondered why.

The young woman brushed a long slender hand against her nose, then straightened her shoulders as if she were going to face a firing squad. She stepped forward. Her high heels clicked on the linoleum floor and Fred wondered when that floor had last felt the steps of a woman.

"Excuse me," she said. Her clear, soft voice seemed to fill the old hotel with life.

She stopped and glanced around, as if startled by the sound of her own words. "I'm.... I am looking for a Mister Fred Thorpe."

Fred thought he was going to swallow his tongue. She was looking for him, as if he actually existed to someone outside of these walls besides the retirement department at the city. He had retired early when his time came up and had regretted it, but not enough to go look for another job.

"That's me," he said, sort of waving a hand in her direction. His voice sounded really odd following hers.

She seemed relieved and took another step forward. "Would it be possible for us to talk?"

He shrugged and pointed to the vacant chair that had been Jamison's chair.

She shook her head. "In private, if you don't mind."

Again Fred shrugged and without looking at the others pushed himself up from his chair in the most dignified manner he had managed in years. He nodded toward the hall that led past the old front desk cage.

"We can talk back in the kitchen."

She said fine and he walked ahead of her distinct and firm footsteps down the hall and into the kitchen.

After they were both settled at the old wood table she took a deep breath. She started out saying that he wasn't going to believe her.

She was right.

He didn't.

CHAPTER EIGHTEEN

About two years later…
June 10th, 2020
Central Wilderness Area, Idaho

TALIA FLAT ENJOYED the incredible top sirloin steak with mushrooms marinated in butter. And the rolls seemed to just melt in her mouth. Amazing meal, just amazing.

They were seated in a fairly small private room off the main dining room. As with everything in the lodge, the room had polished log walls and a huge window looking out in a different direction than the valley. But the view was almost as spectacular, especially as the sun slowly set coloring the hills with reds and oranges.

The conversation before and during dinner had been light and fun.

She relished the time and realized just how lucky she was to be sitting here in the company of three of the great math minds on the planet. She wasn't sure if she belonged in their company, but for the time being, she was going to push that thought aside and enjoy the moment.

And enjoy the laughter with Ryan. Now that he was relaxing as well, his sense of humor was coming out more and more. And she loved that. Not only was

he smart and good-looking, he was funny and clearly enjoyed life.

As the last plates were cleared, Duster stood and pulled over another chair to the table, then went out into the lobby area.

When he got back, he smiled. "We have a special guest to help us talk about this next thing we want to talk about. Actually, we want to offer both of you a long-term job."

Talia was surprised at that, honestly. She taught at the University of Wisconsin Madison and she knew Ryan taught at Berkley. She made enough money to be happy. Not great money, but enough to allow her to enjoy her life.

And for the most part, she enjoyed teaching. But her real love was in the research and she always sort of felt the class time took away from that far too often.

Ryan seemed surprised as well, but before he could say anything, Duster held up his hand to indicate no questions.

"What we are going to talk about tonight is why we had you both sign those nondisclosure agreements. Are you both still all right with that?"

Talia nodded and noticed beside her that Ryan did as well.

"Good," Duster said. "While we are waiting for our guest, I want to be clear about this offer. The moment you come to work for us, you will never worry about money again. Ever. You will both become independently wealthy very quickly. And we will have at your disposal the best libraries, equipment, and computers in the world."

Talia started to ask how that was possible, but again Duster stopped her.

"You know that Bonnie and I are fantastically rich?" Duster asked.

"We give some money to universities to fund chairs and help in remodeling,"

Bonnie said. "And we have a major historical research institute in Boise."

"The mathematics wing of that institute in Boise is in a large building downtown," Duster said.

"And the job is a lifetime job," Bonnie said. "You can still teach when you want, but we have a hunch that joining us will keep you more than busy and challenged for longer than you can imagine."

Talia was so shocked, she didn't even have a question left. And she had a hunch that the surprises were just starting because at that moment the woman who had been behind the front desk of the lodge came in and sat down.

"This is Dawn Edwards," Bonnie said, introducing her. "She and her husband, along with Duster and I, own this lodge."

"The Dr. Edwards?" Ryan asked before Talia could even get out a complement about how much she loved it here.

Dawn laughed.

"The historian?" Ryan asked.

"I am that Dawn Edwards," Dawn said, shaking Ryan's hand, then reaching over and shaking Talia's hand.

Talia had no idea what Ryan was talking about, but he was clearly impressed by her credentials beyond the fact that she and Bonnie and Duster owned this place.

Ryan glanced at Talia and must have instantly seen that she didn't understand, so he smiled and said, "Professor Edwards is the world's leading writer on the history of old mining camps in the West."

Dawn nodded. "My first major-selling book was about that town down in the valley that you visited earlier today."

Talia nodded and forced herself to take a deep breath. Duster had been talking about a major job offer and now another

very smart person had just joined them. Talia was feeling more and more out of her depth with every passing moment.

So after a few more minutes of small talk and Dawn and her research, Ryan turned back to Duster and Bonnie. "I want to know more about this job. But first I want to know how you managed to buy this wonderful lodge."

Silence.

Talia didn't much like that silence.

Duster glanced first at Bonnie, then at Dawn.

"You're going to offer them the jobs, aren't you?" Dawn asked, smiling at Duster.

Duster nodded. "Without a reservation at all. We need them both to figure out the nature of that sound."

"Then we need to tell them the entire truth from this moment forward," Dawn said.

Duster nodded.

"Let me," Bonnie said, leaning forward.

She looked first at Talia, then at Ryan. "You both know that we are mathematicians focusing on the relationship with time, matter, and energy? Correct?"

Talia nodded. She would never have even thought of coming out here for a special project without knowing and being in awe of their minds and the work they had done.

"So this next part is going to be very hard for you to believe," Bonnie said. "But if you just listen tonight and then allow us to show you tomorrow, we can prove everything we will tell you tonight is real."

"This flat sounds scary," Ryan said.

Talia agreed.

"Not scary," Dawn said. "Exciting once you change your perceptions."

"So to answer your question honestly about the lodge," Bonnie said. "We didn't buy it. We all built this in 1901 and 1902."

Talia just sat back. Her mind was not accepting what Bonnie had said.

"The old home site we stood on this afternoon to take readings," Duster said, "was the former site of a home we built as well."

"You did find the Nexus," Ryan said, his voice soft.

"We did," Duster said, nodding.

"Holy shit," Ryan said. "And you figured out how to manipulate it?"

"In a manner of speaking," Duster said.

Talia just felt numb.

Bonnie and Duster and Dawn were all very, very serious.

Ryan seemed to understand instantly what they were talking about.

And that scared Talia more than she wanted to admit.

CHAPTER NINETEEN

December 24th, 2018
Boise, Idaho

THE KITCHEN OF the Golden Dream Hotel smelled of the hot dogs Fred and the other two had had for lunch. The dirty pan and plates were still in the sink. Fred couldn't remember if it had been his turn to do dishes or Hank's.

It was Christmas Eve.

What did it matter?

"My name is Sandy Reeves," the good-looking young woman said across the kitchen table. "I am a private investigator and I was hired to find you by a Mr. Radley Stout."

Fred laughed and leaned toward the woman who looked like she might be barely old enough to be out of high school. "Right. So what is the gimmick? What are you selling?"

She didn't seem bothered by his rude question at all. Calmly she reached into her large purse and pulled out at small, black pistol. With a thump, she placed it on the table between them.

"I have a permit for that," she said, smiling slightly.

All Fred could do was stare at the black gun while she pulled her wallet out of her purse, flipped it open, and slid it across the table. Then she scooped the gun back into her purse.

Open in front of him was her driver's license and her private investigator's license from the state. He glanced at her birth date. She was twenty-six.

He nodded and slid her wallet back at her. "So what does this Mr. Stout want from me?"

She sort of shrugged. "Actually, I am not exactly sure. He owns a place called the Garden Lounge, down on Main. He said he just wanted to buy you a Christmas Eve drink."

"That's all?" Fred shook his head. "He hired a private investigator to find me to buy me a drink?"

She nodded, almost looking embarrassed. "I am just supposed to take you down to the Garden Lounge. And Mr. Stout gave me strict instructions to not force you in any way. He knows nothing about how you are living or even that you are alive. So are you interested in having a drink?"

Fred glanced at her and then around at the old kitchen and the dishes in the sink. It was Christmas Eve and he had absolutely nothing better to do.

"What the hell," he said. "I've always believed that you never look a gift horse in the mouth."

"True," she said. "You just never know when a miracle might happen."

He stared at her, but she only smiled, not explaining at all.

Slowly he pushed himself back from the table and stood. "I could use a drink tonight."

She nodded. "So could I."

CHAPTER TWENTY

About two years later…
June 10th, 2020
Central Wilderness Area, Idaho

RYAN WAS NOT believing that Bonnie and Duster had found the Nexus they theorized was possible in their work. Mathematical theory saying that all time and energy had to meet in one physical location was one thing, but converting that theory into a reality seemed impossible to even imagine.

And then being able to use the Nexus to travel in time just brought up so many questions, nothing seemed likely.

But Ryan had no idea why these two major math minds would even suggest what they were suggesting. They had no reason at all to prank in any fashion Talia or him.

"I think we need to start from the beginning," Bonnie said.

"Please," Talia said.

"It started back in the 1870s when a distant relative of mine worked a gold mine," Duster said. "The mine played out but he went back and tried it again and around 1878 he punched the mine

into a large cavern and then deeper into a cavern filled with what look to be rose quartz crystals. The mine from that point forward remained shut down and in my family."

"The cavern is massive," Bonnie said and Ryan could see Dawn nodding. "An entire massive football stadium could fit inside it easily."

Ryan was having a hard time imaging that size of cavern.

"And that's only a small side cavern of an infinite number of even bigger caverns," Duster said, "all covered completely in the crystals."

"So what are these crystals?" Talia asked.

Ryan had a hunch he knew the answer, but he let Bonnie and Duster explain.

"Each crystal represents a timeline," Bonnie said.

"Every time anyone makes a decision," Duster said, "an alternate timeline is created, thus a new crystal is formed. Most decisions don't change anything and the crystal is absorbed back into the larger timeline crystal. But if the decision has major impacts, then the crystal and that timeline remain."

"An infinite number of timelines," Ryan said, nodding.

"Thus an infinite number of massive caverns," Duster said.

"The crystals close to the mine entrance," Bonnie said, "represent timelines that, for all intents and purposes, are identical to this timeline."

"So we actually fibbed a little when we said we built this lodge," Duster said. "Our counterparts came to this timeline from another and built it while we were building this lodge in another timeline."

"An infinite number of you went back in time and built an infinite number

Now Available
from all your favorite booksellers
in trade paper and electronic editions.

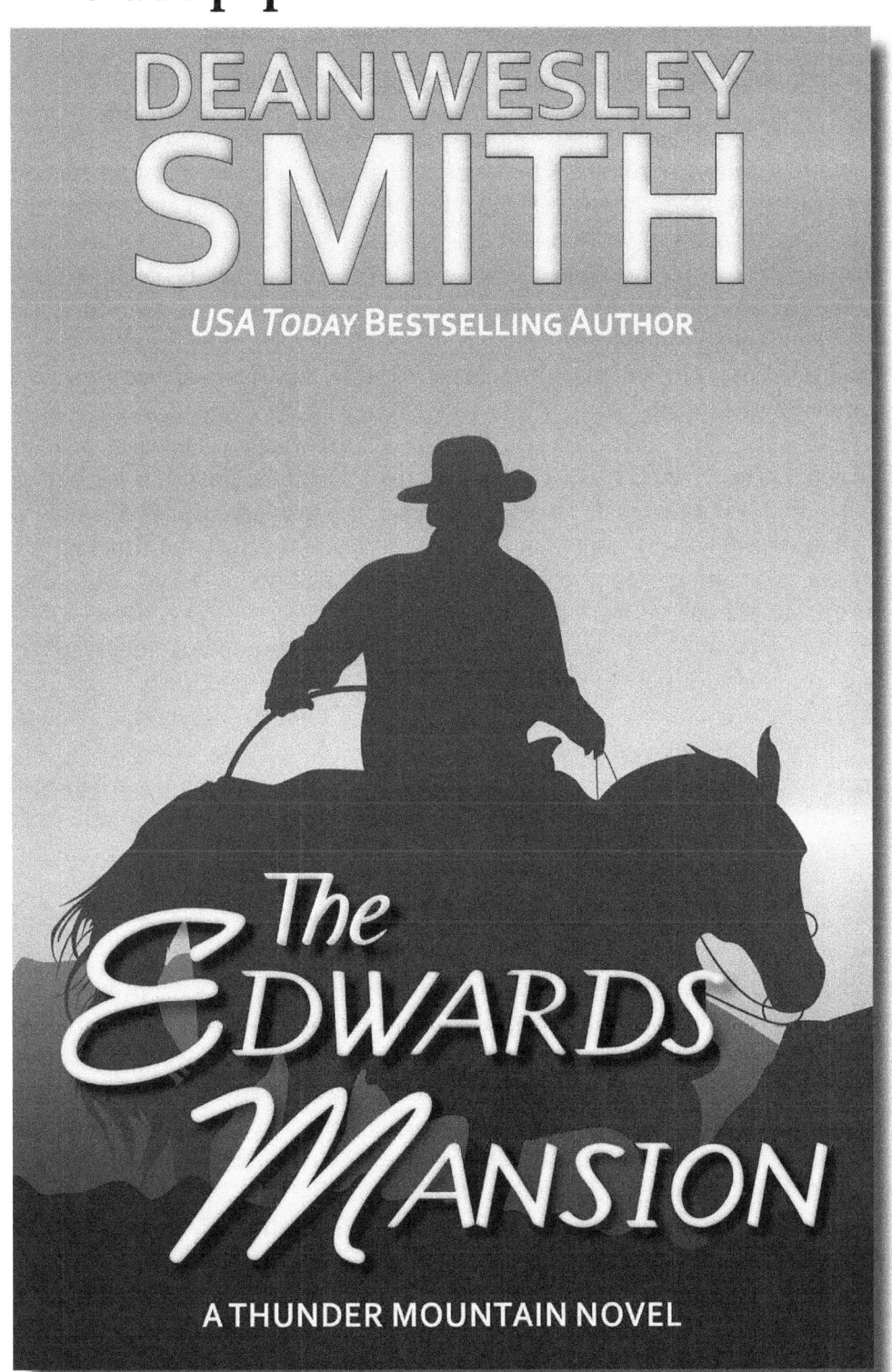

of lodges in an infinite number of timelines," Ryan said.

"Basically," Duster said. "Yes."

"So keep going with your story," Talia said. "How do you do this 'going back in time'?"

"After Bonnie and I were shown the mine by my father," Duster said, "when we were still finishing our first doctorates in mathematics. We had a hunch we knew what it was, but nothing in the math of physics showed it to be possible. So we spent the next four years working out the basic mathematics on time and energy and mass and how time and energy meet and form a physical item."

"The crystals," Talia said.

"Exactly," Duster said.

"After that," Bonnie said, "we used the math to develop a very simple device that allows us to simply step into another timeline using the energy from the crystal."

"We can control it now almost to the hour," Duster said.

"Only two minutes and fifteen seconds pass in this timeline when we are in another?" Bonnie said. "But we cannot go back into any time that we are alive in any timeline. The universe won't let us."

"We can spend entire lives in the history of other timelines," Dawn said, "have kids, grow old, die, and when we return only two minutes and fifteen seconds will have passed."

"So you have used this to get your incredible research detail," Ryan said.

"Living in the time you are writing about sure helps," Dawn said, grinning.

Ryan felt like his head was about to explode. This had to be a dream he would wake up from at any moment.

"So how old are you?" Talia asked, leaning forward. It seemed to Ryan she was getting a slight grasp on the real world issues of this entire thing faster than he was.

Duster shrugged and glanced at Bonnie.

"I stopped counting," she said, "but it's many, many thousands of years we have lived."

Dawn laughed. "I stopped counting when Madison and I went past ten thousand years. And you two were thousands of years older than us when we started."

"You have lived that long?" Ryan asked, his mind now gone.

Talia had just sat back in her chair. She was gone from her eyes.

"Died a bunch of times as well," Duster said. "Mostly accidents, some old age, but each trip just lasts over two minutes."

"Does it affect the timeline you are living in?" Ryan asked. "Or does the timeline reset when you leave it?"

Duster pointed at the walls of the lodge room around them.

"Of course," Ryan said, shaking his head.

"If you have a family in another timeline, that family stays," Bonnie said. "All your actions in that timeline create other timelines as well, of course."

"An infinite number of timelines," Ryan said to himself.

"So tomorrow, we'll head back to Boise and show you the institute," Duster said. "But the job we are offering, the challenge we are offering, is finding out why sound waves can travel through time. And what else can cut through time as well?"

"Will we be able to also travel to another timeline?" Talia asked.

"Actually, if you accept the job, we will insist on it almost immediately," Bonnie said.

"Why?" Ryan asked. That made no sense at all.

"We will jump you a hundred years into the future," Duster said, "to the institute of that time. Then bring you right back."

"Holy shit," Ryan said again. "You want to set us in that future time, as if we were born in the future, so anything we do in this time is just lasting slightly over two minutes in the future."

"Exactly," Duster said.

"I don't understand," Talia said.

"By jumping you to the future and then bringing you back through another crystal," Bonnie said, "if an accident happened say in a year to either of you and you died, you would end up in the future just two minutes and fifteen seconds from when you left."

"You are offering us unlimited money," Ryan said.

Duster nodded. "You will both be rich beyond anything you could ever spend."

"And you are offering us basic immortality," Ryan said.

Bonnie and Duster and Dawn all nodded.

"Just for us to do the mathematical research," Ryan asked, "on how sound can travel through time?"

Again Bonnie and Duster and Dawn all nodded.

Ryan just shook his head, not really believing what they were saying, but knowing in his heart and mind they were telling the truth.

"So we assume you would like time to think about this," Bonnie said. "And either of you can say no if you like. You just have to abide by the nondisclosure agreement."

Ryan couldn't imagine saying no if all this was real.

He glanced at the stunned expression on Talia's face, then looked at Bonnie and Duster. "Think you might sweeten the deal a little?"

They both instantly looked puzzled.

Ryan smiled. "I always wanted an espresso machine."

With that, everyone laughed.

Even Talia.

CHAPTER TWENTY-ONE

December 24th, 2018
Boise, Idaho

SANDY REEVES, Miss Private Eye with the Big Black Gun, held the front door of the Garden Lounge open for Fred to head through. He had passed by the Garden a hundred times and always thought about stopping. Never had. It had just not been the right time. He never expected Christmas Eve to be that right time.

The place smelled of ancient smoke and green plants and he immediately felt at home.

Much more than at the hotel.

Empty tables cluttered the center of the room and booths filled both side walls. Christmas candles were lit on every table. An old-looking polished-wood bar filled the wall opposite the front door and three men sat on stools near the bar's center with their backs to the door. They were the only three customers.

A medium-sized man in a white apron was standing behind the bar. He looked up and said, "Holy Shit."

The three men at the bar turned around as if pulled by the same string as the bartender put a glass on the bar and headed around the end.

He dodged around a few tables with ease. He grabbed Fred's hand and shook it as if he was seeing an old friend after many years.

Fred studied the bartender's face. He looked to be in his early fifties, with thinning gray and brown hair. His eyes were green and his smile seemed to fill his entire face.

After what seemed like a long moment, the bartender took a breath and sort of shook himself. "I'm sorry. I'm Radley Stout. I own this place. And I'm really glad you came."

All Fred could do was shrug. "Not as if I had much else to do. And you did offer a free drink."

Stout just laughed and patted Fred on the back. "Come on up to the bar. I have a few friends I want you to meet."

Stout had Fred take the stool on the left of the three men and the lady P.I. took the open stool to their right.

Stout went around behind the bar as he did the introductions.

Dave was the closest. He was an airline pilot and his daughter was the private investigator.

Next to him was a big guy named Carl who did construction and beside him was a convict-looking man by the name of Billy.

"All right," Fred said to Stout. "Why bring me here?"

Again Stout laughed. "As you said, to have a Christmas drink. Give me a moment and I will explain."

He rummaged in the drawer under the cash register and came up with a key. Then he went to the end of the bar and unlocked a glass case that was mounted on the wall over an old jukebox.

Everyone at the bar watched in silence as he pulled out three of the four glasses that were in there and walked back to the sink. He rinsed out one of the glasses and held it up for Fred and everyone to see.

It was a crystal-type glass, with the Garden Lounge logo etched near the center and the name Fred over the logo.

Fred now understood why he was here. Damn silly reason. "So you needed a Fred to join the toast this year. That it?"

Stout shook his head, set the glass down on the mat above the ice and started to rinse out the other glasses. "No, actually that glass was yours three years ago."

No one else said a word. They either watched Stout wash the glasses, or they stared down into their own drink, as if slightly uneasy about something.

Fred had never seen that glass before and had never met Stout before or been in this bar before. This gift horse was starting to look like a bust, just as most of them had in his life. He laughed for a short moment and then said, "Not highly likely."

"That's true," Dave said. "It isn't highly likely. But I think it's true."

Fred turned to Dave.

Dave was a clean-cut sort, with short hair and wrinkles on his forehead that cut lines across his tanned skin.

"Were you there when I supposedly owned that glass?"

Fred pointed in the direction of Stout and the glass. He had just finished washing out a glass that had the name Dave over the logo.

"In a manner of speaking," Dave said. "I was. But I too do not remember the first time. However, I do remember the second."

Fred just stared at him for a moment before shaking his head and pushing himself back off the stool. These people were all nuts. Free drink or not, this was just a little too much.

"I knew this entire thing was crazy, but you folks are all a bunch of loonies."

Stout put the third glass on the rubber mat. It had the name Carl etched on it.

"Fred. Please just hold on for a moment. I just want to buy you a drink and tell you a story. I know you won't believe me, but what can it hurt? It's Christmas Eve."

Sandy looked down the bar and sort of smiled. "I told you that you wouldn't believe this."

Fred stopped with one hand still holding onto the back of the bar stool and looked down the line of faces staring at him. It seemed clear that everyone wanted him to stay and everyone was taking this craziness very, very seriously. He took a deep breath and let it out in a noisy sigh.

Sandy laughed. "You said never look a gift horse in the mouth. So stop looking."

At that he laughed. "All right. One drink and then Miss Private Investigator there can take me back."

"And a story, too," Stout said. "Don't forget."

Fred nodded and climbed back up on the stool. "A story too. As long as you don't want me to buy anything."

Stout nodded and smiled. "I promise. Now what would you like to drink?"

Fred ordered a vodka tonic and for the next half hour the conversation was light and fun. He could feel the heaviness and gloom of the Golden Dream Hotel lifting from his shoulders as everyone laughed and talked and sipped their drinks. There seemed to be a friendship among these people that he had not felt before. A closeness that went far beyond customers in a bar.

Some Classic Dean Wesley Smith Stories
Available at your favorite booksellers.

Fred ended up asking for a second drink and Stout refilled the special glass. As he placed it on the napkin in front of Fred he said, "I think it's time for the story."

Everyone nodded as Stout went back to stand in front of the well where he was sipping on a glass of eggnog. He leaned against the back bar and raised his glass. "First, at toast. To friends again united."

Fred drank to the toast not knowing what Stout was talking about.

"I had the Garden for just over a year," Stout said. "And I had some really good, regular customers. But four of those customers had become my good friends. Dave. Carl. You, Fred. And Jess."

With each name Stout tipped his drink in the person's direction. With the last name he tipped it in the direction of the glass case that still held one glass over the jukebox.

Fred assumed the name on that glass was Jess.

"Fred," Stout said, "you see that jukebox there? Everyone here except you knows just how special that jukebox is. This is the part of the story that you will not believe no matter how hard or well I explain it, so just think of this part as fiction. All right?"

Again, Fred just nodded, so Stout went on.

"That jukebox can take a person back to a memory. Not just in your mind, but in real flesh and blood. It's a sort of time machine."

"Fiction is right," Fred said and Stout just held up his hand.

"I discovered how the jukebox worked by accident before I ever opened the Garden. Three years ago on Christmas Eve I decided I would give my four friends a chance to go back into their

pasts. A special Christmas present from me. At that time, you were divorced from a woman by the name of Alice and you had a kid."

Suddenly the bar felt very warm. Stout was assuming that Fred had been a regular in here for almost a year and once been married to Alice. But he knew that wasn't true. He must have had too much to drink with just two drinks, since it felt as if the room was spinning. How could Stout know about Alice? And Stout was saying that Fred had married her and divorced her after having a kid.

Stout was watching and after a moment he went on. "You had been divorced from Alice for ten years and you hated her. Completely and totally hated her. It was a standing joke among the five of us. You also had a daughter by the name of Jenny."

"So what happened to her in this crazy world of yours?" Fred asked. His voice had more anger in it than he could remember feeling in recent times.

Stout just shrugged. "I assume she was never born. When you left here through the jukebox, you said the song reminded you of the night you and Alice first made love. The night you conceived Jenny which forced you two to get married out of high school."

Again the room felt too warm.

The night he and Alice first made love was the night her parents were gone to a Christmas Eve party. Right before going over to her house, he had gone to the drugstore to buy some rubbers. He remembered almost chickening out and then the next thing he knew he had a pack of them in his hand and was heading out of the store.

He and Alice always used one every time they made love. She met another guy a year later and left because she said he was never going to ask her to marry him. She was right. He never did.

"You all right?" Stout asked.

Fred glanced up. Everyone was looking at him. He tried to laugh, but it sounded sort of weak. "You did your research real well. Sandy there must be a really good investigator."

"She's good all right," Stout said and Sandy held up her glass in a thank-you gesture. "But she didn't find any of this information out. I knew about Alice and your divorce because you told us over and over for almost a year."

"So how come I didn't live any of this?"

Stout just sighed. "Because you lived a different life after you changed whatever it was you changed that evening. The only reason I remember you is because I was touching the jukebox when the song ended. For some reason that allows me to remember the old timeline. I remember you being in here, but no one else does."

He pointed at the glass. "I was holding onto the glass, too, when you didn't come back."

"Didn't come back? What do you mean I didn't come back?" Again he was trying to keep the anger out of his voice. But all of this was making him mad. And damn tired.

"You changed something while you were back there," Stout said. "And whatever you changed did not lead you to the Garden again in your new life. At least not until now. If you had not changed anything, you would have come back when the song ended."

Dave was nodding. "That happens every year to me. This year I plan to go back and watch Sandy being born. It will be a Christmas present to myself. Trust me, I will be very careful to not change anything."

Fred looked at Dave for a moment and then shook his head. "So why bring me back here now. Assuming that all this is true, which I find not likely, why now?"

Now it was Stout's turn to look slightly embarrassed. "I guess I just wanted the old group back together again on Christmas Eve. Selfish, I guess."

"Looks like you didn't pull it off," Fred said. "What about that other glass? Didn't your P.I. there find the guy?"

Stout took a sip of his eggnog and then looked up. Fred could see the pain in Stout's eyes and the sadness that coated his face. The silence in the bar seemed to fill the room with a thick, heavy feel.

"Sandy found him all right," Stout said. "He changed something, also, when he went back that Christmas Eve three years ago. In the new world he created he was killed by a drunk driver two years before I opened the Garden. We found him up in Memorial Cemetery."

Fred shook his head in disbelief and looked down at his name in the old glass. "So what did I do in the previous life? Be a lawyer or something?"

Stout took a deep breath and then laughed. "Not hardly. You worked for the city. I think you had something to do with streets or something like that."

It was Fred's turn to laugh. "I did that in this life, too. Fancy that. So how come, if that machine can change someone's past, you just don't go back and stop that guy from getting killed?"

Stout shook his head. "I am actually glad it doesn't work that way. Way too much responsibility. No, you can only go back to your own memories. You can't change other people's memories. Or their lives."

Dave stood. "Tell you what, Stout. Plug in that jukebox and I will go watch my daughter being born. That might just give old Fred here a new outlook on life."

Stout shrugged and walked down the length of the bar to the jukebox. Dave downed the last of his drink and joined him.

"You got the record I brought on there?" Dave asked as Stout reached around behind the jukebox and plugged it in. The colored lights flickered for a moment and then held steady. It was a beautiful old Wurlitzer, with the chrome arch, red, green and blue colored lights, and bright red buttons. Inside Fred could see the disk full of forty-five records all waiting to be played.

"Just punch up B-4," Stout said and handed Dave a quarter.

Everyone at the bar had swung around on their stools and were watching intently. Fred felt uneasy and nervous, even though he knew the only thing that would happen was that the song would start playing and that would be that.

Dave dropped the quarter into the slot, punched the two buttons and then stood back as the machine clicked and whirred. Inside Fred could see a record being picked up and placed on the turntable.

Stout saluted Dave.

"Don't go changing anything, Dad," Sandy said. "I want to be here when you get back."

Dave laughed. "Don't worry. Just going to watch."

The jukebox clicked and the song started. Fred recognized it immediately. An old Rick Nelson song called, "It's Up To You."

That song reminded Fred of...

The bar shifted and was gone. For a quick instant he felt dizzy and then everything went black.

And then came back to a bright white spotlight.

Right in his eyes.

CHAPTER TWENTY-TWO

About two years later…
June 10th, 2020
Central Wilderness Area, Idaho

TALIA HAD NO doubt she wouldn't be sleeping anytime soon, so when Ryan suggested the two of them get coats and go sit on the deck, she suggested instead that they just sit by the fire.

Dawn showed them where they could get hot tea or soft drinks in the kitchen and then she excused herself and headed off to bed. Duster and Bonnie had already retired for the night, and no lodge employees were left at all.

So it was just the two of them with a slightly crackling wood fire in a large stone fireplace in a lodge that felt more comfortable than almost any place Talia had been in before.

She could easily see herself living here at times. Easily. And she didn't consider herself any sort of mountain person. But this lodge was that special.

They pulled two of the thick overstuffed chairs closer to each other in front of the fire and turned them so they slightly faced each other. The chairs were the most comfortable Talia could remember, not too hard, but yet soft enough to feel like she was being embraced by the fabric.

Talia had made herself a cup of tea and Ryan was sipping on a Diet Coke. The orange of the flames gave his face a sort of deeper color that made him look even more handsome than he already was. And the light from the fire caught his dark eyes at times and made them almost look as if they were twinkling.

She had read far too many romance novels in her time to not realize what this situation was, and she didn't mind that at all.

They sat in silence for a few minutes, both lost in their own thoughts. And it felt comfortable.

Very comfortable.

Talia could have never imagined sitting and just thinking (without saying anything) beside a handsome man. And she wasn't the slightest bit nervous and trying to think of something to say.

Finally, Ryan took a sip of his Diet Coke, set it on the wood coffee table in front of the chairs and turned to look at her fully. "What do you think of their offer?"

"Too good and too crazy to be true," she said. And she believed that almost to her core. But at the same time, she wanted it to all be true and she was still in awe of Bonnie and Duster, even after spending a day with them and the crazy talk.

"I agree," Ryan said, nodding. "But I don't see a downside in letting them prove to us tomorrow that they are either joking or that what they are saying is true."

She agreed with that. She would have no idea why two major scientists would tell such a tall tale, but she wanted to find out why.

But mostly, she had to admit, she wanted to spend more time with Ryan.

A lot more time.

"So if we agree to this," she said, "we're going to be working with each other and spending time closely together. You all right with that?"

"It's what I'm hoping," Ryan said, smiling at her. "How do you feel about that?"

"Completely the same," she said, returning his smile.

Silence as they stared at each other in the firelight.

Damn, she just wanted to kiss him.

It didn't get any better than this on the romantic scale of things. She was alone with a handsome, smart man, in a giant log lodge, high in the mountains, in front of a soft wood fire.

If this didn't end up in mad, crazy sex, something was wrong with both of them.

But she had no idea how to bridge that gap between the two chairs without standing and going over there and just sitting on his lap. That was a consideration and if something didn't happen soon, she was going to do just that.

"Well," he said, after they had looked at each for a very long time in the flickering light. "There is something I really need to do."

He stood and she could feel her heart sinking. She should have just stood and moved over and sat on his lap. Damn, why had she hesitated?

He reached for her hand and pulled her out of the chair and then into his arms.

And then he kissed her before she even realized what had happened.

After a moment, she kissed him back, holding him and pushing into him.

He felt wonderful. Very strong, and he kissed better than any man she had ever kissed before.

They kissed like that for a very long time until she suddenly realized how warm she was getting, both from his kisses and the close fire.

She needed to get out of these clothes and get him out of his as well.

She pushed back from him and said, "We're going to have a really interesting day tomorrow."

He nodded.

She took his hand and turned both of them toward the staircase. "We need to get some sleep, don't you think?"

He started to say something and then stopped.

At the bottom of the stairs, she stopped and turned and kissed him again. Then she said, "I think we should sleep in my room, don't you? Your room is beside Bonnie and Dusters' room and I would hate to wake them with our sleeping."

He laughed and then said, "So you snore?"

"Oh, I can be much louder than that if the time and place and motion is right."

That time he just coughed.

She led him up the stairs and to her bedroom, which was (as far as she was concerned) exactly how that scene in front of the fire should have ended.

CHAPTER TWENTY-THREE

December 24th, 2018
Boise, Idaho

"GOD DAMN IT!" Stout shouted as the song started.

Sandy, Billy, and Carl had all been looking at Dave and Stout. But as one they turned to look at the bar stool where a moment before Fred had been sitting.

"Oh, no," Carl said.

Sandy just shook her head. "Every year we do this and every year something weird happens."

Stout moved down the bar and put his hand on Fred's barstool, as if that would help bring him back.

"Damn it! I forgot to ask him if he had a memory with that song. What the hell was I thinking?"

"Don't worry about it, Stout." Sandy said. "He'll be back."

Stout picked up Fred's glass and looked at the name. "He didn't come back last time he left here through the jukebox."

Stout reached over and picked up Dave's glass. Then he headed back for the jukebox. "I want everyone holding onto the jukebox when the song ends. If he doesn't come back this time, I want someone besides me remembering him."

Sandy laughed. "Boy won't Dad be in for a surprise when he gets back."

CHAPTER TWENTY-FOUR

About two years later…
June 11th, 2020
Boise, Idaho

RYAN AND TALIA didn't get much sleep that night, and the morning shower together made them late for breakfast with Bonnie and Duster and Dawn.

Ryan didn't care in the slightest. It had been a flat wonderful night. And at that moment he wanted to take any job, it didn't matter, that would keep him close to Talia.

But while they were getting dressed, they talked a little about the coming decision and it was clear to Ryan that both of them had come to the same conclusion.

They both wanted to see what Bonnie and Duster had been talking about and have it proven that all that they said was real. And if it all turned out to be real, by some strange chance, both Ryan and Talia would take the jobs in a heartbeat.

So at breakfast, they had told Bonnie and Duster they wanted to see what they had to show them.

Bonnie and Duster and Dawn all applauded.

After a short breakfast and packing, Duster decided to leave his car at the Institute and all four of them flew in the helicopter back to Boise. What had been a long seven hour drive on twisting mountain roads turned out to be a thirty-five minute beautiful flight over the mountains.

They flew close by the main downtown area of Boise that looked like it had more trees than people and then to the airport.

Fifteen minutes after landing, Duster pulled a large Cadillac SUV, just like the one he had left in the mountains, into the driveway of a large mansion. Bonnie had driven that one to the airport and when Ryan asked how many of the big Cadillacs they owned, Duster laughed and said simply, "Enough."

The road the mansion sat on was called Warm Springs and Ryan was stunned at the beauty of the street. Huge old towering oak and cottonwood trees seemed to line the entire length, forming a dark green sky over the pavement.

The mansion they pulled into after an automatic gate opened was a massive Victorian-style building with a wide front porch and a couple of tall towers stretching up seemingly into the trees. The base was made of large stone and parts of the building were brick.

Ryan could count at least four chimneys as Duster took them past the massive home and into a large parking garage in the back. Down the hill from the parking garage was a river, lined by a paved path on both sides and tall trees.

"This is just amazing," Talia said.

Ryan couldn't have said it better.

As they climbed out of the Cadillac, the large garage door closed. Duster moved over to a door in the sidewall. "There will be plenty of time to explore the main mansion." He opened the door and stepped into what looked like a storage area for tools.

He eased one tool forward slightly on a wooden bench and the entire wall slid aside revealing a staircase going down.

Ryan just shook his head and smiled at Talia.

As Duster started down the stairs he said loud enough for Ryan and Talia to hear, "The underground caverns extend not only under this property, but under the properties to either side, which the Institute owns as well."

"What exactly is this institute?" Talia asked.

Behind her Bonnie answered. "Historical Studies Institute is the official name. It is dedicated to helping research of different times in history."

"As Dawn has done?" Talia asked.

"Exactly," Bonnie said as Duster reached the bottom of the very long stairs and punched a combination into a key pad and the big metal door clicked open. Ryan was very impressed. Clearly money was not a consideration for anything.

He had no idea how Bonnie and Duster intended he and Talia to get rich as they said, but it seemed to Ryan to be more and more possible the more he saw.

Duster led them into a large cavern that seemed to stretch into a distance. It had been carved out of solid rock and had a very high ceiling. The floor was smooth stone and ahead he could see a large living room area with a dozen couches and chairs in various groupings around a massive stone fireplace. The fireplace had a real wood fire going, burning softly.

The air seemed dry and comfortably warm.

A huge kitchen ran along one wall and a bar divided it from the living room area that could sit a dozen people. There was no one else around at all but the four of them.

Ryan just stopped near a couch and stared around, trying to take it all in.

"Is this the Nexus you were talking about?" Talia asked, staring around at the huge cavern.

"No," Duster said as both he and Bonnie went into the kitchen area and opened a large fridge there. "Something to drink?"

"Water," Talia said.

"Water is great," Ryan said, moving over to the large counter and sitting on a stool before his knees gave out from just the surprise of seeing this.

"How big is this place?" Talia asked as she sat on the stool beside Ryan.

"It goes down two more levels and a pretty good distance in both directions," Bonnie said, giving both of them a plastic bottle of cold water.

"Some of it isn't used in this time period," Duster said. "It was built for expansion. We'll explain all that later after we show you what is possible here."

"When did you build this?" Ryan asked, still trying to gather his thoughts.

"We brought crews in from the East Coast in 1880, when this was still way out in the country," Duster said. "And we switched the crews out every few months so no one would really know the extent of what was down here."

"And we paid them well for their silence," Bonnie said, smiling.

"Yeah," Duster said. "We did that as well."

"So how many people know this is down here?" Ryan asked, looking at the furniture. It must be a vast number.

"You two are number twenty-one and twenty-two," Bonnie said. "There are more in the Institute in the future, of course."

Ryan looked at the dark eyes of Bonnie and then at Duster, who seemed like all this was normal.

"Why us?" Talia asked, softly.

"Because we need you two to solve this math problem with the sound and time," Duster said. "And we figure together, with our help and the help of a few others, you can do it."

"And if we don't solve it?" Ryan asked, "Do you erase all this from out minds or something?"

Both Bonnie and Duster laughed. "Not hardly," Bonnie said after a moment. "Once you are in, you are in."

"I'm sure that you two will be solving more math and sound problems than the one we want as the years go by," Duster said.

"So you really can travel in time?" Ryan asked. "Are we going to get to see this Nexus?"

"We can travel into other timelines," Duster said, smiling. "And go into those other basically identical timelines at various points, which gives the sensation of traveling in time. But we cannot go back into the past of this timeline, so technically, no, we cannot travel in time."

Ryan nodded. He actually understood all that.

"And we don't need to go to the Nexus to do so," Bonnie said. "Not since we built this place."

"So you two ready to see the past of another timeline?" Duster asked, putting his water bottle on the counter.

Ryan glanced at Talia and she nodded slowly.

Ryan felt more scared and more excited than he had felt in years.

He stood and helped Talia off her bar stool and the two of them, hand-in-hand, followed Bonnie and Duster toward a side entrance to the cavern.

"Scared?" Talia asked softly.

"Terrified," Ryan said, smiling at her.

"Oh, good," she said. "That way both of us will be shaking at the same time."

He just squeezed her hand as they headed forward toward a trip into the past.

CHAPTER TWENTY-FIVE

December 23rd, 1998
Outside Boise, Idaho

THE SPOTLIGHT HIT Fred square in the face and he moved to cover his eyes. Only his arm hit the steering wheel of his '57 Chevy.

"What...?" He said out loud as he glanced around like a frightened deer caught in a hunter's sights.

The car's engine and lights were off and the windows were rolled up tight. Rick Nelson belted out the song on the oldies station on the radio. Sweat trickled down the side of Fred's face and down his bare chest. The temperature inside the car must have been that of a steam bath and the spotlight was coming through the fogged-up front window.

"Oh, no!" A young woman's voice said from beside him.

He turned to look at her. That was when the memories flooded in like light pouring through an open door between a dark room and a lit one.

Marcy was struggling to get her bra back on. The two of them had dated for two years after Alice left him. Marcy worked at the department store downtown in the men's section and wanted him to be her husband more than almost anything.

That fact had suited him just fine because it made parking with her a lot of fun. She ended up marrying a guy from the appliance section of the store and had three kids last Fred heard.

Tonight was their first anniversary of going out and they were parked on the canal bank behind an orchard to the south of town. It was the only night they ever got caught parking by the police.

"This can't be," Fred said. He looked completely around the car. It was his classic restored '57 Chevy all right. The one he wrecked in 1999 while driving drunk on New Year's Eve.

A moment ago he was sitting in the Garden Lounge with a bunch of people who he thought were nuts and now he was back here parking with Marcy.

He held onto the steering wheel with sweaty hands.

He could still freshly remember getting here and what they had been doing just a few short moments ago. He remembered taking her bra off and almost putting his hand up her skirt. In fact, he was still aroused from all of it and he hadn't had anything but a piss-erection in years back at the old Golden Dream Hotel.

He had said he never looked a gift horse in the mouth. The Private Investigator's words now echoed back through his mind: *"You just never know when a miracle might happen."*

So this was what she was talking about.

Marcy smacked his arm. "Hurry! Get your shirt on."

Outside he heard the car door close and a vague shape through the fogged window started toward the door.

He had a clear memory that they had gotten dressed before the cop got to the window and the cop let them go with a strict warning to be moving along. They had laughed about it for days.

Stout had warned David not to change anything when he punched up the song. And Stout had said that the reason Fred didn't end up back at the Garden was because he changed something when he did this music/time-travel thing the last time.

If what Stout had been saying back there at the Garden was true, and it looked like it was, he had better do some fast dressing.

Real fast.

Marcy was already buttoning her blouse as he turned around and grabbed his shirt off the back seat where his younger self had tossed it a short time before. He had it on and buttoned, in what seemed like impossible speed to his older brain, just as the cop tapped on the window.

Marcy straightened her hair as Fred rolled down the window and looked into the cop's flashlight. "Wow, that's bright."

He remembered that was the exact same thing he had said when he didn't have years of memories to draw upon.

The cop shined his light on him, then on Marcy.

She smiled at the cop.

Fred turned and smiled at him as well.

Then the classic Ricky Nelson stopped singing.

And Fred was back on his bar stool at the Garden Lounge.

Stout, Sandy, Carl, and Billy stood around the jukebox, touching it.

Dave stood in front of the jukebox staring at them.

"Wow," was all Fred could say.

All four cheered and Stout held up an empty glass as if in a toast.

It felt really good to be back.

Real good.

CHAPTER TWENTY-SIX

About twenty-two years later…
June 11th, 2020
Boise, Idaho

TALIA HELD ONTO Ryan's hand as much as he held onto hers as Duster opened a large door into another cavern. As the door opened, the lights came up bright and illuminated a vast warehouse of clothing and supplies that seemed to span most of the last century in styles and looks.

"Amazing," Ryan said softly.

"Bigger than a couple dozen Wal-Mart stores," Bonnie said. "Anything you would need for any time period.

Duster moved over and handed Ryan a brown cowboy hat and a long brown oilskin coat like the one Duster wore.

Bonnie helped Talia into a dress over her blouse and jeans. The dress buttoned up the back and had a long skirt, but Bonnie said there was no point in buttoning it more than one button. They were just taking this much precaution in case they were seen from a distance

by anyone. They needed to look the time period.

That scared Talia more than she wanted to admit, because up until this point, she hadn't really believed any of the time travel stuff at all.

"What date are we going to in the other timeline?" Ryan asked.

"December 27th, 1889," Duster said as he turned and led them through another door on the other side of the massive supply cavern.

Inside the other door was a very wide hallway going in both directions in the rock. And there had to be a good fifty or more doors, all closed, on one side of the hallway.

"This looks like a bad nightmare," Ryan said.

Talia had to agree with that completely.

Duster laughed. "They are all numbered from one end to the other. Seventy doors."

Talia didn't even know what to think of that. This underground complex was just huge.

Duster pulled one door open about twenty steps down the hallway to the right. It was numbered 29.

On the other side of the door, the room looked like another long hallway that went deep into the rock. Along the right side were wooden tables with small wooden boxes on them. Then a floor-to-ceiling chain-link fence next to the table divided the long narrow room right down the middle.

Nestled in the rock wall on the other side of the fence was what looked like large rose quartz crystals with a flexible band around them and two wires leading from the band on each crystal to one of the wooden boxes on the table.

"Only a few of us are allowed into the area with the crystals," Duster said, pointing beyond the fence wall. "Never touch one. Extreme high energy, more than we have been able to measure."

"What are they?" Talia asked, staring at the beautiful crystals along the wall. There had to be sixty or more in this narrow long room. They seemed like a quartz crystal and all were slightly different shapes and sizes.

"Timelines," Ryan said softly.

Duster again laughed. "Exactly. Each crystal is a timeline. We took all these from the Nexus and brought them here."

"Every decision of every person creates a new timeline," Bonnie said. "A new crystal is formed with every decision. If nothing changes, the timeline is absorbed back into the original crystal."

Talia took a deep breath and tried to focus. "So we are in a crystal somewhere like one of those?"

"We are," Duster said.

"And if I decided to walk away now," she said, "a new crystal would form from that decision?"

"In an almost infinite number of timelines, you do walk away," Bonnie said. "And in an almost infinite amount of timelines you stay."

"So if we go back into another timeline," Ryan said, pointing at a crystal on the wall, if we change nothing, a new timeline is not created? Correct?"

"No, it is created by you simply going into the timeline," Duster said. "But if you change nothing, it absorbs back into the original crystal."

"So how does this area not instantly fill with crystals from the infinite number of decisions being made in all those timelines?" Talia asked.

"The new timelines form in the Nexus," Duster said. "We had to prove that mathematically before we even dared remove a crystal from the Nexus."

Ryan nodded and Talia just took another deep breath.

"Will you stay here and pull the plug in fifteen minutes?" Duster asked Bonnie.

"Glad to," she said, smiling, as Duster took one of the wires coming from the crystal and hooked it onto what looked like a battery pole sticking from the side of the wooden box.

He pointed to the pole, then the wire. "Red to red."

Then he adjusted three simple wooden dials on the front side of the wooden box. "Year, date, and time," Duster said.

Then as Talia watched, Duster picked up a thick work glove and put it on his right hand.

"Touch the top of the wooden box," Bonnie said, smiling at them. "And then keep looking at me."

Both Ryan and Talia touched the top of the smoothly polished wooden box. She had never given time travel much thought, but she never would have thought a time travel machine would be wooden on the outside.

Then Duster hooked up the second wire and Bonnie simply vanished.

There was no sense of movement.

Nothing.

"Where did she go?" Talia asked, glancing around at the long room.

"She didn't go anywhere," Duster said. "We did. Welcome to 1889."

CHAPTER TWENTY-SEVEN

December 27th, 1889
Boise, Idaho

RYAN TOOK TALIA'S hand for comfort and the two of them followed Duster and his swirling long coat and cowboy hat back through the large supply room.

The cavern seemed almost empty compared to a moment before. Clearly they didn't need as much stuff at this point in time and brought many things from the future. But it still had a lot, more than any large store, from saddles to coats and dresses and boots and hats.

They went back out into the large area with the kitchen and couches. Now all the furniture was period pieces and the kitchen looked more like a saloon bar than anything.

"How often do you upgrade this room?" Talia asked.

Ryan was impressed she could even get out a question. He was so stunned that jumping to other timelines was real, his brain was on mush mode.

"Every ten or so years," Duster said without slowing down. "But behind some of that time-appropriate decorations are hidden more modern features."

Ryan could understand that. He would have to ask Duster how they brought larger items back and how often they had to do that, considering the timeline problems.

Duster led them to an old elevator and opened the door for them.

"Don't worry," Duster said. "We modernized this as well.

Talia had hesitated getting onto the elevator that looked like it was made out of metal fence and Ryan was about to ask where the stairs were. The door to the elevator was nothing more than an ornate metal gate painted black.

"Elevators were fairly new in 1889, right?" Talia asked.

Again Ryan was impressed that her brain was working at all, let alone that she had that kind of information.

"A decade or so," Duster said. "But I wouldn't get on one until the 1920s."

That just made Ryan shake his head again. This was real.

It couldn't be, but it was.

The elevator was smooth and stopped in a small room with wood-paneled walls and ornate trim.

"Secret room on the main floor of the mansion," Duster said. "You'll learn all the ins and outs of the Institute mansion over time."

He looked through a peephole in the wood, then nodded and pushed open a hidden doorway.

Colder air hit Ryan at once as they stepped into the ornate front room and parlor of the mansion. Two overstuffed cloth chairs and a large couch faced a massive stone fireplace in one corner. A fire was burning and that seemed to be the only heat in the room.

Brown carpets covered some of the hardwood floors under the chairs and everything in the room was done in brown tones.

Ryan instantly liked the feel of the room.

"Nice," Talia said softly.

A large, ornate wooden desk sort of dominated an archway between the front parlor and a second room. A large guest book was open on the desk for people to sign.

The windows in the room were tall and the ceilings high, with an ornate chandelier hanging down in the middle. Heavy cloth drapes covered the windows and were closed. Three glass lanterns were lit on tables and two more on the desk, but even with the help of the fire, the room seemed dim.

Duster gave them a moment to look around, then he went to the front door and pulled it open. "If you don't mind," he said, "I'll stay here."

Ryan looked at him funny and then pushed open the screen door and stepped out into the extreme cold of the front porch.

Talia was right behind him.

He made it two steps and stopped, stunned.

The cold snapped at his face and it was snowing lightly. It was clearly still in the middle of the afternoon, but the light was dim because of the storm.

The huge oak trees that had been beside the mansion when they drove in were now much smaller and where the driveway had been was a wagon track.

There was no Warm Springs Avenue, either. Nothing more than a wagon track, quickly getting covered by the blowing snow, went past the front of the mansion.

The mansions on either side looked new and there were no other structures at all within sight through the snow.

"We really are in the past," Talia said, again taking his hand.

"In another timeline's past," Ryan said.

They stood there, shivering for a moment, then Ryan realized what he had been thinking. "Bonnie and Duster have been telling us the complete truth."

"Yeah," Talia said.

"And they are giving us the opportunity," Ryan said, "to travel in time, be basically immortal, rich, and work on the most challenging project I could ever imagine."

"Yeah," Talia said again, her voice almost taken away by the wind and blowing snow.

"So are you going to say yes to their offer?" Ryan asked, turning to look at her.

"If you are," she said, looking up at him. "I can't imagine learning all this on my own. And I could never imagine myself saying that ever."

He laughed and nodded. "I feel the same way."

"So let's do it," Ryan said.

Talia nodded. "But first, let's get out of this cold."

"If I understand this correctly," Ryan said, "that's going to happen any moment."

"Good," Talia said, "because this dress is a damn poor excuse for a coat."

At that moment, Ryan found himself back underground, his hand next to Talia's and Duster's on the wooden box, and Bonnie smiling at them, holding the wire she had just disconnected from the box.

"Welcome back to 2020," Bonnie said.

All Ryan could do was shiver. And beside him, Talia's teeth were actually chattering.

CHAPTER TWENTY-EIGHT

December 24th, 2018
Boise, Idaho

FRED HAD ANOTHER drink as he told them about his adventure with Marcy, getting caught parking, and who she was to him and his life now. He explained that his two years with Marcy had mostly been trying to forget about being in love with Alice. It had been a fun time, but nothing really important, or life altering.

After he got done telling his story, and Dave told his about how great it was to watch his daughter being born, Sandy went back through the jukebox to visit her senior prom.

She came back smiling and laughing and told everyone all about it, right down to where she and her girlfriends spiked the punch to get the guys drunk.

Carl went back to visit his mother and when he came back he didn't say much and no one really pushed him.

It shocked Fred both times when they just sort of popped out of existence and then back again when the song ended.

And before each song Stout asked Fred if he had any memories associated with the song.

Stout and Billy both declined to play a song, so when Carl returned and dropped back onto his bar stool, Stout moved down the bar and stood in front of Fred.

"Usually," he said, "we only go back once, but since your first trip was an accident, are you interested in giving it another try this year?"

His question surprised Fred, for some reason. "Give me just a second to think about it." He slid his glass toward Stout. "How about a refill?"

He nodded and moved down the bar with Fred's special glass as Fred thought about Alice. She had turned out to be the one woman, over all the years, that he truly had loved. Now he had a chance to go see her again. And maybe tell her how he really felt.

Maybe keep her from leaving him.

Stout was offering him another gift.

And this was a very special gift.

Fred turned on his stool and looked out over the empty Garden Lounge. This evening had been one of the nicest, and wildest, he had spent in more years than he cared to remember. He enjoyed the people and he enjoyed the place.

Why leave it at the moment?

Besides, if Stout was right, he and Alice had ended up in a really ugly divorce that he hated enough to change once. Maybe he was just cut out in this life to live alone, as he had done. Maybe on this gift, this year, it was better to look the old horse in the mouth.

Stout set the glass on the napkin.

Fred turned around to face him again. "Thanks for the offer," Fred said. "But I think I will pass this year. One was enough. Maybe next year if you want me back."

Stout broke into a huge smile. "Every year. You are always welcome."

Stout moved down the bar and unplugged the jukebox. "That's it for another year," he said.

They all toasted the jukebox and then spent the next hour laughing and talking about anything and everything, including what Stout could remember of Fred's previous life, including how really unhappy he had been with Alice.

At a little after midnight on Christmas morning, Sandy dropped Fred off in front of the Golden Dream Hotel for Men.

He almost bounded up the front stairs, feeling younger and more alive than he had in years. He wasn't sure why a few drinks and a trip into his own past would make him feel that way. But it did.

And for the moment that was all that mattered.

He unlocked the front door and went into the front foyer.

The place was dark, the only light the one over the old front desk cage. Hank and Michael were long asleep. In fact this was the latest Fred had stayed up in years.

He looked around at the deep shadows and the worn furniture. It was as if he was seeing it for the first time. Seeing the age and the stagnation. Nothing had changed in this room for as long as he had lived here.

He patted the back of Hank's chair and a small cloud of dust rose in the dim light. Maybe it was time to bring some life back here.

Fred wandered over to the open area beside the cage and looked up at the high ceiling. Twenty feet, maybe. More than enough room for a Christmas tree.

Tomorrow the three of them would stop down at the Garden to have a Christmas drink with Stout. He had promised he would fix them his special eggnog.

And then Fred and Hank and Michael would go buy a Christmas tree for the hotel. It was time they started a few traditions of their own. The guys would piss and moan, but they would enjoy it. They retired sure, but they weren't that old.

And then maybe the following week he might find an old jukebox. A real one

that only gave you memories instead of trips through time.

A person didn't always have to go into the past to change the present. As he discovered tonight, with a very special gift from the strangest gift horse he had ever met, sometimes you can do it right now.

PART THREE
The Power of Music

CHAPTER TWENTY-NINE

About one hundred and thirteen years earlier…
May 30th, 1905
Monumental Summit Lodge, Idaho

TALIA COULD NOT believe how identical the lodge looked in 1905 from when she first saw it four months before in 2020. Almost every detail had been preserved. Same style of 1900 cloth furniture, same polished logs for the walls and ceilings, same wide wooden staircase, same types of wooden tables and chairs in the dining area.

The air in the lodge smelled wonderfully of new timber and a wood fire. She loved it more the second time than she had the first time.

Even Dawn Edwards greeted them behind the counter when they arrived with big hugs. They had just finished building the lodge in this timeline.

The only difference Talia could see clearly was outside the scars of construction of the lodge three years earlier still showed. And Talia hadn't come in on a helicopter, but instead on a three-day horseback ride from Boise.

And this time, she and Ryan shared a room. The same room they had made love in for the first time.

Since they had accepted Bonnie and Duster's offer, they had both been working nonstop after taking a quick trip forward in time with both Bonnie and Duster to 2120.

She didn't get to see anything there because Bonnie and Duster just wanted to anchor them in that timeline. So they had turned around, hooked up another crystal near the back of one of the long crystal rooms, and jumped back.

Now, the entire life she would live in 2020 and forward would only take two minutes and fifteen seconds of her life in 2120. In other words, she was basically immortal. Thinking of that just made her head hurt.

Ryan had tried to explain it with math one night and she actually had understood most of that, even though it was out of her area.

And now they were spending two minutes and fifteen seconds of her life in 2020 on years in the past. After four intense months of math research plus learning how to ride a horse, learning how to dress in 1905 women's clothing, and learning how to act as a woman of means in 1905, they had made the trip back.

The four months had allowed both her and Ryan to really get to know each other.

They spent morning, noon, and nights together. As every day had gone by, she had fallen more and more in love with him.

And the research they had done had allowed them to just start to put her knowledge of sound waves with his knowledge of the physics of time and space. Bonnie and Duster had both worked with them to jump them in quick order to a working knowledge of the math of alternate timelines. That also had helped.

Now she and Ryan planned on spending most of a lifetime together running tests and continuing to work on the math in the past.

In other words, she had committed herself to spend a lifetime with a man she had only known four months and she was happy about that.

Very happy about that.

And from everything he said, he was as well.

Even with the months of practicing riding a horse, that first day from the Institute in Boise and up over some ridgelines had gotten her very sore.

The four of them had camped at a hot springs and the soak had helped, so the second day was easier and on the third day leg up to the lodge, she had felt fine.

And it was a beautiful ride. Snow still filled most of the areas under the trees and in many places the trail went through deep mud and over streams at full runoff levels. But the weather for all three days had been perfect, with temperatures in the low seventies during the day and cold at night, perfect for sleeping in a tent next to the man she loved.

They had each led two packhorses on the trip, stocked with supplies and modern equipment. Bonnie and Duster had made an exception on the hard rule of taking modern equipment into the past.

Talia and Ryan just flat needed it to re-cord over decades the sounds of the pia-nos from Roosevelt. Especially after the town went under water.

Talia wasn't so sure about watching a town be destroyed and doing nothing about it. Bonnie and Dawn had both assured her that no one was killed or even injured. That helped, but she had no doubt it would be a tough spring that year.

That night, in the same bed in the same room in the lodge they had stayed in 115 years in the future, she and Ryan again made love. Then, as they were both trying to catch their breaths, Ryan looked at her with that serious expres-sion he often got. His handsome face seemed to become like a rock and his eyes got intense.

"Sure you want to spend a lifetime with me in that valley below?"

"I honestly can't think of anything I want more," she said, cuddling against him and letting his arm hold her. "Why? You getting cold feet?"

"My feet are always cold," he said, putting his very cold feet against her leg. "I just can't believe someone as beautiful and smart as you are wants to spend decades with me in a cabin."

"And I can't believe," she said, push-ing against him, "someone as handsome and smart as you are wants to spend the time with me."

"Well," he said, "that sounds like a perfect basis for a long-term relationship. Complete disbelief."

She laughed. "Don't forget the sex."

"Another area of disbelief for me," he said, raising up and looking into her eyes. "I can't believe how great the sex is."

"And just think," she said. "We have lots of time to practice."

With that, she kissed him and they started into the second practice session of the night.

CHAPTER THIRTY

July 20th, 2020
Boise, Idaho

STOUT LOCKED THE front door of the Garden Lounge with a loud click and turned up the lights slightly so that it didn't feel like a normal time in the bar. Then he turned back to the six friends sit-ting on the bar stools, drinking and laugh-ing, with their backs to him.

This was going to be very, very hard to tell them.

Outside, the July sun was beating down on the afternoon streets, sending the temperatures to almost a hundred. But inside the Garden, he kept the tempera-ture at a cool seventy-two. But even with that, he was sweating and worried about what he was going to say.

The old jukebox that had changed so many things for so many sat in the corner, dark as always, sort of tucked away be-hind a planter full of natural-looking fake plants.

He seldom plugged the jukebox in and turned it on for anything but the spe-cial Christmas Eve gathering. The back-ground music in the bar came from an old stereo system tucked under one end of the bar.

The last thing he wanted was to have customers playing songs that took them to memories that they changed and then not come back to be customers. He didn't have enough customers as it was.

Now Available
from all your favorite booksellers
in trade paper and electronic editions.

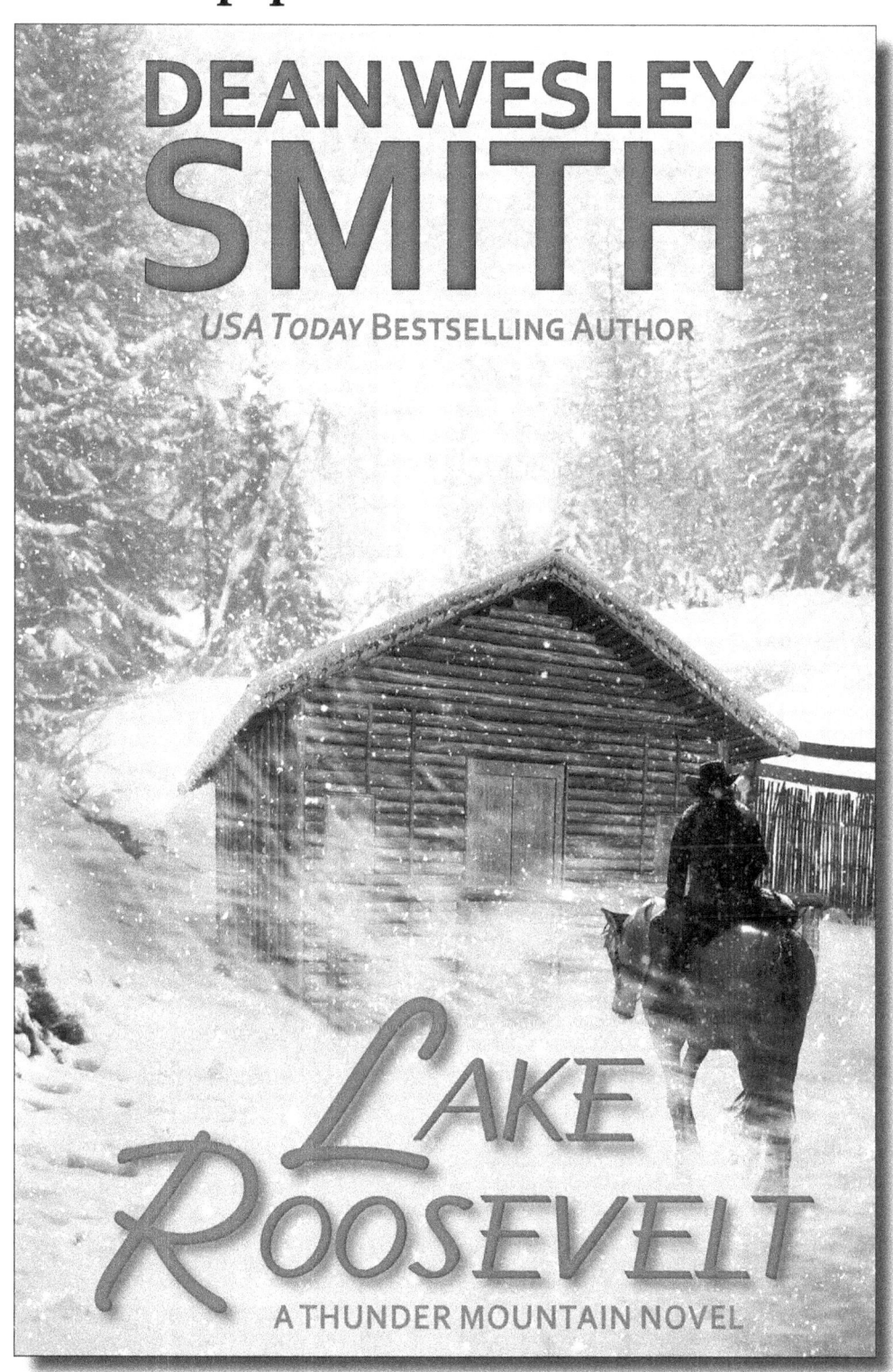

But today he needed to turn it on one more time, just for himself.

So as he walked toward the bar, he moved around the planter and plugged in the jukebox.

All six regulars turned as one, all stunned.

"Stout?" Big Carl said, frowning. "What are you doing?"

Carl was a giant of a man and as gentle as they come. He worked as a contractor and had skin as tanned and leathery as shoe leather.

Dave sat next to Carl on Carl's left. Dave was still in his airline pilot's uniform and he looked suddenly very worried. He had managed to get here by changing flight assignments this afternoon. It was the only time Stout had ever asked him to do something like that, so he already had a hint about how serious this was.

Sandy sat to the left of him. Beside her, Fred stared at Stout as well.

Next to Fred on that end was Billy, a rough-looking man with even a rougher past. Billy had moved into Fred's hotel about six months ago, and the two had become like a couple, always seen together and bickering half the time.

Closest to Stout and the jukebox on Big Carl's right was Richard Cone, a manager of a local factory and the only one of the group besides Stout who didn't drink. Richard also ran the bar when Stout couldn't make it or was out of town for some reason. He was the only help Stout had, and he only worked when Stout wasn't around.

Stout's six closest friends.

All very different people.

And all but Richard had experienced the effects of the jukebox. Richard just kept declining to go back to a memory, stating his life had turned out just fine and he was happy with where he was. But he loved to watch others disappear back into their memories from a song and then come back with stories.

"So what's happening, Stout?" Richard asked, as Stout moved around behind the bar.

"Just a little announcement is all," Stout said. "But before I do it, I need to take a little ride back in time."

"Not to change anything I hope," Sandy said, clearly almost panicked.

Stout laughed. Sandy existed because Dave had gone back through the jukebox and saved his wife. Without the jukebox, Sandy would have never been born, and no way was Stout going to take a chance on changing that.

"Nope," Stout said. "Not changing a thing. Just need to go have a look at someone one more time. Then I'll tell you all what this is all about."

"Jenny?" Dave asked.

Stout nodded, took a quarter from the cash register, then passed out earplugs as he moved over to the very special Wurlitzer jukebox and dropped in the quarter.

"Stay focused on the bar while I'm gone," Stout said. "I don't want any of you jumping by accident."

They all nodded. They all knew the drill.

Stout didn't dare let himself hesitate. It had been years since he had taken this ride, years since he had discovered the jukebox, and he didn't dare hesitate now or he would never do it. But he had to know for sure if his feelings for Jenny were still there before he made his final decision.

And the only way to discover that was go be with her for a few minutes.

The length of the song.

Stout punched A-1, the place on the jukebox where the special song had sat since he found the jukebox.

"Have a good visit," Richard said.

All his friends looked very worried. The next two minutes were going to be a very long time for them, of that he had no doubt. He had done his share of waiting the length of a song while someone was gone, wondering if they would return.

Those two or two-plus minutes could be an eternity.

Behind him the jukebox clicked the 45 record into place. The first note of The Mindbenders song "A Groovy Kind of Love" started and the worried faces of his friends and the Garden Lounge vanished.

And he was facing Jenny across the hard, polished-Formica top of the table at the university student union.

CHAPTER THIRTY-ONE

About one hundred and thirteen years earlier…
June 6th, 1905
Roosevelt, Idaho

FOR RYAN the ride on horseback down the narrow trail and into the Monumental Creek valley had been far, far, far more frightening than the ride down to the valley floor the first time in Duster's big Cadillac.

The trail didn't seem much wider than a horse and Ryan could almost reach out and touch the hillside on his left while on his right the slope dropped a good thousand feet almost straight down into rocks and pine trees.

One slip and he was doomed. Of course, he would wake up back in 2020 in theory, but he sure didn't want to test the dying thing this soon on his first trip to another timeline.

The four of them rode for almost an hour in silence until they reached the valley floor and Bonnie and Duster called a halt and a rest, moving them away from the trail about fifty paces and to a group of rocks.

Ryan's legs were shaking and he swore he had lost ten pounds in sweat under his shirt and long coat, even though the morning air still had a sharp bite to it. The four of them had started so early, right at first light from the lodge, so in the deep valley the sun was still hours from warming it up.

Talia got off her horse and staggered for a moment, then knelt down and just kissed the ground, which sent both Bonnie and Duster into gales of laughter.

"I would have done that as well," Ryan said, "if I hadn't been so frozen in fear and relief."

"That is a nasty stretch of trail," Duster said, shaking his head and taking out his canteen. "Especially with a couple packhorses behind you. One horse slips and it's all over."

Ryan knew that, which was why he had been so scared the last three hours, and hearing Duster say it just made it worse.

"The other three trails any easier?" Ryan asked, hoping the answer would be yes.

"About the same, actually," Duster said and he worked on giving the horses water and checking each pack horse to make sure their supplies were still solidly in place.

"And they don't have that wonderful lodge to stop and rest at," Bonnie said.

"You get used to it after a few times up and down it," Duster said.

"Speak for yourself," Bonnie said.

Ryan got out his canteen and took a long drink, then stared back up at the trail slicking across the rocks above them. He could see two other horse trains working their way slowly along.

This was a long, long ways from his classroom in Berkeley.

"How far to Melody Ridge?" Talia asked.

"Another three miles or so," Duster said. "All easy flat trail."

"We'll have lunch there," Bonnie said. "Right after I take a shower."

"The cabin has a shower?" Talia asked.

"Two, actually," Duster said. "And a couple great tubs as well in the two bathrooms."

Ryan was shocked. "How do you manage that?"

"Cold showers I assume," Talia said.

"Actually, no," Duster said, smiling. "We cheat a little with some future help, well hidden. "We'll show you."

"I think I'm going to like this cabin," Ryan said.

"We hope you do," Bonnie said, "Considering how long you hope to stay in it and do research."

"Yeah, good point," Ryan said, not really wanting to think about being in this valley for decades, but knowing that was what they faced.

"We can always go up the hill to the lodge for dinner and drinks," Talia said.

Ryan glanced back up at that trail. "On special occasions."

"Very special," Talia said, looking up at the trail as well. "Very special."

CHAPTER THIRTY-TWO

May 13, 1992
Boise, Idaho

JENNY HAD BEEN the one true love of Stout's life. She had long, brown hair, very straight, as was the normal fashion at that point in time. She wore jeans and a white blouse tucked in with a cloth belt.

He and Jenny were sitting at their favorite table in the old university student union. She had just told Stout she was transferring to a university in Southern California and would have to leave in three weeks to get to a promised job and get settled before the fall semester started. It was the best school for her music degree, and was a great opportunity for her.

The oldies Mindbenders' song played softly over the student union sound system, which was why the jukebox brought him to this moment.

She had just looked at Stout and asked what he wanted to do. And what he wanted her to do.

He had just stared at her and not said a word, and eventually in a day or so the decision became that she should go and take the job and get the degree and he would visit as often as he could.

He just didn't want to leave the job he had at the moment. She had married someone else six months later.

Now he sat there in that student union once again, staring at her, his stomach twisting just as it had all those years before. His young-self and his old-self memories were all locked into the same brain.

When he was young, he hadn't been willing to give up a job to go with her, and he had lost her. Would he be able to give up the Garden Lounge and all his friends in Boise this time around?

That was the reason he had taken the trip through the jukebox, to try to get an answer to that question.

His young self loved Jenny more than anything. And it seemed his older self did as well. But not just the young girl sitting there, but the woman Jenny had become over all the years.

As he had done when he was young, he just sat there silently and stared at her.

Then the short song ended and he was back, standing in front of the jukebox and the worried looks of his friends.

CHAPTER THIRTY-THREE

About eighty seven years earlier…
June 6th, 1905
Roosevelt, Idaho

BONNIE AND DUSTER and Ryan and Talia reached Melody Ridge while the sun was still only about halfway down the mountains. The ride in, as they got closer and closer to Roosevelt, the sounds of the valley had gotten louder and louder. All kinds of construction sounds punctuated by shouting at times. And all the while the piano music filled the background, echoing off the sides of the steep slopes.

They had come to study sound and it was clear they were going to have a lot of it to study.

Talia could not believe the size of the cabin, as Bonnie and Duster called it, on Melody Ridge just up the valley from the booming mining town of Roosevelt, Idaho. Made completely of logs, it had four bedrooms, two bathrooms, a main stone fireplace in a huge living room, and a kitchen and dining table that seemed like they might fit in any modern home, except no fridge and no electrical stove.

But the wood-burning stove looked pretty amazing.

After walking around the place with Bonnie giving them a tour, Talia had no doubt she could be very comfortable in this cabin.

A stable had been dug into the hillside behind the house big enough to hold all twelve horses they had brought with them. Dug in behind the stable Duster had shown them a deep storage cellar that stayed a set temperature and would be good for supplies. It was also well hidden.

Then Duster had taken them into one of the bedrooms and opened up a hidden area that seemed to be the back wall.

"Solar panels are hidden on the hillside above the stable," Duster said, "up in the steep rocks where no one would ever see them, and they are colored as rocks. Even if someone spotted one of them, they wouldn't know what they were."

"The metal flashing around the roof and along the roof line are also solar panels," Bonnie said.

"This is amazing," Talia said. She was wondering how the small batteries in some of her equipment would last, and when she had asked, Duster had just said it would be taken care of.

"And everything runs to large batteries," Duster said, pointing downward, "dug into a storage area in the ground here and vented out the back."

"They have to make it through long stretches in the winter without sun," Bonnie said.

"And even in the summer on clear days," Duster said, "the sun doesn't spend much time on that hill, so caution on extended battery use."

Talia nodded, suddenly understanding something. "That's why there is no sign of this cabin in 2020. You come in and remove everything at some point."

"Clearly we will," Duster said, smiling. "But we haven't yet because before now, this was just a regular cabin without all the hidden modern elements. We had no reason for them before you two joined the crew."

"Who knows," Bonnie said, "maybe when we get back the cabin will still be sitting here and maintained in 2020."

"Won't happen because of the primitive area designation of this area, remember?"

"Right," Bonnie said, shaking her head. "Looks like we will tear it out at some point in the future."

"Oh," was all Talia managed to say. Sometimes the reality of time travel into alternate timelines just twisted up her mind and this was one of those times.

"So we got a lot of equipment and supplies to unload," Duster said, closing the hidden area in one bedroom and turning for the back.

"Then showers, lunch, and a tour of the town below," Bonnie said.

"We have some more members of the Institute down there we want you to meet."

"There will be other time travelers here in the valley with us?" Ryan asked a moment before Talia could.

The idea of having others here after Bonnie and Duster left in a month or so pleased her.

"There will be," Duster said, "up to the point the town goes under. After that, you'll be on your own."

For some reason, that scared Talia more than she wanted to think about right now. This valley was a long physical distance from anywhere with other people.

And in time she was a long ways from home.

Suddenly the reality of what she and Ryan had decided to do started to sink in.

Really sink in.

CHAPTER THIRTY-FOUR

July 20th, 2020
Boise, Idaho

"YOU ALL RIGHT, Stout?" Dave asked.

Stout nodded, then unplugged the jukebox and went around behind the bar.

"Not really, huh?" Big Carl said.

"Not really," Stout said as he refreshed everyone's drinks, then leaned back against the back bar with the orange juice on the rocks that he sipped during the summer.

The Garden was as silent as a tomb, so he moved over and turned the stereo back on for background noise. Music was so much of a person's life, it didn't feel right to not have some music playing while he talked with his friends.

H couldn't think of how to start into this, so as he moved back to his position leaning against the back bar facing his friends, he just decided to start from the beginning.

"You know computers can be dangerous things."

"I'll drink to that," Dave said. As an airline pilot, he had told them more horror stories about computers than Stout wanted to remember. Especially the next time he had to fly.

"About six months ago, I decided to see how Jenny was doing," Stout said. "So I looked her up on that Google-thing that Sandy showed me how to use when she installed that computer in my office."

Sandy laughed. "That computer was for bookkeeping, not surfing the web."

Billy just shook his head. "Stout surfing. Now I've seen it all."

"Hey," Stout said, laughing. "I used to surf when I was down in Florida for those jobs."

Billy snorted. "Yeah, decades and fifty pounds ago."

"Forty-three pounds," Stout said, laughing even harder. Amazing how good friends could make a person feel better even when trying to tell them bad news.

Billy raised his glass in defeat.

"So you found Jenny," Sandy said, getting him back on his story. "What was she doing?"

"I actually didn't find her at first," Stout said, his stomach twisting. "I actually found an obituary for her husband. He died of cancer two years ago. She was mentioned as surviving him."

"Oh," was all Sandy said.

"I searched some more, and discovered she had an account on something called Facebook, so I joined up."

"The world has ended," Billy said.

"My hero is lost," Big Carl said.

Fred just shook his head, saying nothing, while Sandy looked proud and Richard and Dave looked worried.

"So I contacted her and we've been in touch for six months now."

"No wonder you've been in such a good mood," Richard said.

Stout let them chatter about his mood for a second until Dave said, "Let him finish his story."

"Jenny has two grown kids and a couple of young grandkids. She's living just south of San Francisco and doing fine. Retired from teaching at the university there."

"Is she going to come up and visit?" Fred asked. "I could clean a room in the Golden Dream if she needs a place to stay."

Billy just smacked him on the side of the arm and everyone laughed.

"Thanks," Stout said. "She actually will be in tonight, and I've got her a room at the Comfort Suites down the street from here."

Now smiles lit up on everyone, and they all started talking at once about how they were looking forward to meeting her.

Finally, after the conversation eased, Dave looked at Stout and asked, "So, how come the trip through the jukebox?"

"I wanted to see if the feelings were still there just from the old memories, or if these new memories were building new feelings."

"Getting serious it seems," Richard said.

"Skype will do that for you," Stout said, smiling.

"The world really has ended," Fred said, shaking his head. "Our Stout is doing the nasty with a woman on the computer."

Stout just laughed. "Only talking. Honest."

Everyone but Richard laughed. "So what's the upshot of this, Stout?"

Stout took a deep breath and looked at Richard. "Remember when I had you run the bar for a week two months ago? I was down seeing Jenny and getting to know her family. And that went well, which is why she's coming up here this time. To see my life and meet all of you."

"And if this goes well?" Richard asked.

Stout smiled. Richard was one of the sharpest people Stout knew. And since Richard never took a drink, he often caught stuff others missed.

"We might get married," Stout said, smiling. "We've talked about it, but nothing firm yet. Waiting to see how this trip goes."

Everyone cheered and Stout quickly hushed them. "Jenny is looking forward to meeting you all, but not a word of that marriage stuff, all right? Promise?"

Six hands went up as one, promising.

"And if you decide to get hitched," Richard said, "you'll need to move down there with her. Right? She's the one with the grandkids and family."

Suddenly even the background music didn't help the dead feeling of the Garden. Stout made a note to hear the Beatles song playing on the radio to anchor this moment.

"Actually, we're planning on living both places," Stout said. "And doing some traveling. But it will be tough to own a bar and not be here six months of the year."

Stout glanced at all six of the sad faces on his friends. The Garden was as much of a home to them as it was to him. Just like he couldn't imagine shutting this bar down, they couldn't imagine being without it and all the friendships. And that's what they were all thinking at that moment.

No one said a word, so Stout went on with his plan.

He moved down in front of Richard. "Mr. Richard Cone, sir," Stout said,

acting very formal. "I know you have a great job managing that plant, but I also know you have always wanted to own your own bar."

Richard's head snapped up and he looked Stout square in the eyes.

A Beach Boys song called "Good Vibrations" was now playing.

"If this works out between me and Jenny, which I have a hunch it's going to, would you be interested in buying the Garden Lounge and running it in any manner you see fit?"

Stout watched Richard swallow hard, his eyes slightly misty.

Except for the background song, the bar was dead silent.

Dave leaned over and touched Richard on the shoulder. "I'll back you if you need the help."

"Yeah, me too," Sandy said.

"Count me in," Carl said. "I got some extra if you need it."

"Me too," Fred said.

"Not me," Billy said. "I barely got enough to drink and eat and pay my rent to Fred here. But I'll buy drinks if you'll serve me."

Everyone laughed then, including Richard. Then Richard turned to them. "Thanks. But with my job and low expenses, I've been saving for something like this for a very, very long time."

He turned back to Stout and extended his hand. "Mr. Radley Stout, if things work out with your new girl, you've got a buyer, as long as that damned jukebox stays with the bar. We can't be changing traditions now, can we?"

Stout and Richard shook hands as everyone cheered, and it felt as if a huge weight had just lifted off Stout's shoulders.

CHAPTER THIRTY-FIVE

About one hundred and fifteen years earlier…
September 26th, 1905
Roosevelt, Idaho

RYAN WATCHED with his stomach twisting as Bonnie and Duster waved goodbye and rode off along the trail and back up the valley toward the Monumental Lodge. They both had three empty packhorses with them, leaving four horses behind for the first winter in the valley.

The day had dawned cold, with a dusting of frost on everything. Above the mountain peaks the sky was a bright blue, promising another nice fall day, but the sun had barely hit the tops of the mountains so far. Bonnie and Duster just loved getting early starts.

Talia stood beside him, holding his gloved hand with her gloved hand. Both of them were dressed in heavy clothes, boots, and jackets insulated with future technology, but made to look like 1900 clothing. From what Ryan had heard about the coming winters here in the valley, they were going to need all the warmth they could muster.

"You as scared as I am?" Talia asked without looking at him as they watched their two bosses ride away. Her breath left a cloud of white frost in the air in front of them.

"Petrified," Ryan said.

"Oh, good," she said, turning to go back inside.

Ryan followed her, shedding his coat as he went since the inside of the large cabin was nicely warm and designed to stay that way with just the heat from the fireplace and a few hidden fans and ducts.

The summer had been amazing. They had spent the months since their arrival setting up their equipment, getting in supplies for the winter, and exploring the valley.

They had met Janice and Steven, two historians from the future who had owned the general store here since the town started. Both of them were part of the Institute in the future and two of the founders. They promised to help if anything happened over the winter.

Ryan had liked them both and all six of them had had many a great meal in their cabin, enjoying the laughter and each other's company. It seemed that Janice could really cook. So for the winter, they set up a regular Thursday and Sunday dinner together to check in with each other. Their cabin was directly across the valley from Melody Ridge and also had many hidden features to help through the long winters.

Having them here made Ryan feel a little less worried about the coming winter. But in a number of years, after the town went under water, unless they could solve their math problems, it would be most likely he and Talia would be the only living beings in the valley in the winter.

That scared Ryan more than he wanted to think about, since even though they could see the Monumental Lodge from their front porch, in the winter it would not be possible to reach.

Their work on the music had gone well once everything was set up and they were settled. They had managed to record the sounds of the valley all summer to get a baseline for it all.

And wow was the valley a noisy place. It seemed the extremely steep slopes covered in sharply shaped rocks held the sounds down, including the ten pianos playing every night from open saloon doors.

Every so often Ryan could actually recognize a song, but that was always fleeting. Mostly the valley just seemed to be filled with music and noise day and night all summer.

The four of them had made some progress on the math of sound through time, but not enough. Ryan had a hunch it might take them years, if ever, to solve this problem of sound cutting through time.

They had set up a hidden area lab behind a small empty bedroom that had no windows. And they had wired instruments all over the entire area around their home.

Twice Duster had made a ride for the lodge with packhorses to get more supplies and equipment they had stored there. They had a large pantry and cellar full of food supplies and enough firewood cut and under shelter near the stable to build a small mountain.

They were ready, but Ryan just didn't feel ready.

He took off his coat and hung it on the peg near the door, then moved to where Talia was putting a kettle on the stove for hot water for tea. He put his arms around her and she turned so she could be in his arms, looking him in the eyes.

"This will be an adventure," he said.

"I know," she said, kissing him lightly.

He knew that kiss already, even after only knowing Talia for a few months. Something was wrong.

He smiled and looked into her wonderful green eyes. "And…?"

"I'm just worried?"

"About surviving?" he asked. He was too, but they were far, far more prepared

than anything he could imagine and they had this wonderful cabin as well.

"Sure, a little," she said.

He knew that wasn't the problem, so he said once again, "And…?"

She shook her head, then looked him in the eyes. "I'm afraid after being so close to me for so long, you won't love me anymore."

Somehow, he did the correct thing and didn't laugh. But he did smile and she could see he was amused.

"I'm serious," she said, trying to twist out of his arms, but he held on and she didn't try very hard.

"I love you," he said, again staring into those intense green eyes. "As every day goes past, I love you more. I am looking forward to being alone with you, working with you, making love to you, for years and years. I just hope you won't get tired of me."

Now it was her turn to smile at him.

"And if we have issues," he said, "we are certainly going to have the time to work them out."

"Yeah," she said, laughing. "You have that right. Time is on our side at this point."

Then she kissed him hard. And if the kettle hadn't whistled to say the water was boiling, they might have just gone back to their big feather bed.

CHAPTER THIRTY-SIX

July 23rd, 2020
Boise, Idaho

JENNY FIT IN perfectly with the regulars at the Garden. She and Dave and

Richard hit it off perfectly, and after just a few evenings, she told Stout she felt like she had always been sitting at the bar joking with everyone.

And at one point or another every one of his friends told him in private that if he lost this woman, he was dumber than a post.

Stout had to agree with them, even though Jenny sure didn't look much like the thin, long-haired girl he had fallen in love with all those decades ago. Just as he had done, she had filled out, and now her once-brown hair was short and silver. And she tended to wear dresses more than jeans. And she wore glasses, those thin kind that professors wore.

She actually had been a professor for years, teaching music theory and history before she retired to care for her husband in his last year.

Her husband had been a building contractor, so she and Big Carl seemed to sometimes talk another language that most of the regulars just didn't understand.

After four days, it was clear they were going to be together for a lot longer if Stout could just get past one more hurdle.

Dave reminded him that he needed to tell her about the jukebox.

Stout had to agree with him. It was important that a future partner would know that he owned—and was about to sell—a time machine.

So once again he passed the word to his closest friends to come in early in the afternoon to help him out in case he needed it. And he asked Jenny to come with him to open the bar. He said he had something he needed to show her.

"This sounds serious," she said, looking at him with those wonderful brown eyes of hers. Those eyes hadn't changed at all, and her ability to really see him hadn't changed either.

"It is," he said. "And I hope nothing serious. Just something you need to know about."

The night before they had talked about him selling the bar to Richard and how happy he was about that.

And sad at the same time.

She double- and triple-checked that he was telling her the truth. After the last few days, she could see just how special the Garden Lounge was to him, and how hard it was going to be for him to let it go.

He told her he didn't plan on leaving the Garden forever. They would be regulars when they were in town. And he told her that every Christmas Eve they had to be there, no matter what. They could fly back to her kids for Christmas Day.

He told her she would understand why after he showed her what he had to show her at the bar.

Christmas Eve at the Garden Lounge was a special time for all the regulars. It was the only time he ever turned on the jukebox and let customers go back to their memories. Richard had said he planned on honoring that tradition, and hoped Stout would be back every year to run the party.

So as he finished getting the bar opened, everyone sort of showed up at once, laughing with Jenny. All of them knew what this was all about, and they were all determined to help if they could.

So with Jenny sitting between Dave and Richard at the bar, Stout stood against the back of the bar and had no idea where to start. He just sort of stood there as everyone looked at him. He hadn't bothered to turn on the stereo yet, so the weight of the silence made starting even harder.

"Tell her about the glasses first," Dave said, pointing at the case over the bar.

Stout looked into the eyes of the woman he loved and then said simply, "You are not going to believe most of what I'm about to say, but for now just trust me. Okay?"

She frowned, clearly suddenly worried.

"Trust him," Dave said. "He's not totally nuts, only slightly."

Everyone laughed and Stout took the key for the cabinet out of the register drawer and went to get the four glasses.

He took three down and left the other in the case.

Then he walked the fine drinking glasses down the bar, putting the one etched with the name Dave in front of Dave, another in front of Carl, and another in front of Fred.

"I made these glasses for these men years ago for a special Christmas Eve party. I served them drinks in these glasses, and none of them remembers that night. Except Dave, who came back after I closed the bar. Long story, but what this is all about."

"If you are trying to explain something," Jenny said, "remind me to never let you in a classroom."

"Now that's a deal, Professor," Stout said.

He pointed at the old jukebox, dark and sitting in the corner. "You understand the power of music. Music can take a person back to a memory, to an emotion, to an experience."

Jenny nodded. "There have been many studies on the power of songs to trigger memories to try to help some patients with different forms of brain injury and diseases."

Everyone was deadly silent, which wasn't a normal state for the Garden Lounge, so he just blurted it out. "That jukebox actually takes a person *physically* to a memory associated with a song."

Jenny looked at him frowning. Then she smiled. "Okay, what's the joke?"

"Toss me a quarter, Stout," Dave said, climbing off his stool. "She's not going to believe you; no one does, until they see it. I'll go visit Sandy being born again."

Without looking at Jenny, Stout tossed Dave a quarter and moved around the end of the bar and plugged in the jukebox.

"Give us a minute to get earplugs in," Stout said.

He quickly dug out the earplugs and handed each person a pair. When he handed the pair to Jenny, he smiled. "You said you trusted me. Just hold on for one more moment and you'll understand what I'm talking about."

She was really frowning now, but she did as everyone did and put in the earplugs.

"Ready," Dave asked, smiling.

Stout nodded, and Dave dropped the quarter into the machine and after a moment hit the number to the song that would take him back to the moment when Sandy was born.

Stout looked into the eyes of the woman he loved. "Cover your ears," he shouted so she would hear. "And think of this moment right here and right now. Think of this bar. Okay?"

She nodded, and then the music started and Dave was gone and they were all still here.

"How?" Jenny said, but he could barely hear her through his ear-plugs.

He just held up a finger for her to wait and pointed toward the jukebox. Then he put his hand on hers, holding her solidly in the Garden Lounge.

The two minutes of the song stretched into an eternity.

Then, faintly, he could hear the song ending and Dave shimmered back into being, smiling.

Everyone pulled out the earplugs and Dave rejoined everyone at the bar. "You know," he said to his daughter, Sandy, "you sure were a damn pretty baby."

"You all right?" Sandy asked, just before Stout did.

Seeing his wife again had to hurt some. She had died a couple years back from cancer and everyone missed her.

"I'm fine," he said, taking a drink.

"So what the hell just happened here?" Jenny said. "What kind of magic trick was that?"

"No trick I'm afraid," Stout said, pointing at the jukebox. "That thing really takes people back to their memories. You end up inside the body of the person you were, only with old memories. When the song ends, you come back, unless you have changed something."

Dave held up his glass. "One Christmas Eve, years ago, Stout gave four of his best friends a very special Christmas gift. He let us go back and change something in our pasts we wanted to change. I went back and saved my wife from being killed in a car wreck; as a result, Sandy, here, and her sister were born."

"That's why we only turn that thing on for Christmas Eve," Stout said. "And why we're very careful. It's very dangerous and can change a person's life."

He stared at Jenny for a moment, then said, "You still don't believe us, do you?"

She looked him square in the eye and he could tell she was angry. A deep-down angry.

He wanted to throw up. This couldn't be happening.

"You have to admit this is hard to swallow," Jenny said. "And I don't see why you would play this sort of trick on me, Stout."

The silence in the bar could be cut with a knife. He could hardly breathe. Was he going to lose the only woman he had ever loved for the second time because of the jukebox?

"No trick," he said, softly. "That really is a time machine."

Again the silence became thick and smothering. He had to do something and do it quickly.

"Do you remember the song that was playing right after you told me about your job while we sat in the student union?"

She nodded. "Longest song ever," she said. "I was waiting for you to say something and you didn't say anything."

"Do you remember the name of the song?"

"It was a classic old Mindbenders song about love. Why?"

Stout took a quarter out of the cash register and went around the bar to her side. He took her hand to indicate she should get down off the barstool. "Let's go for a ride."

She walked hesitantly to the jukebox. "Earplugs everyone," he said.

Then he turned to the woman he loved. "You can't change anything while we are there. Nothing. Our older selves will be in control of our younger bodies, and our younger selves won't remember our little visit. But change *nothing*, all right? Please. A lot of lives depend on it, including your wonderful children and grandchildren."

She glanced around at the people at the bar, then nodded, suddenly clearly very afraid.

He dropped the quarter into the jukebox and once again punched A-1.

A moment later he was sitting again across from the young Jenny.

Only this time Jenny's eyes didn't stay focused on the table in front of her as they had done the first time. They looked up at him, panicked.

The older Jenny was in there this time.

Then she looked around, listening to the song over the sound system of the old student union, smelling the greasy fries and smell from the two jocks sitting far too close.

Finally she looked back at him. "Is this real?"

He nodded. "Can you remember your life with Stephen? Your kids being born? Your grandkids?"

She nodded, still looking around. "How is this possible?"

"There's some kind of very advanced equipment in the jukebox I've never had the courage to touch. Somehow it lets the power of a memory from a song take the person listening to their memory."

"And our young selves won't remember this?"

"Do you?"

She thought for a second, then shook her head.

"This was our turning point the first time, wasn't it?" she asked

"It was," he said.

"If you had said you wanted to marry me, I would have stayed."

"But sometimes things work out the way they are supposed to," he said. "We weren't ready that first time around."

She nodded. "I would have been angry at you for making me stay."

"I know," he said. "And I would have been angry for you making me leave."

"You've sat here before from the future, watching me, haven't you?"

He nodded. "A number of times. It's how I discovered the power of the jukebox."

"And you never said anything? Never changed our future? Why not?"

"I loved you too much," he said. "And then, after a while, I knew if I changed my future, a number of people wouldn't be alive right now. And that was before I knew about your wonderful family."

The song was slowly nearing its end.

"You are a very special man," she said, smiling.

"Then will you stay with me this time? In the future, of course."

"I want to more than anything. In the future, of course."

He smiled. "Would you marry me the second time around?"

She looked around at the old student union and laughed as the song finished and they appeared back in the Garden.

She put her arms around him and said, "Yes, you stupid fool. Of course I'll marry you."

Then she kissed him in a way he knew he would never forget, song or no song.

And the friends in the Garden Lounge cheered.

This time, it was *his* life the jukebox had saved.

PART FOUR
The Failure of Music

CHAPTER THIRTY-SEVEN

About one hundred and eleven years earlier…
May 30th, 1909
Roosevelt, Idaho

TALIA AND RYAN stood in the front window of their cabin looking out over what they could see of the Monumental Valley below Melody Ridge. The rain pounded the valley with a constant drumming sound and Monumental Creek was flowing over its banks, not only from the rain, but the snowmelt up the valley.

Talia and Ryan had shut down all recording equipment and covered everything. It had been a long winter and only a few miners and suppliers had managed to get in over the trails so far this spring. Unlike in years past, the gold rush was starting to wear down and the push to come into the valley early was fading.

For the last three springs, Talia and Ryan had been happy when new arrivals started to show up for the summer. But this year was different.

Very different.

Today would be the start of the end for the town below them. None of the other thirty people who had stayed this last winter in the town area knew that. Just below the Dewey Mine up Mule Creek to the right, a mudslide would start.

That would be the beginning of the end of this entire area.

In the last three and a half years, she and Ryan had made amazing progress on the mathematics of sound and waves through time. And every summer Bonnie and Duster joined them and continued the progress on the math.

The summers had been wonderful, but Talia had also come to enjoy the winters with just her and Ryan in the cabin.

During the three years, they had only had a few minor problems. Ryan twisted his ankle one January afternoon two years before when he slipped on a rock going out to the stable to take care of the horses. That had kept him on the couch for a few weeks, but luckily it had been no more than that.

Both of them had managed through a number of colds, usually in the spring when others started arriving. And Janice had gotten sick with some intestinal virus and she and Steven had shut down the general store last fall and headed out.

So this last winter, even though the town was still below them in the valley, was their first winter really alone.

Even the pianos had fallen silent this last winter, which made the valley seem even more desolate.

Her initial worries about the relationship with Ryan were completely unfounded. She loved having him there, depended on him more than she wanted to admit, and had grown to love him even more in the last three years than she thought possible to love another human being.

And she really loved his intense mind. He seemed to see things in ways mathematically that would have slipped right past her. And her knowledge of the math of waves seemed to add in and expand the boundaries of physics they were pushing. Even Bonnie and Duster were impressed and sometimes had trouble following where the math went.

Talia and Ryan together were a very, very powerful team and they had talked about that over dinners.

Each summer they had also spent a full week in the Monumental Lodge, being fed wonderful breakfasts and dinners and having a great time with Dawn and her husband Madison.

The three years had been eventful, yet quiet. Talia couldn't believe it was now May 30th. The day of the landslide that would put this entire town under water.

Outside the rain just kept coming.

She turned to Ryan. "It's going to take most of the day for the front edge of the mudslide to reach the edge of this valley. You want to go watch it arrive?"

He stared silently into the rain for a moment, then nodded. "I think we need to, since we're going to be staying here for some years."

"I agree," she said.

They stood there in silence for a moment. She knew she needed to see the landslide arrive. She needed to see what would finally kill this mining town she had come to love.

For the last three years it had been in steep decline. There was no doubt that Roosevelt, in time, would have become just another ghost town. This area was so remote and without the mining, which was almost done, there was no reason to be in this valley.

But the landslide just sped up the death.

So later in the afternoon they would go watch the mudslide arrive and start across the valley right in below the main part of town.

It would be like watching a slow-motion bullet entering someone's body.

No way to stop it and death a certainty.

CHAPTER THIRTY-EIGHT

December 24th, 2020
Boise, Idaho

STOUT WAS EXCITED. This was his and Jenny's first time back to the Garden for Christmas Eve. Richard had decorated the place in what Dave called "Standard Stout" which meant no real decorations, only red Christmas candles on the ten tables and a few beer signs with Christmas on them.

Stout couldn't believe they had actually made it for the party. Tomorrow morning early, Christmas morning, they were flying down to the Bay Area to have Christmas Day dinner with one of Jenny's sons and their family. Stout was actually looking forward to that almost as much as spending a few hours here in the bar with his adopted family.

Sandy and Dave were both there, along with Fred and Carl and Billy. And Richard was standing behind the bar where Stout had been all those years. And honestly, Stout didn't mind not being back there at all.

He liked his new place sitting at the bar with his wonderful wife Jenny just fine.

"So who is going back this Christmas Eve?" Carl asked as Richard closed up and locked the front door right at 10 p.m. as was the custom

"I'm going to see Sandy being born," Dave said. "Then he glanced at Richard. "If you don't mind, dear barkeep."

Richard laughed. "As long as I don't have to go along, fine by me."

Carl said he wanted to do his regular trip and everyone nodded to that.

Billy and Fred both passed.

And Stout knew that Richard would never go back through the machine. He never had.

"So how about you two?" Carl asked, looking at Stout and then at Jenny.

Stout shook his head, as did Jenny beside him. They had talked about it and neither of them wanted to see anything in their pasts. They were both very happy with the moment in time right now.

"Not this year," Stout said.

Richard nodded.

"So I'll start this off," Dave said, holding up a quarter.

Richard headed around the end of the bar and as everyone watched, he plugged in the jukebox.

The lights came on in rainbows of colors, as always. Sometimes over the years, Stout had just wished that jukebox had been a regular jukebox. The customers would have liked it and it would have made a little extra money as well.

Then Richard went back behind the bar and dug in the drawer near the cash register and handed out earplugs for everyone.

Stout sure understood that. Especially now that David had played this song a few times in the past. No point in all of them jumping to previous Christmas Eve memories. That would be just too weird.

When everyone was set and Stout had hold of Jenny's hand, David dropped in the quarter, took a moment to search for his song, then punched it in and turned to face everyone as the record exchanger pulled up the record.

Stout expected a moment later for David to just fade away, as normal.

But he just stood there. Then, after a few seconds, he looked back at the jukebox, then back at Richard and Stout and shrugged.

Then David just shook his head.

Clearly the jukebox didn't work for him anymore.

Or maybe it didn't work for anyone anymore.

So for the entire length of the song, David just stood there, because no one dared take out the earplugs.

CHAPTER THIRTY-NINE

About one hundred four years earlier…
April 16th, 1916
Roosevelt, Idaho

TWO MONTHS BEFORE tragedy struck, Ryan and Talia had worked out the final parts of the math on how the sound waves had the power to punch through time.

Actually, they didn't jump back or forward in the same timeline, but jumped timelines to basically identical timelines. Just as Bonnie and Duster had all of them doing. Just moving around in identical timelines.

But the final solution actually hinged on the power of the human brain. And that had both surprised Ryan and Talia.

And excited them.

Since time and energy and matter all acted as fluids, waves could move through that fluid mix if at the correct frequency and power. So could light waves and such, which explained things like deja vu, because an image could come back to a person from a certain timeline future giving the person the sense they had been somewhere before.

It seemed the sound waves easily traveled through the fluid state of energy, time, and matter. Talia and Ryan had proved that a few years earlier with mathematics that Bonnie and Duster had both confirmed. But the final problem had been why the sounds from the past could be heard.

It wasn't until a snowy night in January as Ryan sat with his feet up near the fire listening to recordings in earphones that the solution had dawned on Talia. She had been stretched out on the couch, just staring at the fire and thinking. The two of them spent a lot of time in silence and they both loved that, something Ryan was very grateful for.

Talia had suddenly waved her arms to get his attention and he had clicked off the recording and sat up straight, taking off the headphones.

"We are missing the critical element of all this," Talia said. "The receptor."

Ryan had no idea what she was talking about.

"Our brains are powered on forms of chemical impulses as well, correct?"

Ryan honestly didn't know, since that had not been his area of study in the slightest. But he tried to add what little he did know. "Chemical impulses moving along like a wave from cell to cell is what I remember from a very early class."

"Exactly," Talia said. "Our brains, through our ears and eyes get sounds and images. So why don't they also hear and see what is coming through time? And translate them?"

"And magnify them?" Ryan asked, starting to get an idea of where she was headed with this.

"Just as our equipment can pick up certain wave patterns coming through time and clean out the other sounds and amplify the ones we want," Talia said, "Our brains work in the same fashion."

Ryan was starting to understand where she was going.

"And experiences of the person doing the observing can amplify or deaden the reception as the case might be," he said.

"That's why songs can bring back such vivid memories," Talia said, almost bouncing on the couch. "Our brains pick up and filter the actual sounds from the past in a way to bring the memory the song has attached into sometimes clear focus."

"Like a scope looking back through time," Ryan said, smiling. "That's the one element we have been missing."

"We're going to need research and massive computer power to crunch all this math," Talia said.

"Looks like this is our last winter here at the moment," he said, smiling and moving over to kiss her.

He didn't realize at the time just how accurate that statement would be.

On April 7th, Talia went out into a slight snowstorm to get some firewood. Ryan was studying some sound wave recordings of the valley they had recorded two days before and didn't realize for a good fifteen minutes that she hadn't come back in.

He found her, in her light coat, blood oozing from a gash in her head where she had fallen and hit her head on the edge of some cut firewood. She was covered in snow and almost blue.

Her breathing was shallow and she wasn't awake.

He got her back inside in front of the fire and out of the wet clothes and wrapped in a blanket.

In all his years alive, he had never, ever felt so panicked and alone.

He got the gash in her head cleaned out and bandaged.

He got her body temperature back up to normal and sat with her for the next day on the couch, wanting to be there when she woke up.

Two days later she had a fever and still hadn't come to. He gave her more antibiotics that seemed to help for only a short time. Her wound was healing but something inside was clearly wrong.

Six days later, on April 16th, 1916, she died in his arms.

And he became the last person living in the Roosevelt area.

CHAPTER FORTY

December 24th, 2020
Boise, Idaho

THE SILENCE IN the bar seemed like a big thick weight as Stout pulled out his earplugs.

Stout glanced at Richard who was shaking his head. He clearly had no idea what had just gone wrong.

"Looks like I wore out that memory," David said, looking sad as he moved back to his spot at the bar. Sandy touched his shoulder.

Stout understood completely. That memory allowed David at a safe point to go back and see his wife Elaine. She had died of cancer a few years before and they all missed her. He looked forward every year to seeing her again for even the length of a song.

Carl stood and said, "Let me see if it's just you or if this thing is broken."

Everyone scrambled, at Richard's insistence, to get the earplugs back in as Carl dropped a quarter into the jukebox and punched a selection.

Then he turned to face everyone as the record loaded and started to play.

Nothing.

Just nothing. He shrugged as well and headed back to his spot at the bar.

Stout pulled out his earplugs, as did David. Stout had a clear memory of the first time he heard that song on Christmas Eve a long time ago.

But he didn't jump to the memory.

"Looks like we have a regular old jukebox now," Carl said, finishing off his drink. "Can't say that I'm sorry."

Everyone took out the earplugs before the song ended and no one vanished from the bar.

Richard silently picked up the earplugs and put them back in the drawer, then he quickly refilled everyone's drink, including Stout's eggnog.

Finally, it was David who raised his glass.

"A toast to the jukebox," he said. "It saved my life, my wife's life, and gave me two wonderful daughters."

"And it gave me Jenny again," Stout said, raising his glass as well.

"It allowed me to live," Carl said. "Really live."

"And it gave me good friends," Fred said.

"I'll drink to that," Billy said.

"To the jukebox," David said.

And everyone drank.

Then, as Stout set his glass down, he asked, "I wonder what happened?"

Richard just shook his head and moved around the end of the bar to unplug the machine. The bright lights and colors went dark and Richard quickly covered it with a special cover that Stout had had made years before.

"It's a machine," Carl said. "Machines wear out."

And with that, Stout could only agree.

After a few more minutes, they were back enjoying each other's company and the jukebox was forgotten for now.

And even without someone jumping back in time from the bar, Stout's first Christmas Eve back in the bar since he sold it was a wonderful time.

CHAPTER FORTY-ONE

About one hundred and four years earlier…
April 30th, 1916
Roosevelt, Idaho

RYAN SOMEHOW managed to chip away at the frozen ground for three days after Talia died, working to dig her a grave on the ridge above the frozen waters of the lake. He moved like a sleepwalker, stumbling around and not realizing sometimes how he managed to get from one place to another.

He couldn't make himself sleep in their bed, so just stayed on the couch in front of the fireplace.

He had to believe she would be standing beside him when he pulled the wire on the crystal at the Institute, but believing that mathematically and actually having her die in his arms were two different things.

So he kept repeating over and over that she would be there as he worked to dig her grave.

And he kept visualizing her smiling face and those wonderful green eyes.

They had talked some about what they would do if one of them died here. But he honestly hadn't given it that much thought. Not having her beside him never seemed to be any reality he wanted to think about.

They had lived together for eleven years in this cabin, and up until the end, he had loved every minute of it.

But now he had to bury Talia and figure out what to do with the cabin and everything and somehow get out of this valley and back to the Institute.

Up the valley, on the clear days, he could see the huge Monumental Lodge. He knew that Dawn and Madison, two other travelers from the Institute and their kids were living there through the winter, but it might as well have been light years away for all the good it did him now. The trail up the side of that mountain would be snow-covered and impassable.

By April 18th, he had Talia buried. He left her fully dressed and wrapped in her favorite blanket. Her grave was right beside the trail leading away from the cabin, a place he knew she would have approved of.

After he finished getting her covered in the frozen dirt, he went back inside and drank himself to sleep in front of the fire.

The next morning broke clear and he was hung over, but ready to get to work. Talia would be standing beside him when they unhooked the crystal for this time-line. Bonnie and Duster and Dawn had said they had died many, many times in the past. The key now was to get back to the Institute.

And he had to figure out what to do with a cabin with far too many things in it that were far, far ahead of the time period. If someone else stumbled on this cabin, and found some of its secrets that had allowed he and Talia to live in almost modern comfort, there might be problems.

And, at the same time, he had to try to get all their notebooks back to the future with him.

For the next twelve days he worked at packing saddlebags for the two horses they had in the stable, trying to get any-thing into the saddlebags that might be taken out of time if found.

Then he slowly and carefully de-stroyed all the remaining equipment, pulled down all the recording devices, and buried all the remaining parts in the ground in the back of the stable that was dug into the hill.

Duster had given him a pretty accu-rate valley weather forecast for every day of every winter. They had the records in the Monumental Summit Lodge after many, many timelines of staying through the same time. Ryan knew that April 30th would be the first possible day he could get over the trail leading out past the Dewey Mine and down onto the Middle Fork of the Salmon.

That trail wouldn't take him up to the lodge, but instead out of this valley and eventually south to Boise. The lodge trail would be just too dangerous until late May or early June. And he didn't want to stay here without Talia for an-other month.

He wasn't sure he could, actually.

So on the crisp, cold morning of April 30th, he loaded up the two horses and led them down the trail a short distance away from the house and stables as to not spook them.

He tied them up right near Talia's grave.

Then he turned and went back to the house he and Talia had both loved.

The mountains were showing the first rays of sunrise reflecting off the bright white snow, and the lake below the house was starting to show cracks in the ice, but was a few weeks from thawing yet.

The snow around the house now was only a couple feet deep and melting fast. Spring and summer were on their way.

He stood for a moment looking out over the valley that had held ten thousand people at one point in the not too distant past. He was the last person living in the valley full time.

He glanced up at the Monumental Lodge and waved. He was sure they would see what he was about to do and understand.

He took a deep breath and went in the front door of the house he had come to love. He had piled blankets in various places near walls and a lot of straw covered many areas to work as extra fuel.

He walked through the place once, making sure he had missed nothing. Under his coat, he had strapped a vest with Talia's main notebooks and his main notebooks.

For the last week he had slept with that vest in his hand. He wanted to make sure the math they had done ended up back in the future with him if he died on the way out. He was sure that he and Talia could recreate it, but he didn't want to take any chances.

The home was full of wonderful memories. It was hard seeing it ready to be burnt to the ground.

He might suggest to Talia at some point that they build it again and live here again in another timeline. They both had loved the peace and the quiet and the time together.

He took a deep breath and then moved quickly around the house, setting fire to each pile of material, making sure it was going full.

Then he went out the back door and to the stable.

In the back of the stable he had what dynamite they had bought in the general store when they first arrived. He had set it in two places to bring down the mountainside on the stable. He would have the fire he was going to set ignite the explosives.

He checked everything quickly, then lit all the piles of feed and straw he had stacked earlier and moved out into the cold morning air.

The house was already fully engulfed and the flames were crackling and shooting into the clear morning sky, filling the air in the valley with a black smoke.

He paused just long enough to make sure the fires in the stable were going, then headed quickly along the trail, got the horses and mounted up, then with one last look at Talia's grave, he moved along the trail leading the one packhorse.

Three minutes later an explosion rumbled through the valley.

He didn't look back.

There was no reason to look back.

His future, the woman he loved, would be waiting for him in Boise in 2020.

He had to believe that.

And he had to get there safely with their work.

CHAPTER FORTY-TWO

October 17th, 2020
Boise, Idaho

TALIA WAS SURPRISED to find herself standing with her hand on the wooden box in the cavern under the Institute.

Bonnie and Duster and Ryan were standing beside her, also touching the box. She was wearing her normal clothes and had a blanket wrapped around her.

And she was so cold, she was shivering.

Duster had the wire in his hand from where he had unhooked it and brought them all from the past back to 2020.

Ryan dropped the packs he had been carrying and hugged her so hard, she almost couldn't breathe.

Then he kissed her and Bonnie and Duster laughed and moved toward the entrance to the long, thin cavern that held timeline crystals.

The last thing she remembered was in the spring of 1916 going out for firewood. It had been snowing slightly, but not that bad.

She pushed Ryan back and looked into his eyes. She could see he was so upset that he was almost in tears, while at the same time smiling the largest smile she had seen him smile since they figured out the sound-wave math.

"What happened?" she asked, her voice shaking from being so cold.

He hugged her, then kissed her again, then picked up the packs he had been carrying and turned her toward the door where Bonnie was waiting. "Come on, we need to get you warmed up some."

"What aren't you telling me?" she asked Ryan, feeling slightly annoyed.

"You died," Bonnie said.

That froze Talia in her tracks. Ryan put his arm around her and hugged her, then got her started again toward the door.

"We'll explain it all and what happened since the day you died," Bonnie said. "But we need to all take showers and get in fresh clothes and get you warmed up and some food in you."

Talia was shaking and shivering from the cold and her mind was swirling.

Died?

How could she have died? What had happened?

It took them only a few minutes to get back to the main area and Bonnie helped her into the showers in the women's locker room area. After a few minutes of standing under the warm water, Talia was starting to slowly feel better.

She put on fresh modern clothes from her locker that felt strange to her after eleven years of living in the past, and combed her more modern haircut. Over the eleven years in the valley, she had let her hair grow long, but it was now back the way she had it when she left.

And she looked younger as well.

Of course, eleven years younger.

Only two minutes and fifteen seconds here had passed in those eleven years. Amazing, just amazing.

And she had supposedly died in the past in that timeline. But she had no memory of how.

Oh, no, poor Ryan.

Bonnie was already finished with her shower and was working on cooking them all some lunch with warm chicken noodle soup and sandwiches. The soup smelled wonderful and made her realize just how hungry she really was.

The large cavern area felt warm and nice, almost like being home again. She sat on a stool at the counter that divided the main kitchen area from the rest of the massive space and looked at Bonnie.

Bonnie looked away from the soup she was stirring and smiled. "Feeling warmer?"

"Much," Talia said.

At that point, Ryan came out of the men's locker room looking younger and smiling like the world was the best place ever.

He came over to her and kissed her hard, then sat down at the counter beside her, putting his hand over hers.

Bonnie smiled at both of them. "When Duster gets here, we'll tell you the entire story."

"I'm here," Duster said, coming out of the locker room with his hair wet and a western plaid shirt and fresh jeans.

"So what happened?" Talia asked, turning to Ryan.

He took a deep breath and for a moment his eyes looked haunted. "On April 7th you went out to get firewood from the stack near the back porch."

"I remember," Talia said, surprised that she did. "It was snowing lightly. It's my last memory until I found myself touching the box."

Ryan nodded. "You slipped and must have hit your head on a piece of the firewood stacked there."

"Oh, my," she said, looking at Ryan. "I am so sorry."

Ryan nodded. "We talked about something like that happening, remember?"

"Talking and having it happen are two different things," Talia said, squeezing Ryan's hand.

"Very different," Bonnie said.

Duster only nodded from his position standing next to Bonnie near the stove.

"I got your wound cleaned out and kept any infection down," Ryan said, "but you must have had internal bleeding on your brain. You died on April 16th, 1916."

"Oh," Talia said, holding Ryan's hand. Hearing her own death date was just damned hard and creepy and a bunch of things Talia didn't have time to even think about yet.

"You are here now and that's all that matters," Ryan said. He kissed her and she kissed him back.

"So go on with the story," Bonnie said after a moment as she moved Duster over to work on sandwiches.

"I dug a grave for you in the frozen ground and buried you, then started working on getting out of there."

"In April?" Talia asked. "How?"

"The weather reports that Duster had given us showed a few clear days at the end of the month. And since it was 1916, I knew that there were ranches and such on the Middle Fork of the Salmon."

"Good thinking," Talia said. Over their years in the valley, they had traveled all three of the routes in and out of the valley during the summer. The Middle Fork route was by far the easiest and the one that would clear the soonest every spring.

"I packed the saddlebags with everything I could get from our modern equipment, strapped your journals and mine to my body, then destroyed the rest of our equipment and put all the pieces in the back of the stable, in the cellar there that was dug so deep under the mountain."

Duster and Bonnie both nodded. Talia was sure they had heard parts of this already.

"Then I set the house on fire and blew up the stable and set it on fire as well, burying any evidence at all that we were there."

That jolted Talia to know the home she had come to love had been destroyed. But of course she knew it had been, since when they stood on Melody Ridge four months ago in this time, there had been nothing remaining there.

"I'm sure Dawn and Madison went down from the lodge to make sure nothing was left after the trail opened," Bonnie said.

"We sure did," Dawn said as she and Madison came walking from the back room toward the main room. They were both carrying packs and both looked like they were dressed in clothes from the 1930s or so.

"Get the kids all grown safe and sound again?" Duster asked.

"We did," Dawn said. "They are a good brood. We got them off to college before mom and pop were supposedly lost at sea."

"So all these years we've been wondering," Dawn asked, looking at Talia and then Ryan, "What happened?"

"Seems I died," Talia said.

Dawn shook her head and Madison smiled.

"Remind me to tell you about when Madison died in the late fall in that valley," Dawn said. "when no trails out would be open for six months. Our first trip back in time as well."

Talia just shook her head. That had to have been almost impossible to survive alone in that valley. No wonder Dawn's book on the valley described how brutal it was, as well as how amazingly pretty it was.

"So after you burnt down the place and blew up the mountain," Dawn said, looking at Ryan, "what did you do next?"

"I managed to get out over the Dewey Mine trail and down onto the Middle Fork," Ryan said. "Took me almost a week to make my way through the snow and out of the mountains and back to Boise."

"Then what?" Madison asked. "If memory serves, Bonnie and Duster were both hooked up to the same crystal with you two."

Talia hadn't even thought of that. Bonnie and Duster would have had lives as well in 1916. Ryan just couldn't go pulling the plug on their lives without warning.

"I was here," Bonnie said. "I had finished up in San Francisco and came back north early."

"It took them a month to find me," Duster said. "I was in Denver playing some cards. I was just about to head back here to go visit you two and the lodge when I got word to come as soon as possible. And what had happened."

The First Two Ghost of a Chance Novels
Available at your favorite booksellers.

Talia looked at Ryan. "That had to be a hard month, just waiting."

"Knowing you would be there when we unplugged the crystal made it easier," he said.

She kissed him again.

"So what happened to all our stuff you rescued?" she asked, after a moment.

"It's in a time vault locker in the back," Ryan said. "All our books, all our recordings, everything I couldn't easily carry, stored and sealed to last through the years until now."

"And speaking of that," Duster said, "did you two figure out the math on how sound travels through time?"

"We did," Ryan said, smiling.

And Talia found herself smiling right along with him. "And even more."

"Oh, this is going to be fun," Dawn said, laughing. "Don't start until we get out of the showers." And then Dawn looked at the soup and turkey sandwiches with a longing eye.

"You want me to make you two some as well?" Bonnie asked.

"Oh, please," Dawn said.

With that, Dawn and Madison headed for the locker rooms and Talia turned to Ryan. "Thank you."

"For what?" he asked.

"Just for everything and for being you," she said. "I don't think I could have done what you did. And bring all our work forward at the same time."

"You could have," Ryan said, smiling at her.

"How about we don't test that for a few hundred lifetimes," she said.

"Deal," he said.

Then she kissed him as Bonnie and Duster laughed.

CHAPTER FORTY-THREE

February 19th, 2021
Boise, Idaho

FOR THE LAST four months, Ryan and Talia, working with Duster and Bonnie in the Institute, had gone over and over and over the math that proved that sound could actually move through time and matter and energy. Ryan had loved every moment of it.

And they all did a massive amount of research on the aspect of human brains having an ability to pick up the sound moving through time in one direction or another.

For Ryan, not only had the work been wonderful, but being with Talia again was something he treasured every day. He loved having her beside him, having her laugh at his silly jokes, and challenge his assumptions. It was going to take some time to have that moment she died in his arms move into the past, but he was managing it.

The massive Institute computers had just finished their final run on the math and Bonnie and Duster and Talia were sitting with Ryan in the large cavern living room area. A fire was crackling in the fireplace and both Ryan and Talia were sipping on hot chocolate.

Ryan and Talia were on one couch, Bonnie and Duster were on a facing couch. Bonnie also had a mug of hot chocolate, but Duster had warm apple cider.

Ryan hadn't been outside the Institute in a few days, but he knew it was cold and snowing slightly. All the more reason to stay inside and drink hot chocolate.

The silence in the large room was comfortable and Ryan finished his reading of the results about the same time Duster did. The results were as Ryan had expected. The math was right. They had proven that sound waves did travel through time and that the human brain was a perfect receptor at times for those sound waves, depending on the recipient.

Ryan sipped on the warm and sweet hot chocolate while both he and Duster waited until all four had finished.

Then Duster said simply, "I think it's time we run a test, don't you?"

Ryan shook his head. He didn't like that idea at all. What they had figured out with the last math was that a person actually did hear sounds inside their own timeline.

Not from another timeline.

The sound waves remained along a timeline, so a person could, in a sense, go back inside their own timeline, following the sound along to a point in their own memories like a lifeline back into time.

And thus their own life.

And in so doing, that person might be able to change something and alter the base timeline in ways that could not be predicted. This was very, very different from going into the past of another timeline. The original timeline here still remained and as Ryan had proven, even with Talia dying in one timeline, she was still very much alive in this one.

"Far too dangerous," Bonnie said, "for any of us to do, or anyone else in the Institute to do."

"I agree, Talia said.

"I agree as well," Duster said. "This discovery just scares hell out of me to be honest."

Ryan was very glad to hear that and agreed. The more he learned about this, the more he wanted nothing to do with actually using the discovery in any fashion, or even publicizing their results in any way.

"So what are you thinking of as a test?" Bonnie asked Duster, giving him a long look that Ryan could only guess had a vast amount of meaning.

"A jukebox," Duster said. "We set it up with popular music, plant it in a small bar, and let others ride back on their memories to test it for a time before pulling it out."

"People not associated at all with the Institute?" Talia asked.

Duster nodded.

And everyone went silent in thought.

Ryan wasn't sure he liked that idea either, since they would have no way of knowing how someone else might switch the timeline into a very different road.

"We would have to have an observer from the Institute on the jukebox at all times," Bonnie said.

Ryan agreed with that as well.

"We pull it and destroy it at the first signs of a problem," Duster said.

Again silence.

The idea scared Ryan more than he wanted to admit, but at the same time, it felt right to at least test the theories he and Talia had worked on for over a decade in the past.

Duster looked around at everyone. After a moment Ryan nodded, then Talia nodded.

"So we build a jukebox," Bonnie said.

"We build a jukebox," Duster said.

"When?" Ryan asked.

"1980," Duster said. "Before any of us were born."

"And not until we have a remote connector developed on it," Bonnie said.

Ryan wanted to ask Duster why 1980, but Bonnie's mention of a remote connector puzzled him even more. Talia asked what that was before he could.

"A remote connector would be a device in the jukebox that allows us here and now to know when a new timeline is set by someone going back into the jukebox and changing something in their lives," Bonnie said. "Like touching the wooden box to remember a timeline, but from a distance."

"Is that possible?" Ryan asked. The entire idea surprised him.

Duster laughed and nodded. "We've been working on the math of that for some time now. It is pretty much developed and this will be a perfect test for it as well."

"So when that works," Bonnie said, "then we build the jukebox. I want to remember both timelines if there is a timeline switch."

Duster nodded. "We need to get that connector on board for everyone anyhow."

Bonnie laughed and waved off a question that Talia was about to ask. "The reason the connector came up is a long story involving saving the world from a dictator. Ask us about it at some point later on."

With that, all Ryan could so was sit and stare at Bonnie and Duster and hope that he and Talia hadn't opened Pandora's box with their discovery.

He had a hunch they had.

CHAPTER FORTY-FOUR

May 8th, 1980
Boise, Idaho

TALIA JUMPED BACK to 1980 with Ryan and Duster and Bonnie. The time was a few years before Bonnie and Duster had been born. Just looking out at the cars on the street, she was amazed at how just forty years made such a huge difference. She had no intention of going out into the town at all while here.

They were met in the Institute by a man by the name of Richard Cone. Richard had thick, wavy brown hair and a smile that seemed to light up his eyes. He was actually an historian doing human studies on regular people in this time period and was looking forward to being embedded with the jukebox.

Talia was surprised that Richard was actually from 2120, but had jumped back to 2020 and then back to 1978 to establish a life in here.

They had decided to build the jukebox in 1980, then store it for at least twenty years, if not longer. The remote connectors would work fine over a twenty year span from 2021, but not much farther back.

Richard then was supposed to get the jukebox into a small bar somehow without anyone knowing he was doing it and then become a regular in that bar.

With the connector running, from the Institute in 2021 Ryan and Talia would be able to trace its use and timeline shifts when they got back.

They also set into the jukebox a limit on how many times it could be used before it shut itself down. A final safety feature that Talia really felt good about.

Talia still wasn't sure of the saneness of this idea overall, but like Ryan and Bonnie and Duster, she really wanted to see if their theories actually worked.

Duster found them an old Wurlitzer Bubblier jukebox built in the late 1940s and they completely tore it apart in a workshop area near the main living area in the cavern under the Institute.

They used a small crystal from one cave, worked to develop a way for it to power the time jump of the person along memory lines, but at the same time not cross into the timeline in the crystal. Luckily both Bonnie and Duster had been working on that math problem for a lot of years and had it solved.

Talia watched as they set the crystal inside a closed box, then shut it and sealed it, then set the safety to shut off the entire thing after one hundred trips into the past. All of them figured that would be more than enough data.

For some reason, Talia was very, very relieved when they returned to February 2021 and the world there was the same as they world they had left.

She wasn't sure what she was expecting, but the relief of it being the same seemed to give all of them a moment's pause.

The data were waiting for them.

The jukebox had already allowed one hundred people to travel back to their own pasts. And even though about a quarter of the trips had resulted in a slight timeline switch, nothing major had changed. Just personal directions for each person involved.

Duster and Bonnie ran a massive program over a two-day period trying to calculate the changes that would affect the future, and from the looks of it, almost all changes to the timeline had just been absorbed back in. Only a couple of children that would not have existed without the jukebox and one child that didn't exist because of the jukebox. All those changes turned out to be minor as well.

Richard also had a report waiting for them that detailed out each of the memory jumps that he had witnessed, some he had heard about, and so on. He hadn't

gotten the jukebox into a position it was used until just a short ten years ago. The report covered just about eighty of the one hundred jumps, which Talia found amazing. Richard must have spent most of his time in that bar.

Richard detailed out the bar, its main customers who knew about the jukebox and time travel, and how the owner of the bar had used the machine in a very responsible manner. They all sounded like great people to Talia.

And they had told no one about the jukebox. It seemed to have been a very carefully guarded secret among only a few.

Talia found it interesting that Richard now owned the bar with the jukebox. He knew it would no longer work, but he wanted to keep it in place as part of the bar for the regulars.

So they quickly built a replica of the jukebox, right down to the same scratches, and replaced out the dangerous one with a jukebox that would only take a customer into a memory, not into the past.

Richard let them in late at night in early March and was very happy about that switch.

So just a regular old jukebox now occupied the place of the time machine in the small bar on the outskirts of Boise.

And Talia was very, very relieved with that result.

And very happy about the experiment.

All their hard work had been proven accurate.

Then, Duster and Bonnie and Talia and Ryan, on March 15th, 2021, locked all the results and their notebooks and data into a very secure secret vault in the third level underground below the Institute. And they locked up the jukebox with everything as well after they returned the crystal to one of the rooms.

When that secure door slid closed and the wall slid back into place to hide the door, Talia felt a giant sense of relief. Traveling into the past of other time-lines was one thing. New timelines were formed and nothing really changed.

Going back into your own body, your own mind, in your own timeline, was just too dangerous for anyone.

And after getting the data on the juke-box, they were willing to just put it all away now.

Success. The End.

CHAPTER FORTY-FIVE

December 24th, 2023
Boise, Idaho

FOR ALMOST THREE years real time since locking all the data and the jukebox in that safe room, Ryan hadn't much thought about the jukebox or the math on sound through time.

In those three years, he and Talia had taken one hundred and seven trips into the past, and by Talia's count, had lived with each other for just under three thousand years. She had promised she would tell him when they got close to the big number three, since they had celebrated at one thousand and two thousand years along the way.

Ryan found that amazing. He had never expected to find someone to live with for even one lifetime, but it seemed that the longer he and Talia were together, the more they didn't want to be apart.

They had spent thirty-one of those trips into the past living in the same cabin in the Monumental Valley, rebuilding it every time and then destroying it when they left. They loved it there, loved the solitude, loved the ability to work when they wanted and not be disturbed.

They had spent another forty trips into the past living from 1930 into the 1960s being caretakers of the Monumental Lodge because Dawn and Madison wanted someone to keep up the tradition of the lodge through those decades.

Both Ryan and Talia loved that as well. Especially the long winter months when they were the only two in the big lodge.

This morning they had been both working together on solving a sight-wave issue on why sometimes events from the future poked back through time and were caught by human minds in what many called deja vu. Usually the experience was of images of physical spaces.

They had been working on that math together now for two years real time and more years than he wanted to count in the past and had yet to make a breakthrough. Sending various waves backwards in time never seemed to be much of a problem. The problem was in figuring out why light and images came back from the future without bidding.

But over the hundreds of years, they had learned to be very, very patient and they both knew that eventually they would work it out.

"We're going to have a visitor," Richard Cone said as he came into the large living room area in the large cavern.

Ryan and Talia had been sitting at the counter in the kitchen area working on beef sandwiches and chicken noodle soup for lunch. Bonnie and Dawn were sitting beside them at the counter, also eating.

Now Available
from all your favorite booksellers
in trade paper and electronic editions.

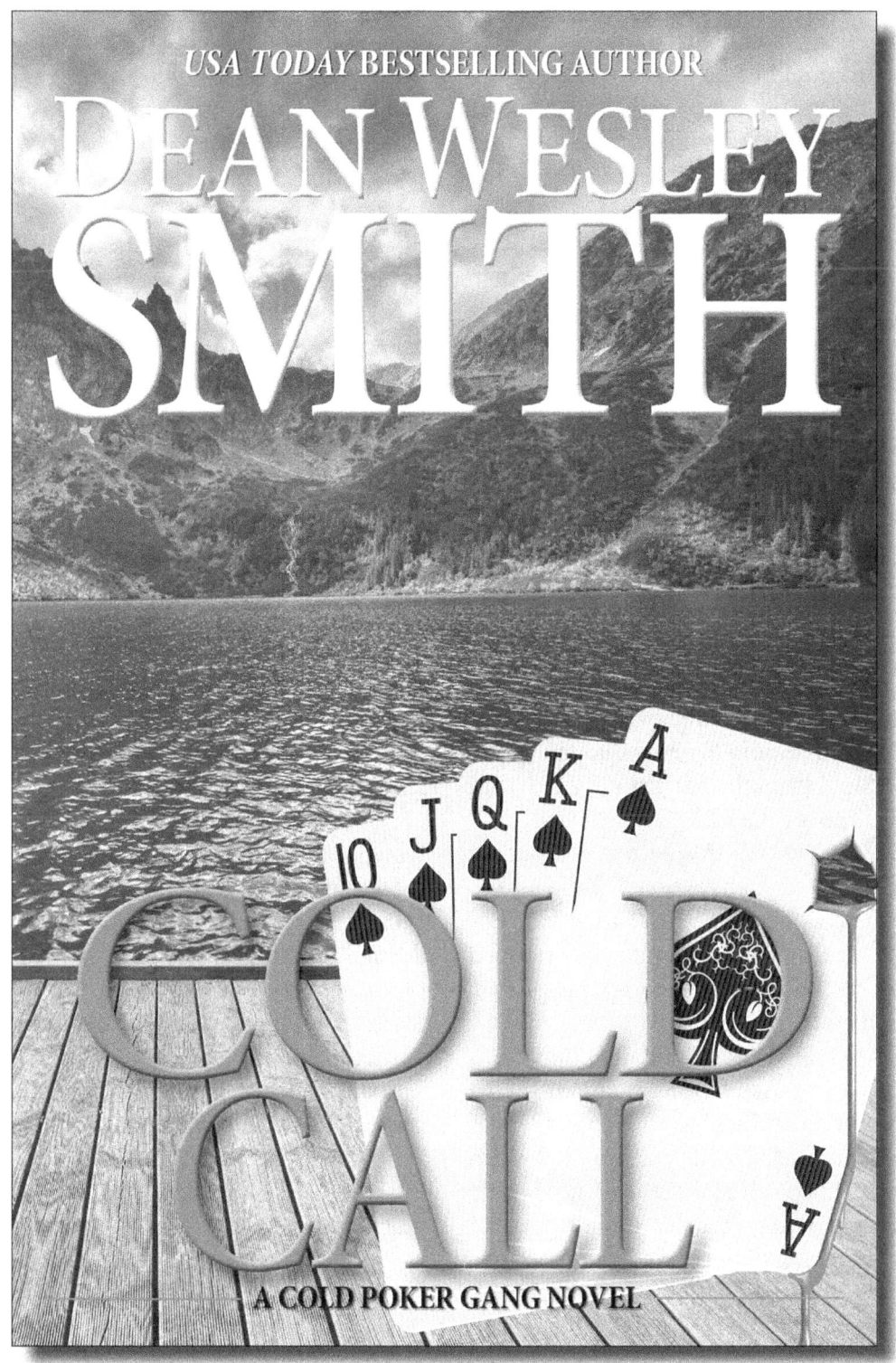

USA *TODAY* BESTSELLING AUTHOR

DEAN WESLEY

SMITH

COLD CALL

A COLD POKER GANG NOVEL

All four of them turned around to watch Richard approach from the elevator through the couches to the kitchen.

Until Richard introduced himself and mentioned the jukebox, Ryan didn't recognize him. The first time they had met, Richard couldn't have been much more than mid-twenties and rail thin. Now he had gray and thinning hair and his face was a mass of wrinkles. He had on a tan jacket and wore a smile like he was used to it.

But that first meeting in 1980 when they built the jukebox had been thousands of years before for Ryan and Talia. Ryan found it amazing his memory worked at all over that length of time. But actually, as the years went by, his mind and memory seemed to be gaining clearness.

From what Ryan had heard in various reports along the way, Richard really loved owning the little bar and was staying on in this time as long as he could before going back and resetting.

"So who's this visitor we are getting?" Bonnie asked after hugging Richard and asking him to join them for lunch.

"Stout from the bar, actually the original owner of the bar," Richard said.

"The guy that treated our time travel machine with such respect?" Talia asked.

"The same one," Richard said. "For three years, since the jukebox stopped working, he's been trying to track down who built it."

"Oh, oh," Bonnie said, laughing.

"Is that possible?" Ryan asked. "That was back in 1980."

Richard laughed as well. "When Duster bought the jukebox, he had it delivered here. Stout is on his way to ask about that delivery and see if anyone knows anything about why a jukebox would be delivered to an historical

institute forty-three years ago or if there are any old records about it."

"Suggestions?" Bonnie asked Richard.

Richard only shrugged as he went around behind the counter and looked in the fridge for something to eat or drink. Clearly Richard was used to this place and Ryan was surprised he hadn't crossed paths with Richard at one point or another. There just weren't that many time travelers using the Institute in this time period.

"Suggestions about what?" Duster asked as he came toward them from the direction of the crystal rooms.

Duster still wore his long coat, cowboy hat, plaid shirt, jeans, and cowboy boots. He clearly had just come from a trip into the past.

He walked over and kissed Bonnie hard. More than likely, for him, he had been gone for years.

Ryan and Talia didn't feel they wanted to start taking separate trips into the past yet. Or ever for that matter.

"How was Delemar?" Bonnie asked, smiling at her husband.

"You back in the Silver City area?" Dawn asked, looking surprised.

Ryan knew just enough of general West history to know that Delemar was a small mining town with a great hotel down the valley from the old mining town of Silver City in the southwestern corner of Idaho.

"Just spending a few years playing some poker," Duster said.

"And playing Marshal as well, I'll bet," Bonnie said, smiling at her husband.

"Sure, why not?" Duster said, shrugging and turning to Richard. "So what's this suggestion thing?"

"We're going to have company in about a half hour," Richard said taking some bread and sandwich meat and working to build a sandwich. He glanced over his shoulder and smiled at Duster.

Ryan was glad to see that it took Duster a moment to recognize Richard as well before moving around and shaking his hand. It seemed that Richard didn't visit the Institute that often, even though he lived in the same town.

"So I was asking for suggestions as to how we want to approach Mr. Radley Stout," Richard said, "the former owner of the Garden Lounge. He somehow traced the delivery of the jukebox to here and is coming by with his wife, Jenny, in about thirty minutes."

"So since it stopped working," Ryan said, "he's been trying to find the original owners?"

"He has," Richard said, nodding before taking a large bite of his sandwich.

"Three years," Duster said, laughing. "That's some pretty good dedication to a cause."

"So any suggestion on how to handle this?" Richard asked. "More than likely it will be best to just turn him away."

"And let him keep trying to find the thing?" Bonnie said, shaking her head. "That doesn't seem to be nice."

"Can he be trusted?" Duster asked.

"Completely," Richard said, smiling. "In all the years he knew what the jukebox could do, he didn't tell anyone until he gave the gifts of changing the past to a few friends. And he and his wife are two of the nicest people you can ever have the pleasure of meeting. They hadn't said a word to anyone about what the jukebox could do."

Duster glanced at Bonnie who just smiled.

Bonnie looked at Ryan and Talia. "You two did the math and helped build the thing. Do you care about how we handle this?"

"I would hate to see him continue searching when he actually found us after three years," Talia said.

Ryan agreed with that completely.

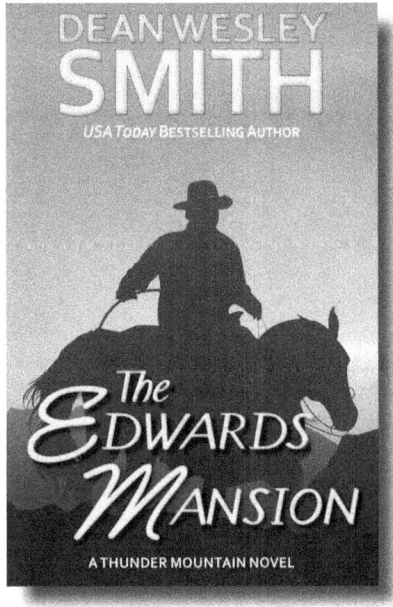

Two Thunder Mountain Novels
Available at your favorite booksellers.

Duster turned to Richard. "So meet them in the main room and get them to sign the standard nondisclosure agreement and bring them down for some lunch. I need to take a shower and change clothes."

With that, Duster turned toward the men's locker room.

"This is going to be fun," Richard said, laughing and pushing his sandwich forward slightly on the counter and heading toward the elevator. "Don't eat my food. I'll be back."

"Actually," Bonnie said, "this just might turn out to be a wonderful Christmas Eve."

Ryan just laughed and went back to working on his soup and sandwich. He remembered clearly, even though it had been thousands of living years before, how shocked he felt when he first saw this place.

Now he was going to get to see it on two other people's faces. And actually get the chance to thank the man who treated his and Talia's experiment with such class and respect.

CHAPTER FORTY-SIX

December 24th, 2023
Boise, Idaho

STOUT WAS STUNNED at the huge mansion that sat in front of him and Jenny as they were buzzed through the gate and into the Historical Research Institute grounds.

There was a cold breeze blowing and both of them were wrapped up tight in their winter coats. The massive old oak trees that surrounded the old Victorian-style home were bare of leaves and the grass still showed the dusting of snow they had gotten a few days before.

There was hope of a white Christmas, but Stout doubted it would happen. But he just wanted to have a report to the gang at the Garden tonight about the jukebox original owners' search. Since the jukebox had quit working, that was about the only mention the thing got now every Christmas Eve.

"This place is something," Jenny said, staring up at the tall spires and old windows.

"I haven't been in this part of town since I was a kid," Stout said. "I didn't remember these old houses were out this way."

They moved carefully up the stone steps onto the covered wooden porch that was massive and stretched along the front of the house and went around one side.

"You sure the jukebox was delivered here?" Jenny asked.

Stout laughed. "I was sure of the address, and the name, but now seeing this place, I can't imagine it. We might as well just head back."

"We got this far," Jenny said, shaking her head at him. "We can ask a few really silly-sounding questions."

Stout laughed and kissed her lightly on the cheek. "It's Christmas Eve, what can it hurt?"

"Exactly," she said.

They turned to the big wooden door with a small typed sign that said, "Push hard and come in. The old door sticks."

So Stout did push hard and the door swung open and he moved aside to let Jenny go in first. Then he followed her and pushed the door closed.

As the door clicked shut, blocking the cold wind and the slight traffic noise from the road in front of the building, Jenny gasped, like she had seen a ghost.

Stout swung around to face Richard from the Garden, smiling at them from near a massive antique desk that sat between the entrance room and a second room beyond.

A wood fire in a large stone fireplace in one corner crackled lightly, the only sound in the room.

Stout started to say something, but not one word came out. Not one.

Richard just kept smiling.

He looked completely wrong not standing behind the bar at the Garden.

Finally Jenny said, "What are you doing here?"

"That's a very long story," Richard said. "And before I can tell you, I need you both to sign a very simple document in which you promise you will never tell anyone what you see here."

Again Stout tried to say something, but his mind just wouldn't connect with his mouth as Richard turned, picked up two pieces of paper and handed them to both of them.

Stout forced himself to look at the simple nondisclosure agreement. Very basic, very simple. It wanted nothing. It was just an agreement to not disclose anything they saw or heard in the Institute.

"If we sign these you can tell us what the hell is going on?" Jenny asked.

"I can," Richard said, smiling.

"And if we don't sign them?" Stout asked.

"Then I can tell you that no one in the Institute knows about any jukebox being delivered here."

"Are you a member of this place?" Jenny asked, indicating the old rooms around them, decorated to look like time had frozen in 1880.

Richard pointed to the documents and handed Jenny a pen.

Jenny moved over to the edge of the desk and signed the paper and handed it to Richard.

Richard went around behind the desk, made a copy, then handed the copy to Jenny and put the original in an empty file basket.

Stout was still so shocked to see Richard, he didn't even know what to say. He had known Richard since he started the Garden, had sold him the bar after all, had trusted him with everything. And yet clearly he knew nothing about the man.

Stout moved to the desk, took the pen, and signed the simple non-disclosure agreement and handed the paper to Richard.

Richard made the copy, handed the copy back to Stout, and then smiled.

"To answer your first question," Richard said, "yes, the jukebox was delivered here in 1980."

"Is your real name Richard Cone?"

Richard laughed. "It is, and always has been. Come on, I have some friends I want you to meet."

"Who is that?" Stout asked, trying to keep the anger he was feeling at Richard out of his voice.

"The inventors of the jukebox," Richard said, touching a button hidden on a panel. "They are wonderful people. I think you're going to like them."

CHAPTER FORTY-SEVEN

December 24th, 2023
Boise, Idaho

IT WAS ALMOST ten in the evening on Christmas Eve when Stout held Jenny's hand as he opened the Garden Lounge door for her. Light snow was falling, giving everyone the hoped-for white Christmas.

To Stout, coming into the warm, comfortable interior of the Garden always felt like coming home.

And now, tonight, it felt even more so. The red candles on the tables were flickering and the faint background smell of old smoke mixed with a faint odor of rum gave the air a slight thickness.

Fred, Carl, Billy, Dave, and Sandy were all sitting at the bar. And two stools remained open for him and Jenny.

Richard stood behind the bar, smiling at them.

That afternoon, he and Jenny had sat in a massive underground cavern, talking with Richard, Bonnie, Duster, Ryan, and Talia, the four inventors of the jukebox, and a world-famous historian named Dawn Edwards.

After a few hours, Dawn had to leave to go be with her husband for Christmas Eve and Richard had left to go open the Garden.

The four inventors had asked if he and Jenny were hungry for dinner and the six of them had gone out for a wonderful dinner downtown in a private room.

Stout wasn't sure about all the stories they had told, and about Richard being from a hundred years in the future, but after owning the jukebox for so many years, he was more than willing to keep an open mind about everything. Owning a time-traveling jukebox could do that to a person.

And besides, the four of them were wonderful and smart and really loved to laugh. And they all seemed very appreciative of how he had protected the jukebox and told very few people about it.

Over dinner, Stout had told them about how he had decided to give his friends the gift of change one Christmas Eve, and how the new group of friends had been very careful with the machine.

He and Jenny both told them about their last trip through the jukebox before it stopped working. And it had helped them decide to be married in this time period.

Then the inventors told Stout how they had retired the original jukebox and that the jukebox now in the Garden was just a replica.

And he and Jenny learned that their only trip together through the jukebox had been the very last trip anyone would ever take through it.

Stout felt very relieved when he heard that.

And Jenny had just said, "Good."

Now, he and Jenny were back where Stout felt he belonged, with his friends at the Garden Lounge. But he and Jenny both felt they had made new friends today. Three years of searching on and off for the creators of the jukebox had turned out better than he could have ever hoped.

So as Stout and Jenny took their spots at the bar, Carl asked, "So where have you two been?"

"Running down the last research on the jukebox," Stout said.

"And having a wonderful Christmas Eve dinner," Jenny said.

"And did you have success on the search?" Sandy asked. She had helped him a lot in his quest to find the owners of the jukebox.

Bonnie and Duster had given him permission to tell the others who knew about the jukebox the truth about it. But not anything about the Institute or the location of the jukebox.

But Stout and Jenny had decided to just invite the four of them for a Christmas Eve drink at the Garden and let them tell what they wanted to tell.

And all four inventors had agreed.

"Before I answer that," Stout said as Richard put glasses of eggnog in front of both him and Jenny, "let's have a toast, as we always do every year to the jukebox."

Stout raised his glass and everyone followed suit.

"To the jukebox," Richard said, raising a glass. "The reason we are all here."

Everyone agreed and drank.

A moment later, the front door opened, letting in the sound of the traffic outside and the blowing wind.

"You forget to lock up, Richard?" Dave asked.

Richard smiled and shook his head.

"Make room at the bar everyone," Stout said as he and Jenny stood and scooted their stools in closer together. "We have very special guests joining us this Christmas Eve."

"Who?" Carl asked as everyone turned around to see who was coming in.

"The inventors of the jukebox," Stout said, moving toward the front door to greet his new friends.

This was going to be the best Christmas Eve ever at the Garden Lounge.

~

#1... October 2013

#2... November 2013

#3... December 2013

#4... January 2014

#5... February 2014

#6... March 2014

#7... April 2014

#8... May 2014

#9... June 2014

#10... July 2014

#11... August 2014

#12...September 2014

#13...October 2014

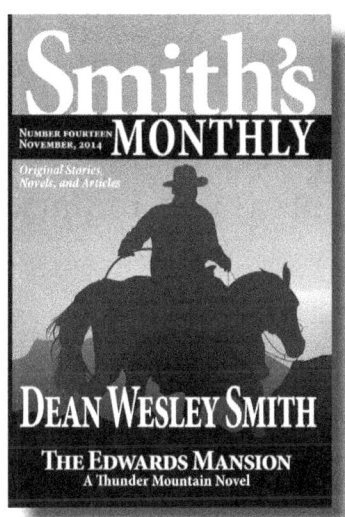

#14...November 2014

#15...December 2014

#16...January 2015

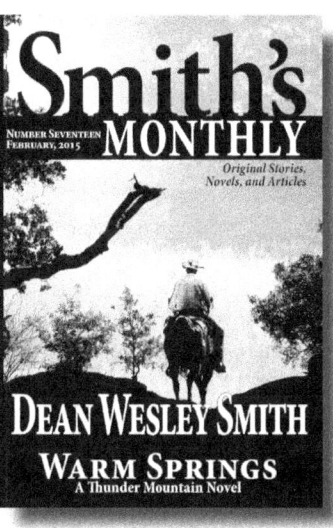

#17...February 2015

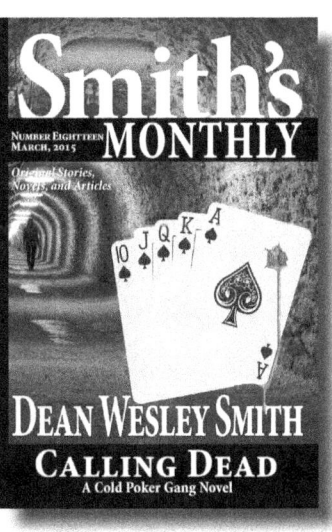

#18...March 2015

Thank You!!

Walter White Cat and I would like to thank
the following wonderful people who support my blog
and my work through Patreon.
Your support is very important to me.
Thanks!

Rob Cornell

Scott Gordon

Erick Lindman

Kathryn Rooney

Christopher Ridge

Sherman Cox

Miguel Angel Alonso Pulido

Fen

Nancy Hendrickson

Livia Quinn

Ryan M. Williams

Amri Ackers

Jacob Proffitt

Robin Brande

Ryan Whiteside

J.R. Murdock

Marian Goldeen

Kathleen McClure

John Connelly

Michael Kelberer

Gary Speer

Gunnar Gunderson

Megan Bryce

F.I. Goldhaber

Michelle Tatam

Mary Jo Rabe

Ann Tucker

John Kilgallon

Kari Wolfe

Dave Hendrickson